The Misadventures of Marjory

by

James Ball Naylor

Dr. James Ball Naylor

Photo courtesy of the Morgan County Historical Society

The Misadventures of Marjory

by

James Ball Naylor

Edited and Annotated

by

Theresa Marie Flaherty

Theresa Marie Flaherty

Pat – Its a good old fashioned story – more than a hundred years old. Good to see you again.

Jerry

TURAS
PUBLISHING
www.TurasPublishing.com

Oct 2014

Photo Credits:
Front Cover Photo: Rick Shriver; inset illustration by Jillian Flaherty
Back Cover Photo: Jean Naylor Finley
Naylor Portrait: Courtesy of the Morgan County Historical Society

The Misadventures of Marjory

by

James Ball Naylor

Edited and annotated

by

Theresa Marie Flaherty

ISBN-13: 978-0-9832342-3-4

Cover Design: Michael Flaherty

www.TurasPublishing.com

Tribute Series

The Misadventures of Marjory
is the fourth book in a Tribute Series
to James Ball Naylor

TURAS
PUBLISHING

Acknowledgements

Preparing this fourth book in a Tribute Series to Dr. Naylor has been a continuation of the labor of love that began for me with Naylor's biography, *The Final Test – A Biography of James Ball Naylor*, a project initially started more than forty years ago under the guidance of my mentor, D.W. Garber, an Ohio historian.

I have been inspired to continue bringing Naylor's works to light by the warmth and acceptance I received from his family, some of whom I had the opportunity to meet in person or by telephone after the release of the biography, including: Richard Robison of Zanesville, Ohio, a grandson, who attended the unveiling of the biography at the Morgan County Historical Society in McConnelsville, Ohio; Doug Weisman, who bears an amazing resemblance to his great-grandfather; Meg Barry and her daughter Kate; Jenny Natali and her brother Curtis; David Heald, his sisters Nancy Hayward and Gail Barker; and Lyn Mayewski, Betty Lennon, Nancy Quaschnick, Tom Richardson, and Gary Weisman.

Additionally, my family serves as a continual source of encouragement. My husband, Gerry, is my most enthusiastic fan and toughest taskmaster. As the man behind Turas Publishing, his unfailing support keeps me going. Our daughter, Vicki Flaherty, provides invaluable editorial assistance with a positive attitude and gentle approach. Our son, Michael Flaherty, transformed a simple book cover idea into a distinctive design for the biography, which serves as the foundation for all of the Tribute Series covers. Our granddaughter, Jillian Flaherty, provided the cover illustration of Marjory.

Special thanks go to Rick Shriver for the use of the photograph for the cover and for sharing so many wonderful contemporary photographs of Naylor's beloved Morgan County. Thanks also to the many folks in Ohio for their help and encouragement, especially to Sara Hurst, Greg and Ellen Hill, Blythe Shubert, Linda Showalter, Dr. Douglas Anderson, Betty White, Dr. James Mason, and Robert and Jacqueline Carter.

Table of Contents

Introduction

The Misadventures of Marjory is dramatically different than any of James Ball Naylor's previous novels in subject, tone, and characterization. The main character, Marjory Dawes, is a young woman about the age as his daughter, Olive Nance, at the time he wrote the book. The story was inspired by his eldest daughter and her circumstances. In May 1907, Olive went away to college and was gone for six months. In his diary, Naylor wrote: "Took Olive to Zanesville, to enter business college. Seventeen years old—and leaving the nest! Ah, so it must be; but it hurts! My baby girl, my comrade! May the fates be kind to her and send her back to her father and mother to still love and comfort them." Writing the book appears to be Naylor's way of coping with his profound loss at Olive's being away.

The story is a romance cleverly peppered with humor and narrated by the delightful and controversial Marjory. While Naylor used first person narration with male characters in his previous two novels, The Kentuckian and The Scalwags, this is his first foray into narration by a female character. Naylor artfully reveals Marjory's attitudes and personality through what she says and thinks and especially in how she expresses herself. Twenty years of marriage and the presence of five daughters in his household no doubt contributed to his ability to aptly interpret a young woman's feelings, opinions, and ideas. Another contributing factor to his deep appreciation for a feminine perspective were his travels with Olive and her sister Nettie Lucile around Ohio when he and the two girls were under contract with the Lycium Bureau of Columbus. The girls sang and played musical instruments, performed solos, provided musical backgrounds for his talks, and gave readings of poems he wrote for them.

The use of Dawes as the main character's last name was a tribute to his warm friendship with Rufus R. and Charles Dawes. Charles served as vice president under Calvin Coolidge, and Rufus became a national banker and industrialist and president of the Century of Progress Exposition in Chicago for the 1933 World's Fair. Naylor tutored the brothers at Marietta Academy when he attended it for five months in 1879 and remained life-long friends with the Dawes brothers.

In 1908, the year that The Misadventures of Marjory was published, Naylor was at the height of his popularity. He was amazingly productive in all sorts of ventures, all while maintaining a medical practice. A short story, A Counterfeit Coin, appeared in the Ohio Magazine that year. A novel, The Scalawags, and a children's book, The Little Green Goblin, were published just the year before, as well as a lengthy book of poetry, Songs From the Heart of Things and two versions of another book of poetry, Old Home Week. His political sketches in verse, Who's You in Ohio, appeared in Ohio newspapers during that time as well, and he made frequent appearances, performing as an entertainer and speaker.

The Misadventures of Marjory is one of his most entertaining novels; it is definitely a favorite of mine.

Theresa Marie Flaherty

Note: Because this story was written more than one hundred years ago, sometimes obscure words occur that are difficult to decipher or an otherwise familiar word may refer to an alternate or no longer relevant meaning. Footnotes identifying such words and their intended meanings are included for the reader's benefit.

Foreword

There is no treatise erudite
    On Martian astronomy,
No essay learned teaching right
    Political economy;
It does not deal, for woe or weal
    With socialist histology,
Nor does it show, or claim to know
    The tenets of psychology.
In short, it is no classic score
    Of faultless style and diction,
Parading scientific lore—
    All in the guise of fiction.

A modest tale, its meager plot
    Is noways allegorical;
It does not lay a claim—God wot!—
    To characters historical.
It has no art to search the heart
    Of every sect fanatical,
Nor feels the need to frame a creed
    From scriptures emblematical.
In fact, the author did not look
    Through musty tomes and hoary,
To glean material for his book—
    It's just a little story.

It does not treat, in any way,
    Of themes and things political;
And may not please—I blush to say!—
    The critics hyper-critical
It does not claim the right to name
    Itself a modern novel,
Nor beg the fate to circulate
    From mansion-house to hovel.
In truth, the author had no thought
    Of future fame or glory;
He simply sat him down and wrought
    A story—just a story.

L'Envoi

Dear Reader, let me just repeat,
    Sans further inventory:
This is no literary treat—
    'Tis but a little story!

JAMES BALL NAYLOR

Chapter 1

WELL, dear old chum and room-mate,—Sweet Nell of old Oberlin!—agreeable to promise given so long ago, I'm writing you of all and sundry that has befallen me since our tearful farewell and sobbing avowal of eternal friendship and fond remembrance; and, knowing myself as I do—knowing my proneness to drivel, to make much of small and unimportant incidents, I must warn you in advance that if you attempt to read this bulky communication at one sitting, you'll probably fall asleep over it,—far in the night,—and miss chapel next morning.

But if you do, Nell Adams, it'll be worth while—indeed I believe it will!

Those were dear days—dear dead days now!—when you were a sophomore in college proper and I was a senior in business-school; when we had rooms together at Mrs. Fram's—sweet motherly old thing!—and took meals at one of the "feed-'alls;" when we dreamed our dreams and planned our plans—and had a royal good time, on the whole, seven days out of the week; when the sun was always shining—in our eyes, and the birds were always singing—in our hearts.

Speaking of our dreams, Sweet Nell, of course you haven't forgotten how you used to laugh me to scorn and point the finger of derision at me because my pet dream, my highest and fondest ambition, was to return to sleepy, Quakerish old Chesterville, the village of my nativity, and live with Aunt Dodo and help Jack run the general store. Of course you haven't forgot! I can hear you right now—this very moment, saying as you used to say so frequently:

1

"Marjory Dawes, you're a goose—a precious little goose! The bare idea of you thinking you'll be content to bury yourself alive in that musty graveyard of a town—after having a taste of real life! The mere thought is preposterous. Child, you don't know yourself; it's time you were forming an acquaintance with your ego. Nay, nay! Mad Marjory! You, the diminutive, the petite,—you of the fluffy brown hair and hazel orbs, were not born for the simple life; you were born for adventure, for conquest and spoils—for a mad and merry career. And—unconsciously, I'll suppose for the sake of argument—you desire it, you want it; and fate has willed that you should have it. I know; I know!"

And then you'd go on and recite in proof of your assertions, Nell, a list of all the madcap pranks and wild escapades I had been guilty of during my stay at Oberlin. I'd bear with you patiently, you remember—indeed I'd have you remember that!—smile complacently, albeit a little superiorly, shudder deliciously at thought that you might be right, possibly, in your predictions; and resolve to outwit fate—if you were right—and end my days in drowsy old Chesterville, with Aunt Dodo and Jack. But rarely did I cry out against the charges you made against my character as a decorous and circumspect young woman; and then it was simply to call your attention to the fact that you had been my first aide, my prime abettor, in every foolish frolic I had indulged in, and that you were much more likely than I to become a fascinating adventuress—much more likely to become an adventuress, in fact, than a blue-goggled blue-stocking, as you proudly anticipated and hoped.

If you're still of the notion, however, dear Nell, that your forte and fate is literature, here's material for your first story.

Well, the months sped—they have the sad habit of doing that very thing, I've noticed!—and we were delightfully, irresponsibly, irrationally happy; happy in spite of tiresome exams and galling restrictions upon our liberties. For we loved each other, chum mine, and were blissfully content in the camaraderie that was ours.

Then—like the slap of a wet towel in the face—came that letter from Jack; from Jack, mein grosser bruder—saying that he was to be married. To whom he did not say—nor when it was to be; it was just like the thickwitted fellow to neglect to mention such very important details. Jack to be married! Jack, who was twenty years older than I—and big and poky and bald; who was everything to me and nothing to any other woman on earth—excepting Aunt Dodo, and she didn't count; who had protected me, provided for me, given me my schooling, humored me and coddled me and spoiled me, and lorded it over me—ever since our parents' death, when I was a tiny tot of two. Jack to take unto himself a wife!—Jack Dawes, whom I had looked upon as the very best man in all the wide world—but an impossible husband to any woman under any sun or set of circumstances; whom I had considered a little lower than the angels but far above ordinary mortals—so far above that the association of his name with the mere thought of marriage smacked of sacrilege. Jack was to be married! And what of my blissful visions of the simple life? Gone like frost-palaces upon a sunlit window! Could I go back home to live with Aunt Dodo and Jack and help him run the store? No! Another woman would have a place in his house and his heart; and there would be no cozy corner for me. Could I endure the sight of Jack—overgrown, unsentimental Jack!—spooning and mooning with an old-maidish wife? No!—several times no! I just knew I couldn't and I just knew I wouldn't. But what was I to do; what could I do?

Though I write of the matter in a semi-humorous way to-day, Nell, you will readily recall that I was quite heartsick over it at the time; that I bowed my queenly head,—think of bowing a queenly head that at best is only five-feet-two from the floor!—and wept, boohooed right out loud; that you tempted me, my beautiful, with hunks of fudge and chunks of toffee—but that I refused to be comforted.

Then, suddenly,—I can see you smiling!— I came out of the depths of my misery; I got mad—furious. I got up and walked the floor, and stamped—and said naughty things under my breath; and straightway resolved to set out for home, to cut the remaining few weeks of the school-year, to forego the reward of a blue-ribboned diploma, to save Jack—dear, blundering, innocent, Jack!—from the smiles and wiles of the arch temptress, whoever she might be, and to save unto myself my dream of a simple and blissful life.

That night you helped me to pack, Nell—and wasted a deal of sympathy and nervous energy upon me, in a vain attempt to comfort me and coax me into a semblance of resigned cheerfulness; and the next morning I was off on the train, bound for my native heath— waving you a tearful farewell from the car window.

And now, old chum, to speed away from the places and things you do know and get to the scenes and events you don't know, I'll state briefly that late in the afternoon I arrived at Stockton, the near- est station to Chesterville—five miles away, across the hills. While waiting for the lumbering hack—that was to bear me to my destina- tion—to get ready to start, I went to the village hostlery, bathed and brushed away all traces of grief and marks of travel, and got a warm supper—thus fortifying myself for the ordeal I knew was before me.

An hour later the clumsy, screaky old hack had left Stockton behind and was bowling and bumping over the gullied roads, up one hill and down another. The sun sank from sight; the evening shadows gathered. I was the only passenger. The driver was old and partially deaf, and uncommunicative; and I was lonely—un- speakably lonely, in a literal sense, Nell. At the top of a red-clay hill I leaned out of the vehicle and looked far ahead and to the west. There shone the twinkling lights of Chesterville, a mile away across the deep valley of Wolf creek; and you can imagine how I felt at that moment—I know you can. I was glad and sorry, happy and miserable; eager to get home, yet anxious over what the result of my home-coming might be.

Down another long hill, through a covered wooden bridge spanning the placid stream, up the opposite slope—turning and zig- zagging, and mounting ever higher and higher, we rolled; and then came the summit—and the suburbs of the village. It was quite dark by this time. I requested the driver—whom I knew, and who knew me—to drive first to my home, and warned him to say nothing of my arrival. I felt sure Jack would be down at the store, and I desired to see Aunt Dodo alone and learn the true status of affairs before I encountered my deluded brother.

"Whoa—ho-ho!" bellowed the driver, loud enough to apprise

the whole neighborhood of my advent, had the inhabitants been on the quivive[1]. The dolt! I could have killed him without compunction or chloroform, Nell. After I had warned him that I didn't want anyone to learn of my arrival, too! Then, not content with the noise he had already made, he jammed down the brake with a rattling bang and surged back upon the lines, grunting and muttering like the wild man in a side-show. And the most-provoking thing about the whole procedure was that it was wholly unnecessary; the tired horses had already come to a stop, of their own accord.

But how good—how deliciously, enchantingly good!—the old frame house looked to me, homesick, heartsick, as I was! The front hall door stood invitingly open; and a warm red light was streaming from the sitting-room windows. I had difficulty in swallowing the lump in my throat; and was so blinded by the moisture in my eyes that I stumbled and almost fell as I alighted from the vehicle—my hands and arms full of skirts and parcels.

"Carry my trunk into the hall, Andy," I said crossly to the driver; "and get away from the front of the house as quickly as you can. And—for pity's sake!—remember what I said: don't tell anybody I've come home."

I stood upon the broad flag step until the dark hulk of the hack disappeared in the darker shadows down the long street. The smell of moist earth, tender grass and fresh-blown apple-blossoms greeted me; the open portal of my home stood ready to enfold me. But, oh, I was wretched—so wretched! At last I entered the hall, moved slowly to the sitting-room door and stealthily pushed it open. No one was in sight; but I heard Aunt Dodo pottering around in the kitchen beyond. Her easy chair and small work-table stood near a front window; her sewing lay upon the floor near.

"Dear old Aunty!" I murmured, gulping hard at the lump in my throat. Then I managed to call aloud, plaintively, breathlessly:

"Aunt Dodo!"

The clatter of dishes instantly ceased, and was immediately followed by the sound of shuffling footsteps crossing the kitchen floor; and there she stood in the doorway, surprise, wonder,

---

1 Qui vive - On the alert or lookout

consternation—almost, upon her wrinkled countenance.

"Marjory Dawes!" she exclaimed, tragically throwing up her hands.

"Aunt Dodo!" I screeched hysterically, in return.

I dropped my parcels, flew to her and flung my arms around her neck, hiding my face upon her bosom; and she enfolded me, drew me to her portly person and rocked to and fro with me, convulsive respirations heaving her chest.

And, oh, I was sad and happy at one and the same time! At that moment I felt that though Jack—dear, stalwart, foolish Jack!—and all the rest of the world might desert me, Aunt Dodo would prove stanch and steadfast; that I could rely upon her to see things as I saw them, could depend upon her to aid me in bringing the perverse and provoking Jack to a sense of the true proportion of things—of the eternal fitness of things. But await the sequel, my Nell—await the sequel!

Aunt Dodo disengaged herself from my clinging embrace, gently pushed me from her, and murmured slowly, huskily, in awesome tones:

"Marjory Dawes! You home!"

"You can see for yourself, Auntie," I giggled, wiping the tears from my eyes and weakly dropping into a chair.

"You sick?" she inquired—with well-assumed solicitude.

But I was convinced from the way she eyed me and nervously patted and smoothed her gingham apron, that she was not as ignorant of the cause of my untimely home-coming as she would have me believe; in fact, I began to suspect that she had rather expected me.

"Jest git homesick?" was her next question.

"No," I made answer.

"Y'r school ain't out, is it?"

I shook my head, looking her through.

"Well, you didn't git done—didn't graduate 'fore the rest, I s'pose, did you?"

Again I shook my head, still gazing at her steadily.

She grew so uneasy under my prolonged stare, that she sought the depths of her favorite chair and vigorously began to fan herself with her apron.

But she pursued resolutely: "What brung you home, then?"

"The train and hack, Auntie."

"Humph!" she snorted, but smiling in spite of herself. "Don't try to be smart, Marjory; you know what I mean."

"And you know what brought me home, Aunt Dodo."

"What?" she persisted.

"Jack's letter, of course."

He wrote you that—that—"

"Yes, he did; you know he did."

"W'y, poor child, you needn't 'ave come home on that account," she replied smoothly, complacently; "Jack's gittin' 'long first rate, makin' the arrangements fer his—his weddin'."

"Indeed!" I fleered[2] scornfully.

Then we sat and looked at each other for several seconds; and I realized, Nell—with a sickening sinking of the heart—that I was to get neither sympathy nor support from Aunt Dodo.

The strained silence grew embarrassing, oppressive. Aunt Dodo fidgeted a moment, then remarked tentatively:

"You hain't had no supper, of course, Marjory."

"Yes, I have."

"You have? Where'd you git it?"

I told her.

"Well, won't you have a cup o' tea, anyhow?"

I declined, and asked: "Where's Jack?"

"Down to the store, I s'pose. He'll be mighty surprised to find you home; an' I don't b'lieve he'll more 'n half like it."

"I don't care whether he likes it or not," I declared stoutly, recklessly; "I've come home to keep him from making a fool of himself."

"You're talkin' 'bout his gittin' married?" Aunt Dodo inquired, smiling frostily—her brows lifted.

"Yes, I am. Now, who's—who's the—the—"

"Who's the woman he's goin' to marry?"

"Yes," I snapped, setting my jaws.

---

2 Fleer - to laugh or grimace in a coarse derisive manner

"W'y, didn't he tell you her name—in his letter?"

"No, he didn't."

"Well, if that ain't jest like a man!"—And Aunt Dodo chuckled asthmatically, her fat sides shaking—"The idee of writin' his own sister that he was goin' to git married, an' never sayin' who he was goin' to git married to! I don't wonder at y'r comin' home—I don't a bit; an' I don't know as I blame you, neither. I know jest how you felt; you was worried to death fer fear he was takin' up with some purty-faced good-fer-nothin'—as so many men does nowadays. But you needn't 'ave been c'ncerned, Marjie; he's showed re'l good sense—Jack has, an' made a good choice."

She paused impressively.

"Well?" I cried impatiently, irritably.

"He's goin' to marry Dor'thy Crewe."

"Dorothy Crewe?" I gasped.

Aunt Dodo nodded, looking me straight in the eyes.

"Dorothy Crewe!" I murmured chokingly.

Again Aunt Dodo nodded, gazing straight at me—and through me.

"Humph!" was all I could say.

Then I arose and slowly began to remove my hat and gloves. Dorothy Crewe! A little faded-out, thirty-year-old, namby-pamby, village school-mistress, Nell—think of it! I wanted to laugh, I wanted to cry; and as I couldn't decide which to do first, I took a grip on myself and did neither.

"Surely you can't say nothin' ag'in her—ag'in Dor'thy Crewe?" Aunt Dodo remarked, defiance in tone and manner.

I did not accept her implied challenge—to, her evident disappointment; but stood viciously thrusting a hat-pin through the crown of my hat and biting my lips, for several moments. Then I tossed the unoffending bit of headgear upon the table in the center of the room, and collapsed wearily into my chair.

"Tired?" Aunt Dodo inquired kindly.

"A little," I admitted.

"You'll be wantin' to go to bed purty soon, an' git a good night's rest," she suggested soothingly. "I'll tell Jack you've come; an' you can see him in the mornin'. He'll understand you're wore out, an' won't think nothin' of y'r not stayin' up to meet him. I'll go up an' fix y'r bed right now—this minute."

She arose to leave the room; but I waved her back into her chair.

"I'm not so nearly exhausted as all that, Aunt Dodo," I said, yawning to hide the smile upon my face—her eagerness to bundle me off to bed, to keep me from pouncing upon Jack, was so patent; "and I want to talk further about—about things. So Jack thinks of marrying Dorothy Crewe, eh?"

"Thinks of marryin' her, Marjory?" Aunt Dodo returned irritably. "W'y, he's goin' to marry her, jest as soon's her school's out— which is sometime 'bout the last o' this month 'r the first o' next. I b'lieve he did mention somethin' to me 'bout settin' the weddin' fer the last o' June—so's you'd be sure to be at home. But seein' you're here now, maybe they'll set it fer a sooner date."

"They needn't consider my whereabouts or convenience," I remarked acidly; "I shan't be present."

"You won't be present?" exclaimed Aunt Dodo, her eyes open wide.

"No, I won't," I said decidedly.

"Why?"

I kept silent.

"You hain't got nothin' ag'in Dor'thy, you said, didn't you?"

Still I maintained a determined silence.

"Marjory Dawes, what's the matter of you, anyhow?"

And then I couldn't stay upon earth any longer, Nell; I went up in the air like a rocket—fizzing, sputtering, scintillating. Such a display of verbal pyrotechnics[3] Auntie Dodo had never before witnessed, I venture. Think of me, Sweet Nell—picture me out in your mind! Me, Marjory Dawes—five-feet-two, striding the stage and playing the tragedienne![4] And here's some—a few of the things I said:

"What's the matter!"—with withering scorn—"You can ask such a question, Aunt Dodo? This is what's the matter: Dorothy

---

3 Pyrotechnics - a fireworks display
4 Tragedienne - an actress who plays tragic roles

Crewe can make a fool of Jack; the two of them can make a fool of you; but all of you together can't make a fool of me! So there! What's the matter, indeed! The idea of Jack—dear big-hearted, ugly, old Jack!—getting married! And to such a little mummified, fish-eyed creature! Bah! Auntie Dodo! Bah!—Although I was so wrought up, so tragic in the intensity of my feeling and expression, I was closely observing the effect of my words and actions upon my very select audience; and I noticed that her seamed and ancient visage[5] was reflecting various and conflicting emotions. Amusement, admiration, wonder—I read there; then something like quick surprise and sudden consternation. I noticed, too, that now she appeared to be looking past me into fathomless space, instead of at me; and I could not understand. But I went on recklessly:—" Jack marry Dorothy Crewe—and without consulting me! Well, he won't! I'll not have it; I'll—"

A slight noise behind me—like a snort of smothered laughter— attracted my attention. I threw a glance over my shoulder. There stood Jack in the doorway, grinning like an inspired wooden Indian!

---

5 Visage - a person's facial expression

Chapter 2

JACK continued his nasty grin; Aunt Dodo chuckled her infinite amusement. Tears of anger and mortification came into my eyes; but I blinked them back, turned and walked to the window and stood peering out into the darkness—saying never a word.

Jack came over and tried to put his arm around me; but I pettishly drew away from him.

"Why, what's the matter, Marjory?" he said in a hurt tone. "Aren't you going to kiss me?"

"No, I'm not!" I blurted out crossly, moving farther away from him, but so blinded by my tears that I was in danger of bumping into the furniture—and so miserable I did not care if I did.

"Why aren't you going to kiss me, Marjory?"—succeeding in getting his arm around my waist, and drawing me to him.

"Because—because you made fun—fun of me Jack; and—"

And then my face was pressed against his shoulder; and I was sobbing heart-brokenly.

He dropped back into a rocking-chair and pulled me down upon his lap; and for several minutes sat and rocked me, smoothing my tousled tresses and patting my cheek—as one would soothe a fretful child. And what else was I, Nell mine—but a spoiled child grieving over a broken toy? But, oh, it was good to have a good cry—especially in Jack's arms! And hope effulgent[1] hope, and wild, ecstatic joy came into my heart!

"Jack," I murmured at last, lifting my head and fixing my eyes upon his homely face, "you're not going to—to get married, are you? Say you're not—please do!"

---

1 Effulgent - radiant splendor

"Don't you want me to get married, little girl?" he questioned, in a tone of infinite kindness.

"Of course I don't, Jack."

"And that's what brought you home—my writing you that I thought of getting married?"

"Why, certainly."

"But why don't you want me to marry, Marjory?"

"Why!"—I felt my anger rising; and I know the red must have flared up in my cheeks, for Jack smilingly, deprecatingly[2] shook his head at me.—"Why! Jack, you're as unreasonable as Aunt Dodo. I don't want you to marry because—because—oh, for so many reasons! And—"

"No, you hain't got no reason, Marjie," Aunt Dodo broke in on me, "why Jack shouldn't git married—if he wants to; but the cause of y'r objections—an' the only cause—is y'r own selfishness."—Wasn't that mean—wasn't that awful, Nell? And from Aunt Dodo, who had always humored me and taken my side in every difference of opinion between Jack and me, heretofore! I was shocked beyond measure; the solid earth seemed crumbling from beneath my feet!— "You're jest like I was when my father married his second wife; an' you're actin' jest as foolish as I did then. Jack's alluz petted you an' spoiled you, an' let you boss over him; an' now you can't bear the thought o' him havin' any other boss—you want to keep him all to y'rself. But he's old enough to know his own business; an'—goodness knows!—he's old enough to git married. The thing fer you to do is to jest step aside an' let him do as he pleases. You'll be wantin' to git married y'rself, one o' these days; an' you won't want him objectin' then. That's all I've got to say; an' I guess I'll go an' finish puttin' the dishes in the cupboard, then fix y'r room fer you an' go to bed."

I sat in speechless wonder—and horror, until Aunt Dodo was out of the room and the door was closed. Then I hastily scrambled from Jack's lap, smoothed down my skirts and flounced into a chair, and exclaimed:

"Well, I'll declare! Jack Dawes, I almost hate her!"

2 Deprecatingly - expressing disapproval

"Don't talk like that, Marjie!" he said coaxingly. "Aunt Dodo means all right—you know that; and she is all right. That is," he hastened to add— "I don't mean she's all right when she says you're spoiled and selfish; I know you better than to think that of you. But she's all right about me being old enough to—to—"

"Old enough to know your own business, old enough to get married—old enough to make a fool of yourself," I sneered.

"Well, yes," Jack returned, nodding and smiling inanely.

"Jack, I tell you I almost hate her," I snapped spitefully; "I do hate her—I do! So there!"

"Tut—tut!" he replied gravely, sternly, pulling agitatedly at his stubby straw-colored mustache. "You mustn't talk so, Marjory; you'll be sorry when you've had time to consider, and—"

"I won't, Jack!"

"Yes, you will."

"I say I won't! Now!"

"Aunt Dodo has been very good to us all these years, little girl."

"I don't care."

"And she loves you."

"She doesn't; and I don't care if she does."

"Why, Marjory Dawes!"

I could see that my perversity hurt him; and that hurt me. But I didn't care, Nell; I had been hurt so much, a little more didn't matter—and I wanted to hurt somebody. So I reiterated vixenishly:

"I hate her, Jack; I don't care what you think of me."

The merest semblance of a smile quivered the corners of his wide mouth, as he murmured half-pathetically:

"I guess you do hate her, little girl. And why? Just because she holds I've a right to marry—if I so desire?"

I nodded, angrily tapping the carpet with the toe of my swinging foot.

"Well, haven't I the right?"

"Oh, I suppose you have the right, Jack—if you've so little sense as to have the desire!"

"You consider me foolish to think of marrying?"

"Yes, I do."

"Why? I'm old enough—eh?"

"Old enough!" I fleered scornfully. "You're too old."

"I'm only thirty-nine, Marjie."

"Only thirty-nine!" I cried aghast. " Jack Dawes, are you already in your dotage—not to realize that you're getting old, when you'll be forty your next birthday? Why, your hair's turning gray—what little you've got left; and your face is wrinkled; and—and you're old."

He smiled—actually smiled, very complacently, I thought.

"You offer my age as a reason why I shouldn't enter into wedlock, Marjory?" he inquired.

"To be sure I do," I made reply.

"Well," he drawled provokingly, "I can't look upon that reason as valid, seeing Miss Crewe, the young lady who has honored my suit—and who is the most-interested party, offers no objections to my age."

"Miss Crewe—a young lady!" I sneered. "Jack, she's every day of thirty."

" And I don't object to her age," he grinned.

"You're both fools!" I cried snappishly.

"Perhaps," he laughed; "but we're happy in our mutual foolishness, and have no desire to be saved from our plight."

Apparently I was not winning my big brother from the error of his ways—not swiftly, at any rate. I must try another procedure.

"Jack," I asked after a moment's thought, "why did you send me away to business college?"

"Why did I send you away to business college?"—with a perplexed stare.

"Yes."

"Why, to fit you for office work—that you might the better assist me in the store and help me in running my business, of course."

"That was your idea—your intention?"

"Certainly. But what are you driving at, Marjory—what prompts you to ask such a question? "

Unheeding his query, I continued: "And you meant for me to come home and live with Aunt Dodo and you, and help to look after your business?"

"I meant you to graduate first—not to come home as you have, Marjory."

"I know. But you meant the other, too?"

"About your living with me and helping me in the store?"

"Yes."

"Why, of course."

His perplexity was evident—and amusing.

"What led you to change your plans, Jack?" I asked innocently.

"Change my plans?"

"Yes."

"I haven't. I still desire and expect you to live with me—with us, and help me that is, us—in the store. I won't send you back to graduate—as you've seen fit to come home without consulting me; but you've probably learned all that's needful—a diploma of itself amounts to little. No, I haven't changed my plans in a single particular, Marjory; my marriage will make no difference, whatever."

"Jack, my brother," I said with all the earnestness and solemnity at my command, "it will make all the difference in the world."

"What do you mean?"—quickly, concernedly.

"I can't stay here, Jack—if you marry."

"You can't?"

"I can't——and won't."

"Why?"

"Oh, Jack, how can you ask such a question!"—My voice was tremulous with emotion, my lips were quivering and ever-ready tears were in my eyes. Really, Sweet Nell, I felt all I expressed; and Jack must have realized the fact, for his face reflected the momentary compassion he felt.—"Do you think I can live in this house with her—work in the store with her? After all you've been to me, Jack—father, mother, brother, everything, do you think I can stand it to see you making over her, and—and neglecting me? There's no use talking, I can't—I can't! And, oh, Jack, I've dreamed of the good times we were going to have—just you and I! You'll break my heart, if you get married!"

He shrugged his round shoulders, and screwed his rugged features into a serio-comic expression.

"There'll always be room in my heart and my home for you, little sister," he muttered huskily.

"No, there won't, Jack—no, there won't; I'll be crowded out! And I—"

He raised his hand, commanding me to stop; and the look upon his face, rather than his gesture, awed me to silence.

"Marjory," he said hoarsely, "you must not—you shall not talk that way! You hurt me. I've tried hard to do my duty by you; and I'll continue to try. I love you just as I've always loved you; and I'll always love you just as I do to-night. But, as you well say, I'm getting up in years; and, if I'm ever going to marry, it's time I should be doing it. You'll get married some day,"—I tried to offer a word of dissent, but he shut me off with a frown and a shake of his head.— "Aunt Dodo will die, and then—if I have no wife—I'll be left all alone. I can't bear the thought of the prospect. No, little sister, my marriage won't make any difference in our affairs; you'll have a home with Dorothy and Aunt Dodo and me, and a place in the store. Be reasonable, now—won't you?"

"Jack, I can't!"

"You can't be reasonable?"—half smiling.

"No—no!"—irritably.—"I can't stay here, if you marry. Promise me that you'll give it up, Jack—promise me you won't get married; please—please do!"

"I can't promise anything like that, sister."

"Why?"—frantically.—"Why can't you—why can't you?"

"Because I must keep the promise I've made to Dorothy—Miss Crewe."

"Then you think more of her than you do of me,"—angrily.

" Now, Marjory!"—reproachfully.

"Oh, you do!"

"Well,"— slowly and stubbornly,— "you'll have to think what you please, I suppose. However, I'm going to marry Dorothy Crewe."

"You are!"—coldly.

"I am!"—frigidly.

"That's final, is it, Jack Dawes?"

"It is, Marjory Dawes."

We sat unwaveringly, unflinchingly gazing straight into each other's eyes. I heard Aunt Dodo ascending the back stairs. Sore with defeat and disappointment, I said at last:

"Then, I'm going away—to-morrow."

"Going away—where?" Jack replied.

"To some city."

"'What for?"

"To get a position."

"Oh!"

"Yes, sir."

"Won't you wait till after my wedding?"

"No, I won't."

"Indeed?"

"Indeed!"

"People will talk, Marjory."

"I don't care; I won't be here to know it."

"But I will."

"That's your business; and you've been at some pains to make clear to me that you're old enough to look after your own affairs." I saw him wince; and, emboldened, I went on:—"And, I flatter myself, I'm old enough to look after mine."

"But you're not."

I started, dimly divining what was coming.

"What do you mean?" I demanded with dignity.—And you know what the word dignity means when applied to my behavior, Nell.

Jack answered composedly: "I mean just this, Marjory—my misguided little sister, you're not going away from this town to-morrow—nor till after I'm married; and you're not going away to any city to hunt work, at any time. Let's have a plain, blunt and final understanding, right now. I sent you away to business college to fit you to assist me in the store; and I need you—and I'm going to keep you. When I've had a fair return from my investment,—say several years from now,—if you don't marry in the meantime, and then desire to go out into the big world to battle alone, you can go. But now you're too young, too inexperienced, too erratic—and entirely too good-looking."—Too good-looking! Think of unromantic, matter-of-fact old Jack saying that! Nell, he almost won me over—with his blarney! "You'll get into trouble. So I don't care to discuss the matter further, Marjory; you can't go."

"That's your decision, eh?"—sneeringly.

"It is,"—flatly.

"Well, it isn't mine."

"Yours cuts no figure."

"What!"

"I mean what I say, Marjie."

"Jack Dawes!"—my voice vibrating with mingled antagonistic emotions.

He nodded stubbornly.

"You mean that you'll—you'll keep me from going—against my will?"

"If necessary—yes."

"Jack, surely—surely you don't mean that!"

"I do."

"Jack Dawes, you're a brute!"

"Call me anything you please, little girl; it's the reward I get for all I've done for you—I suppose."

"I don't mean that, Jack; but you are acting mean—shabby, so you are."

"No doubt you think so."

I saw that he was set, Nell; and when an easy-going, poky fellow like Jack gets set he's "sot."[3] I realized that he was not to be moved by arguments or appeals a bit more than a meeting-house is to be moved by one's breath. But I was not ready to give up, I had no intention of relinquishing my purpose; and I thought it no more than fair to so apprise him.

"You're not my guardian, Jack," I pouted.

"I am—self-appointed," he declared complacently.

"You're not; and I'll do as I please."

---

3 Sot - a habitual drunkard

"You'll do as pleases me—in this, Marjory."

"I won't; I'm of legal age."

He simply smiled a mean, sarcastic smile.

"Do you mean to violate the law, Jack Dawes, by holding me here against my will?"

"You'll find that I'm a law and gospel unto myself; in this case, Miss Marjie."

Did you ever, Nell Adams! Jack Dawes—Jack, that I had always wound around my little finger, acting like that! From that moment I lost all feeling against Dorothy Crewe,—poor, wishy-washy little thing—and profoundly pitied her.

Exasperated beyond endurance by Jack's pigheadedness, I cried tauntingly:

"Oh, yes, you'll keep me from going! How will you do it—I'd like to know? How will you do it? Will you keep me a prisoner?"

"Prisoner is a harsh word," he said; and he had the ill manners to chuckle.

"Yes, it is," I assented readily and feelingly.

"But," he continued heartlessly, "I'll keep you prisoner, in a sense, till you come to reason and promise me to abandon your childish notion of running away. I'll grant you the freedom of the village, but I'll see that you don't leave its precincts."

"Oh, you will!" I cried hotly.

"Yes, I will," he replied coldly.

"But if I give you my promise to stay here and be your meek and obedient little underling—what then?"

A spasm of pain twitched his features—Jack's dear old features, Nell; my words cut him I knew. For the moment I pitied him—pitied him that he was such an obstinate dolt.

"If you promise what I desire, Marjory," he made answer to my question, "you may come and go at will; I've always found you honorable—you always keep your promise."

"Which is commendable—and rare, Mr. Dawes," I laughed bitterly; "and far more than some persons do."—Again he winced, and again I felt a grain of pity for the big stupid fellow; but I concluded: "And I keep my resolves, too; don't forget that."

"And?" he questioned, lifting his shaggy brows.

"And I've resolved to leave Chesterville to-morrow—never to return."

"Very well; I'll see that you don't."

"Very well; I'll see that I do!"

Then I arose and swept out of the room, and up the stairs to bed; and far into the after hours of the night I lay tossing and turning, pondering and wondering, scheming and planning.

Chapter 3

WHEN I descended to the dining-room next morning, cross and heavy-eyed, Jack had already eaten his breakfast and gone to the store. Aunt Dodo was sitting in her accustomed place at the table, leisurely and critically sipping her coffee. She accorded me a cheery good-morning; but I merely nodded and murmured a surly response—half aloud.

When I had forced down a few mouthfuls and pushed away from the board, I inquired carelessly, stiffly:

"Did Jack take my trunk up-stairs?"

She gulped down a swallow of coffee, and nodded.

"Where did he put it?"

"In the spare bedroom," she made answer.

"I guess I'll go up and unpack," I remarked, rising.

I meant to slip a few things out of the trunk and into a traveling-bag, thus preparing for hasty flight.

"You can't," Aunt Dodo said; "Jack took the key with him."

"The key?" I murmured, wondering what she could mean. "The key to my trunk? No, he didn't; it's up-stairs in my pocketbook."

"It was the key to the door he took," she explained.

" O-oh!" I ejaculated.

"Yes," she responded.

"He locked up my trunk in the spare bedroom—and took the key?" I cried, aghast; I had not thought Jack capable of such a questionable act.

"He did," Aunt Dodo replied composedly—the merest hint of ignoble joy in her tone and manner.

"Oh!" was all I could say—and restrain myself; I wanted to fly at her—and scratch her.

Dignifiedly, deliberately, I left the dining-room and ascended the back stairs to my own apartment. There I sat down by an open window, to think.

I was more determined than ever, to leave; I did not need to assure myself of that fact. But what was I to do? How was I to get away? I felt that Jack—the pig-headed country bumpkin!—would not relent and let me have my things; he was too cock-sure that he was in the right—too complacent in his smug holiness. And I had nothing but the clothes upon my back—a traveling-suit, and a few toilet articles in my traveling-bag. Then, how was I to get out of town and to the railroad—at Stockton, say? I couldn't go in the hack—of course not! It had gone already! And I couldn't go in it the next day, even; Jack would be on the watch and make a scene, if nothing more. And I didn't want a scene! No doubt, too, he had barred me from procuring a conveyance at the livery stable; he'd be sure to look after that, I reasoned. Of course I could compel him to hand over my trunk to me and let me go in peace, by appealing to a justice. But I didn't want to do that, Nell; I've some sense of propriety and the true proportion of things fit and seemly. I simply desired to get away from the town—quietly, unostentatiously, immediately—and never come back. But how was I to accomplish my purpose? I thought—and thought; and could evolve no plan.

I felt that I must get out in the open air for a walk, to clear my muddled brain; and I put on my hat and went. Wishing to avoid all friends and acquaintances, I took a quiet lane leading to the cemetery at the far edge of the town. But fate was against me. And who do you suppose was the first person I met—just as I was turning into the narrow byway? Dorothy Crewe! She, too, had been out for a morning ramble, and was on her way to the schoolhouse; and as soon as she saw me she was all giggling cordiality and silly effusiveness. I knew at once that Jack had been to see her that very morning, had told her everything, and had prompted her how to act—what to do and say—when she met me.

Well, I let her do the talking, Nell; I simply called her "Miss

Crewe"—and failed to see the hand she offered me. The poor, in-significant little thing! I disliked to act so rude; but I couldn't help it—I just couldn't!

She was so glad to see me; so pleased to know that I was so in-terested in Jack's welfare, as to come right home to learn whom he was to marry; so desirous of being my friend—and sister; so full of happy anticipations of the pleasant times we'd have together—in our home and our store; so—so— so, ad disgustum, ad never-endum!

When I'd had all I could stand, Nell mine, I just walked on and left her—without so much as a word in reply, or a backward glance. I wasn't hurt—I was past being hurt, I guess; but I was mad, mad all through—and wildly resolved to depart from the mean little burg—that very day, and no later!—if I had to crawl on hands and knees. And I wondered how I ever had tolerated the place!

I strolled on out the lane, apathetically pondering whether I had one true friend in the town, who would understand me and sympa-thize with me; and blundering along thus, with my head down, I plumped right into Colonel Wells—Kate Brown's uncle from the South. I had met him before—but hardly so informally. Kate's an or-phan and a seamstress; and her uncle comes up from Georgia every year, to spend the summer with her. He's a gay old gallant, Nell—a hale old beau of sixty, at least—with soft, drawling voice, and long white hair and fierce mustachios and goatee; and he's blessed with all the courtliness and graciousness imaginable.

"Why—why, it's you, Miss Dawes!" he drawled, as we re-bounded from the impact of our encounter. "I beg a thousand par-dons, Miss Dawes—indeed I do. It was very careless of me to run into you; I was dreaming day-dreams—and not observing where I was going. I do indeed beg your pardon."

And there he stood—his broad-brimmed soft hat in his hand, and pressed against his heart—making me a sweeping bow.

I smiled—a little wanly, a little wearily—and replied: "You owe me no apologies, Colonel. I was as much to blame as you, maybe more; I, too, was heedless of my surroundings."

Again he bowed; but slowly shook his handsome white head.

"No—no Miss Dawes," he insisted: "I do owe you apologies. A

gentleman always owes a lady apologies, after a mishap of the kind that has befallen us—no matter whether anybody's to blame."—I despair of conveying, in cold, insensate black-and-white, Nell, any idea of his quaint and kindly manner of speech—any idea, even the faintest, of his soft and seductive intonation of voice; so I won't attempt the impossible. But I know my heart bounded with relief and gladness; I had met a friend—and I knew it.—"I didn't know you were at home; but I'm delighted to find that you are—and to have this gracious opportunity of talking to you. I just came up North last week; and I made inquiry about you as soon as I arrived. You've always been a great favorite of mine, you know, Miss Dawes. But they told me you were away at school, at business college, I believe they said; and I've been quite lonesome—really quite lonesome. I was walking along, moodily and seriously contemplating a return to the South, when fate threw us together. That is, I don't literally mean that. I mean that I'm pleased, delighted beyond measure, to learn you're at home; and now I'll stay here—perfectly contented and happy. But—but, Miss Dawes—Miss Marjory, if I may make so free as to inquire, when did you arrive in town?"

"Last evening," I informed him.

"Ah?" —scraping and smiling.

"Yes," nodding brightly.

"You came rather suddenly—rather unexpectedly, did you not, eh? I was talking to your brother about you yesterday, down at the store, and he said nothing of your immediate return; in fact, I recall that he told me you would not be home till next month."

"Yes," was all I found to say.

The good Colonel absent-mindedly put his hat on his head, interlocked his fingers under his long, full coat tails, and teetered back and forth upon heels and toes as he said stammeringly:

"Miss Dawes—ah—Miss—Miss Marjory, don't think me inquisitive or impertinent, but you came home to help along the wedding, eh? That is, may I presume that—am I to presume that?"

"No, you're not to presume anything of the kind, Colonel Wells," I hastened to say; "I came home to prevent the wedding."

"Oh!' pursing his lips and nodding sagely.

"Yes, I did."

"I see—I see; in fact, I suspected as much. I thought I knew just how you'd feel about the—the unusual affair. And—and you've"—

"And I've failed," I completed.

"I see," again nodding, and pulling vigorously at his fierce-looking mustachios. "I suspected that, too—from your preoccupation, your moodiness. Now, Miss Marjory, you know I'm your sincere friend, don't you?"

"I do, Colonel," I answered earnestly.

"You don't know how pleased I am to hear you say that," he muttered huskily, feelingly. "I know now you'll understand my motive in questioning you, as I've taken the liberty of doing, is not mere idle curiosity; and I know, too, you'll not take offense if I pursue the subject further—eh?"

"Indeed I won't, Colonel."

The dear, ingenuous old man! He little suspected, Sweet Nell, how eager I was to have him know all about my affairs. Already I was elated; already my heart was beating rapturously at thought that—in some way, I knew not how—he might be able to help me out of my quandary.

"Well, then," he continued, "what are you thinking of doing—seeing your brother has determined to make a fool—that is, to marry? Will you stay here—live with him and his new wife?"

" I—will—not!" I declared with emphasis.

"I thought you wouldn't; and I'm gratified to find that I understand you so well. But what are you going to do, Miss Marjory?"

"I'm going to leave."

"Yes?"

" Yes, I am."

"I'm sorry you have to go; yet I rejoice at the manifestation of your independent spirit. So you'll bid a fond goodbye to old Chesterville, eh?"

"Yes, Colonel; that is, if I can get away."

"If you can get away? Why, what's to hinder you, Miss Marjory? "

"Jack."

"Your brother?"

"Yes."

"He—he—"

"He says I shan't go."

"What!"

"He does."

"Oh, my!" cried the Colonel in genuine astonishment—akin to dismay. "Why, what reason can he have for saying you shan't go, Miss Marjory?"

"He says he has provided for me, educated me; and, that now he needs me in the store, I must stay and help him."

"I see,"—nodding gravely; "all very reasonable, but narrow—illiberal[1]. He oughtn't to look upon the case in that way, in my estimation. It's not my province to criticize, of course; but you're of legal age, and should be permitted to choose for yourself—whether you go or stay. No doubt, however, your brother—he's a reasonable fellow, in the main, I think—will see the thing in the right light, when he has had time to think it over; and will give his consent to your going. Eh?"

I shook my head.

"You think not?"—in evident surprise.

"I know he won't," I said positively.

"Indeed!" the Colonel ejaculated, astounded. Then, after a moment's profound reflection: "Well, you can go without his consent. Of course I wouldn't advise you to do that, ordinarily; but you can—if necessary."

"But I can't, Colonel."

"Eh?" —quickly and sharply.

"Jack says I can't leave the town at all, for any purpose, till I've promised him that I won't go to the city, to hunt a position; and he's watching me."

"You don't say!" gasped the Colonel.

I nodded—with difficulty refraining from smiling at the look of mild amazement upon his clean-skinned old face.

"And he's locked up my clothes," I concluded pathetically.

_____

1 Illiberal - lacking culture and refinement

"What!"—perfectly dumbfounded.

"He has, Colonel."

"You're—you're joking, Miss Marjory," he muttered hoarsely; "you don't mean it—that your brother, your own and only brother, is such a—a brute!"

"I mean every word I say, Colonel Wells," I assured him solemnly.

"My—my!" he growled, almost snatching his goatee out root and stem, so savagely did he pull at it, "That's simply awful—awful! In a free country like this, too! Make a virtual prisoner of an innocent young lady; and lock up her clothing; and exercise surveillance over her actions and movements! Oh, it's unchivalric, inhuman, preposterous! I didn't think it of your brother, Miss Dawes—I didn't! Why—what—can he have any other reason for such radical measures; any real reason why you shouldn't come and go at your own sweet will?"

After momentary hesitation, I said coquettishly:

"He says I'm too young, too erratic, to know how to deport myself—to take care of myself; and that I'm too—too pretty, Colonel, and that I'll get into trouble."

His black eyes snapped; a flash of light from his sunny heart irradiated his countenance. Then a smile twitched the corners of his mouth; and he laughed outright.

"I think he's just about half right, Miss Marjory—Miss Dawes. You are most devilish pretty; that part's true. But as for your inability to take care of yourself—well, I'd put up my money on you every time. Get into trouble, eh?"—again laughing.—"It's my opinion it's the other party will get into trouble, when trouble comes. You're fated to play the mischief with some poor chap's heart—and peace of mind. Why—why, if I were twenty years younger,—and the good Lord knows I wish I were; and never so much as right now!—I'd be making love to you myself, this blessed minute!"

"Oh, Colonel!" I tittered bashfully.

But he said it with all the courtesy and sincerity in the world, Nell; and I'm confident he meant it. I almost loved him—the dear, courtly old soul!

However, his words of praise had suggested an idea to me; and I started, and looked all around to note whether we were observed. No one was within sight or hearing.

"Colonel Wells," I breathed softly, drawing close to him and laying a hand caressingly upon his arm, "I must get away from this town, and to-day—to-night, somehow."

He gulped once or twice, nervously screwed his features into a frown that was patently foreign to his nature, and muttered brokenly:

"So—so soon, Miss—Miss Marjie?"

"Yes, Colonel," I answered sweetly, glibly; "the sooner the better. Don't you think so?"

"Undoubtedly—yes, undoubtedly," he replied in a hoarse, agitated tone.

"Besides, Colonel," I went on, looking up into his face and pouting my lips just the least bit, "I've defied Jack and told him I'd leave to-day—in spite of his edict to the contrary; and I mustn't break my word—or my resolve. Now, must I?"

" No, indeed—of course not," he agreed readily. "But—but, Miss Marjory, I—I hardly see how you're to manage it. To be sure you could appeal to a justice, could replevin[2] your things, and—"

"But I can't do that, Colonel Wells."

"No?"

"No, I can't. Think of the talk—the disgrace."

"True—too true."—And he nodded energetically.—"But what can you do?"—in deep and genuine perplexity.

"Can you suggest no way out of my difficulty, Colonel?"

He shook his white head—slowly, dejectedly.

"None at all?" I persisted.

"None at all, I'm sorry to say, Miss Marjie."

"I'm sorry too, Colonel," I murmured, pouting deliciously and snuggling a little toward him. "For I—I thought maybe you—you could help me; you're so—so chivalric and—and—"

"Heaven knows I'd like to help you, Miss Marjie," he cried;

---

2 Replevin - the recovery by a person of goods or chattels claimed to be wrongfully taken or detained upon the person's giving security to try the matter in court and return the goods if defeated in the action

"nothing would please me more. And I would help you, if only I could think of a way. I'd cut off my right arm for you—if it would do any good."

"Colonel," I said coyly, "you can help me, if—if you will."

"Only show me the way," he muttered, tragically striking his chest with his clenched hand.

"You won't think me bold, no matter what—what I propose?" I whispered hesitatingly, smiling archly at him.

"Never! Never, Miss Marjory!"

"Colonel, I want you to—to—oh, how can I tell you! You will think me bold—awful! But I must tell you; I've no one else to appeal to. I—want—you—to—-elope—with—me!"

I don't know how I did it, Nell Adams! I must have been desperate, I suppose; and I blush yet as I think of it—yes, I do. But—oh, Nell!—if you could have seen that dear old chap's face at that moment! I wanted to scream with laughter; I wanted to cry with shame. But there's no use for me to try to describe how he looked; the nearest I can come to it is to say that his countenance was simply a white death-mask with an open mouth and two staring eyes.

"Miss Dawes!—Miss Marjory!—Miss Marjie!" he panted hoarsely. "You want me—to—what?"

"I want you to elope with me, Colonel Wells," I responded shyly, almost choking with suppressed merriment.

He took a step backward and leaned heavily against the paling fence behind him, weakly letting his elbows rest upon its top.

"Miss Marjory," he breathed softly, solemnly, "you don't realize what you're doing—what you're saying, do you?"

"Yes, I do, Colonel," I answered cooly.

"Asking me—literally asking me!—an old fellow of sixty to elope with you! Is that it?"

"It is, Colonel."

"Why, child—child! You've thrown a great temptation in my way; how great you little know. I—I can hardly resist. If my hair wasn't quite so white—but pshaw! You're joking—you're fooling with me!"

"I'm not fooling with you at all, Colonel; I mean just what I say."

"Is it possible that you desire me to elope with you, and—and marry you?"

"No—no!" I cried in mild dismay, glancing fearfully up and down the quiet lane. "You don't understand me. I said nothing of marriage. I want you just to elope with me out of town. Can't you understand?"

"I—I guess I do—now," he faltered. And, Nell, he really looked hurt and disappointed!—"I must be in my dotage already, to have misunderstood you; and I sincerely beg your pardon. You just want me to help you to escape from the unwarranted restraint your brother is exercising over you, just to bear you away from here—to do the eloping act only."

"That's it, Colonel."

"I see; I ought to have seen at once."

"And won't you do it, Colonel; won't you—please?"

His sweet, hale old face brightened.

"What's to be my reward, Miss Marjie?" he questioned, smiling.

"The satisfaction of having performed one more chivalric and noble deed," I answered.

"And it's enough!" he cried. "Miss Marjie, I'll do it."

"You will—sure, Colonel?"

'Dead sure,"—with convincing earnestness.

"Jack will be very angry at you," I suggested to test his courage.

"I won't mind that," he laughed boyishly, recklessly. "It'll be a great lark; and will take me back to other days—when larks were no rare fowl with me. Oh, I'll do it—never fear!"—chuckling; and slapping his thigh. "We'll wake the sleepy old town up for once. But how far do you want me to take you, Miss Marjory?"

"Just to Stockton."

"I see; and that's all right. We must be circumspect—we mustn't carry the joke too far; people might take it in earnest. I don't care for myself; I'd enjoy the reputation of really eloping with you. But they mustn't have a chance to smirch[3] your good name. As I now understand you, you just want me to get a conveyance at the livery stable and drive you to Stockton, to-night. Am I right?"

3 Smirch - to bring discredit or disgrace on

"That's it exactly, Colonel. And I wouldn't ask you to do it—to elope with me,"—giving him one of my most fascinating smiles,— "if any other way of escape were open to me. But I can't hire a conveyance myself; Jack would know—and stop me. I—I don't very much mind asking you, though, Colonel Wells; you're so chivalrous, so kind-hearted. And—and I like you; and know you don't mind."

"Indeed I don't!" the dear old fellow declared stoutly. "We'll have a great lark; and I'll thoroughly enjoy it. What time shall we start?"

"Be at the fork of the road just beyond our house, at nine o'clock. I doubt if I can steal away earlier."

"Very well; I'll be on hand—I won't fail you. But what will you do about your clothing—your trunk, Miss Marjie?"

"I think I can manage in some way to get what I absolutely need, and pack it in a traveling-bag; if I can't, I'll go just as I am. I'll be ready and waiting at nine o'clock."

"All right," he said briskly—very briskly for him, usually so deliberate. "And now we'd better separate; someone might see us together, and say something that would frustrate our plans."

"Goodbye, Colonel—till to-night," I murmured sweetly, giving him my hand.

"Goodbye, Miss Marjory—and good luck to our venture."

I returned to the house, treading upon air, Nell,—my heart, head and heels as light as thistle-downs, I was going to outwit and defeat Jack!

Aunt Dodo looked me over, and remarked slyly:

"Your walk seems to 'ave done you good, Marjie."

"It did," was all the reply I made.

When my brother came to dinner I was all affability—and sweet humility.

"Jack," I remarked, "Aunt Dodo tells me you've locked up my trunk in the spare bedroom."

"I have," he responded.

"You don't expect me to wear this traveling outfit all summer, do you?"

'No."

'Won't you let me have a few of my things—a skirt and a shirt-waist and a number of handkerchiefs, at least?"

"You can have anything and everything, if you'll promise me what I ask, Marjory."

"But I don't want to—yet, Jack." He eyed me keenly. Then he said:

"I guess you're coming around all right, little girl. Aunt Dodo, take the key and get her what she desires."

The result of my diplomacy was that an hour later I had on a clean and cool shirtwaist and skirt, and had my traveling-bag packed with all that was absolutely needful for my flight; and had secreted it in the wood-house at the back of the lot.

Then I contentedly sat down to read—and await the coming of my cavalier.

Chapter 4

IT WAS half-past eight, and dark—quite dark. The sky was over-clouded; a deliciously cool, damp breeze was rustling the tender green leaves of the trees; lightning was flashing and thunder was muttering low down upon the western horizon. Jack had come home from the store and was reading down in the sitting-room, where Aunt Dodo was sewing. I was up in my room, all alone—and without a light, waiting impatiently for the tall clock in the hall to strike nine.

And I was elated, dejected—glad, sorrowful, Nell Adams! Elated over the thought that I had out-witted dear thick-pated old Jack and Aunt Dodo; dejected over the thought that I was leaving them—and everything most dear to me, forever. Heighho! I look back upon it now, and wonder how I had the grit to do it.

Presently the clock gave a premonitory[1] whirr and rumble; then struck one, two, three—nine big lusty strokes. I nervously started to my feet, and walked out into the hall. Without knowledge on the part of Jack or Aunt Dodo, I had hung my hat and linen traveling-wrap out on the back porch. Now I calmly descended the stairs and entered the sitting-room.

"It looks like a storm coming up," I remarked carelessly, walking to a front window and peering out.

"Uh-huh," Jack grunted, without looking up from his paper.

With assumed aimlessness I strolled on to the kitchen and out upon the back porch, and closed the door behind me. There I hastily donned hat and wrap, and stepped out into the yard. A few big drops of rain began to patter down.

Just then I caught the ring of the telephone in the front hall, and

---

1 Premonitory - giving warning

I paused to listen; and immediately I heard Jack's voice in conversation—his tones loud and excited. Instinctively surmising that the phone call at that unusual hour had to do with my contemplated flight, I hastened across the yard and into the black depths of the wood-house, hurriedly caught up my traveling-bag and slipped out into the blacker alley beyond. Suddenly the kitchen door flew open and a stream of light shot out into the darkness. I smiled and gleefully shrugged my shoulders as I silently made my way along the narrow alley-way.

"Marjory! Oh, Marjory!"

It was Jack calling. I hustled on.

"Marjory! Marjory Dawes!"

By this time I was out of the alley, upon a cross street, and hastening toward the main thoroughfare and the fork of the road a hundred yards away.

" Marjory! Oh, Marjory—please answer!"

Jack's pleading call,—so faint, so far-away, so sad!—almost shook my resolution, Sweet Nell. I wanted to answer him; I wanted to go back. Oh, I did—I did! But I set my teeth and held on my way. For some reason I felt—I knew that haste was now necessary, that someone had warned Jack of my contemplated flight, and that he would follow me.

The storm was swiftly approaching. The whole western sky was of inky blackness. The lightning flashed almost incessantly; the thunder boomed nearer and nearer.

And where was the conveyance that was to bear me to larger life and liberty? I paused and peered ahead—anxiously, fearfully. Ah, there it was! A darker smudge upon the somber surface of the highway!

Again I pushed onward, swiftly, breathlessly. A vivid streak of lightning blinded me, confused me; and a ripping peal of thunder nearly deafened me. I could not restrain a little scream of affright[2]. The rain began to pour down in streams and sheets. I trembled, stumbled, staggered—nearly fell. Then a pair of strong arms were thrown around me and I was lifted gently but quickly into a closed

---

2 Affright - sudden and great fear

vehicle.

"We're going to have a romantic night for it, Miss Marjory," chuckled the Colonel, as he climbed in and took a seat at my side.

"Yes," I whispered gaspingly; and was silent.

My companion tucked the waterproofs around me, caught up the lines and spoke softly to the horses; and away we rolled—out of the semi-gloom of the little town and into the gloom impenetrable of the country beyond.

The lightning continued to flash; the thunder continued to rip and reverberate; the rain continued to pour. We conversed but little; the Colonel's attention was devoted to the team and the darkness and difficulties of the road, and mine was devoted to my thoughts. The frequent flashes of lightning showed us the traveled track— and the muddy water running in rivulets. "Whew-whew!" wailed the wind; "swish-swish!" fell the rain; "splash-splash!" went the horses' feet.

Soon we began to descend toward the Wolf creek valley, stream and bridge—winding and turning, zigzagging this way and that; and moving very slowly and cautiously. The hill was slippery; and the heavy buggy crowded the horses sorely. From one side of the road to the other they slid and sprawled; and I held my breath till my throat ached—expecting any moment to precipitate an accident. But the Colonel, so far as I could judge in the darkness, was cool and collected; and I greatly admired the manner in which he managed the team, bringing us safely out of one threatening situation into another.

However, on reaching a small flat half way down the precipitous slope he pulled up and, feelingly rubbing his arms, remarked with a sigh of relief:

"There! The worst's over. This is a bad bit of road on a night like this, Miss Marjory; but it all goes in the day's adventure. I'll laugh over our escapade when I'm so old I can't remember anything else to laugh about; and you'll tell it to your children, in the years to come. I—"

"Colonel," I interrupted half timidly, "I'm—I'm afraid."

"Afraid, my dear child?" he said kindly. "What are you afraid of? Not of me, of course—eh?"

"No—no!" I quickly disclaimed. "Not of you."

"Of the night and the storm, then?" he suggested.

"Just a little," I admitted. "But what I'm most afraid of is that we'll be followed, overtaken—and caught!"

"Ah?"—sharply.

"Yes, I am."

"Well," he said slowly "we'll not be over-taken and caught; I've got the best team in the town."—Then, abruptly, suspiciously:—"But what makes you fear we'll be followed?"

"They'll miss me at home, and search for me," I explained.

"Yes," he admitted, "they will of course. But they'll hunt the town over for you first; and before they get that done and start in pursuit,—if they're shrewd enough to associate your absence with mine,—we'll be in Stockton, and you'll be on the night train and gone."

"But, Colonel," I objected.

"Well, Miss Marjory?"

"Just as I left the house the telephone rang, and I heard my brother talking in a loud and excited voice. I'm sure, almost, some-one had discovered our secret and was warning Jack."

The Colonel laughed outright—laughed explosively, heartily, immoderately. Irritated by his unseemly hilarity, I cried:

"What amuses you so, Colonel Wells? What have I said or done to cause you to laugh so? I don't see anything to be tickled at so—I don't, Are you laughing at me? Tell me; or I'll be angry at you."

Immediately he checked his risibility[3] and made reply, his voice shaking:

"No-no, Miss Marjory! I'm not laughing at you, I assure you. But I see I've got to make a confession, to set myself right in your estimation; I've got to reveal a secret I never meant you to know. The fact is I was expecting you to say just what you did say—about your brother and the phone call, Miss Marjory."

"You were?"—In surprise.

"Yes."

3 Risibility - the ability or inclination to laugh

"Why were you?"

"Can't you guess?"

"Of course not,"—irritably; "tell me."

"I arranged the whole thing myself, Miss Marjory."

"You—you—what do you mean, Colonel Wells?"

"I mean I arranged with one of the boys at the stable, to call your brother and apprise him of our elopement—as soon as we were started."

Nell Adams, I was so dumbfounded that, for the moment, I could not utter a word. But the sound of my companion chuckling to himself, like a kid that has done something it considers smart, made me furious; and instantly I found my tongue.

"Colonel Wells!" I screamed in a tone of severity. "Surely you didn't do such a foolish, such an idiotic, such an insane thing as that, did you?"

"I did, Miss Marjory," he answered, threatening to go into another convulsion of laughter.

"Well, what on earth possessed you to do it? " I cried in rage and disgust.

"I'll tell you," he said, wheezing and chuckling. "To my way of thinking, an elopement without an irate father or brother or other male relative of the fair lady, in pursuit, would be like playing Hamlet with Hamlet left out. I go in for realism—the real thing; and when I elope with a young damsel, I want to elope."

I was so angry, so disgusted, so fearful and miserable that I burst into tears.

"Yes, and now I'll—I'll be caught" I sobbed; "and—and taken back home—and disgraced forever!"

"No, you won't, Miss Marjie—indeed you won't!" he murmured soothingly. "There! Don't cry; and don't worry. I just wanted to add a little spice to our adventure; I didn't think it would worry you. But we'll not be overtaken; no danger."

"Jack'll be right after us," I pouted—but lifting my head and drying my eyes; "and he'll be so close behind us that he'll catch me before I can get on the train at Stockton. Now!"

"We're not going to Stockton," the Colonel replied coolly.

"We're not?"—instantly concerned.—"Where are we going, then?"

"To Conesville."

"Why that's twice as far. Why are we going there?"

Once more the Colonel chuckled—at thought of what he looked upon as his own smartness.

"Your brother has information that we're going to Stockton; I saw to that—that was a part of the message he got. It's there he'll seek you—and waste time in the search. In the meantime I'll have you safe at Conesville; and you can take the early morning train to Zanesville. But now we must be moving along. Two miles beyond the creek we're approaching, at Dodd's, we'll turn to the left; and—"

"Hark!" I interrupted, catching his arm.

The hardest of the storm had passed over; but in the distant southeast the lightning still flashed and the thunder still boomed and reverberated. The fall of the steady, heavy rain upon the leaves of the trees above us on the hillside gave forth a deep, sonorous murmur.

"What did you hear?" inquired the Colonel, in a tense whisper.

I thought I heard voices," I answered. "There! Listen!"

"I hear them!'" he muttered excitedly, gleefully. "They're at the second turn above—fully a half mile away by the road. There! That's the sound of wheels."

"Yes," I wailed weakly, "and it's Jack—or somebody—after us. Now just see what you've done, Colonel Wells!"

"Tut-tut!" he cried cheerily. "Don't take on, Miss Marjie; you sha'n't be overtaken, or disappointed in your endeavor to escape from your brother."—And he gave me a reassuring, caressing pat upon the shoulder.—"Here's where the race begins—and the fun comes in!"

Then he chirruped to the team, shook the whip, and down the final slope we went at a fair trot, the horses slipping and sliding, the buggy slewing and careening. I held my breath; and held on to the seat as best I could. At that moment, Nell, had I had the courage and strength, I would have pitched my gay old cavalier out in the mud and driven off and left him. Oh, I was provoked!

On reaching the foot of the hill he touched the horses with the whip, and we moved more rapidly. But hardly were we under swift headway when he suddenly pulled up, crying fearsomely:

"Hark! Listen—listen!"

A sullen, awful, indescribable roar—growing louder and rising in pitch, with each passing moment—smote upon my ears.

"Oh, what is it?" I breathed in an agony of wonder and fear.

"It's the water—the flood coming!" the Colonel panted. "And we must get through the bridge and over the bottoms on the other side before it reaches here, or we won't get across at all—for an hour or two, anyhow."

"Oh, do hurry I" I urged. "We must get across, or Jack will catch us."

But my brave cavalier did not need any urging, as I soon realized. Already he was applying the whip to the mettlesome horses and guiding them with firm and steady hands. Along the wet level road we fairly flew, mud and water flying in a splattering shower from the swiftly revolving wheels. And all the while that awful booming noise was roaring nearer and ringing louder.

The covered bridge was but a few hundred yards from the foot of the hill. It rested upon two stone abutments, about ten or twelve feet above the ordinary level of the creek. The roadway, on both sides of the stream, was much lower than the floor of the bridge; and the approaches were short and steep.

The oncoming flood rapidly drew near, roaring louder and louder, until the clamor and din of it absorbed all other sounds. A flash of lightning revealed to me the approaching wall of water—huge, black and tumbling. It was almost upon us; and in terror I shrilled:

"Drive, Colonel! Drive—drive!"

"We'll make it—to the bridge!" he yelled in my ear.

And the next moment the horses scrambled up the steep approach, and stood upon the firm plank floor of the primitive structure—trembling and pawing and snorting; and the mad and tumbling flood was sweeping three or four feet deep over the roadway we had come.

I collapsed against the back of the seat, too weak and nervous and wretched to care much what my final fate was to be. The Colonel jumped out to soothe and control the restive[4] animals.

Another storm was following close on the heels of the first. Again the lightning was sizzling and flashing; the thunder was ripping and crashing; and the rain was falling in torrents. On all sides of our insecure retreat, the foul-smelling flood—black as soot in the darkness, yellow as ochre in the lightning's flash—rolled and surged and boiled. Great logs and other heavy drift bumped against the stone abutments, causing our crazy wooden shelter to quiver and shake dizzily; and the poor scared horses snorted and stamped their protest. As for me, Sweet Nell, I just lay there and shivered and sniveled; my courage was all out—and I was all in. At least, so I thought at the time.

The Colonel came to the vehicle, set one foot upon the step, and thrust his head in and queried kindly—but straining his voice to make me hear:

"How are you, Miss Marjory—all right?"

"Don't speak to me!" I screamed in reply—endeavoring to make him hear.

"Why—why—" he stammered, "what's the matter?"

"What's the matter!"—caustically.—"Look what you've got us into—here on this old tottering bridge, in danger of our lives!"

He leaned farther into the vehicle, put his face close to mine and bellowed—literally bellowed:

"Tut—tut, Miss Marjie! Don't be alarmed; we'll come out all right—we're in no real danger. Besides, you mustn't blame me; I'm not the weather-man. And you chose the night for our elopement."

"Yes," I screeched wrathfully; "and you stopped back there on the hillside, and talked and laughed and palavered[5] till this flood caught us. And now how are we to get away?"

"Oh, we'll come out all right!" he bawled—almost cracking his voice in an effort to lift it above the general uproar. "The water'll go down in an hour or so; then we'll go on our way rejoicing. And this

4 Restive - stubbornly resisting control
5 Palaver - idle talk

is the best part of the adventure, I think—great fun. But say!"

"Well!" tartly enough.

'I can see the twinkle of a light over at the foot of the hill we just left. No doubt it's a lantern carried by our pursuers."

"They'll catch us, too—as soon as the water goes down," I predicted with fatalistic positiveness.

"No, they won't," he asserted sturdily. "The water goes down sooner on the far side of the stream: that is, I mean the road is higher. We'll be gone from the bridge before our pursuers can get to it. Don't worry, now—that's a good girlie; we'll come out with flying colors."

He left me and returned to the heads of the pawing horses. Unreasonable, ungovernable restlessness and dread took possession of me; and I couldn't sit still—I couldn't stay in the buggy. I climbed out, straightened and stretched my cramped nether[6] limbs, and walked to the rear of the vehicle. There I stood, looking afar across the tumbling waters, toward the foot of the hill whence we had come. I could see several lights bobbing and jiggling erratically here and there; and caught—or fancied I caught—the faint and uncertain sound of men holloing and shouting.

The second violent but brief storm was passing, the rain was lessening; but still the lightning played and the thunder rumbled and rolled. All at once I started nervously and stepped aside from my position. Water had splashed upon my foot. I bent and peered closely at the floor of the bridge; but could distinguish nothing. Then I put down my hand and felt the rough planks; and let out a little cry of dismay and terror. Water was bubbling up through the cracks!

Nell Adams I was scared stiff! I thought I saw my finish—a watery grave, an unlovely bedraggled corpse! For the moment I stood spellbound with fear. Then I recovered the use of my limbs and voice, and darted toward where I thought my companion was, screaming shrilly:

"Oh, Colonel Wells! We'll be lost—drowned—killed! The flood's coming up through the bridge!"

And I went on screaming warnings and predictions and proph-

---

6 Nether - situated down or below

esies, at the top of my voice. I guess I must have been just a little hysterical, Nell. The Colonel caught me and put an arm around my waist; and held me firmly—but respectfully.

"Stop that yelling, Miss Dawes!" he commanded sharply. "Stop it, now—stop it!"—I subsided limply; then he continued in a calm, even voice:—"Suppose the water is coming up through the floor, what of it? The bridge is heavily-timbered and anchored to the abutments; it can't float away or break up, unless the flood gets much higher than it is. And the rain's practically over, and the water will be falling soon. Get back into the buggy, now—that's a good girl."

"I don't want to," I pouted perversely.

"Yes," he said sternly, "you must do as I say; you'll get your feet wet. Come on."

"But I won't get back into the buggy, Colonel Wells," I cried.

"But you will," he growled.

"I won't, I say!"

"I say you will!"

And what do you think, Nell Adams? The impertinent, stubborn old dunce caught me up in his arms, carried me to the vehicle and placed me in it; and without another word calmly returned to the care of the team. Did you ever hear of the like! I sat and pondered and pouted; and, provoked and frightened and miserable as I was, came near wishing the bridge would float away with us—just to spite the Colonel.

Presently, however, he came to me and said humbly, contritely:

"Miss Marjie, please pardon my apparent rudeness of a few minutes ago. Perhaps I was a little abrupt in my words and actions; but I didn't mean to be, I assure you."

I maintained a surly and stubborn silence.

"Miss Marjory, do you hear me?" he questioned.

"Yes, I do," I snapped in reply.

"Listen, then. The water's already falling—as rapidly as it arose, almost. Isn't that good news—eh?"

The dear, kind-hearted old fellow! How hard he was striving to regain my favor. A little ashamed of my pettishness, I answered as graciously as I could:

"Yes, it is, Colonel. And what of our pursuers?"

"I'll look and see," he said with alacrity[7].

He walked to the near end of the bridge, and back.

"Their light has disappeared," he announced.

"There was more than one lantern," I returned, "there were several; and I thought I heard people shouting and holloing a little while ago."

"Is that so?"—surprised, and apparently concerned.—"Then they must have been alarmed over our seeming danger. But the lights have disappeared. What do you make of it, Miss Marjory?"

"I don't know what to make of it, Colonel; but I'm glad they're gone. Perhaps they've abandoned the chase."

He was silent for some seconds; then he said thoughtfully:

"I think I have it. The iron bridge a mile below here and the highway crossing it are out of reach of all floods, are they not?"

"Yes," I replied, wondering what he had in mind.

"Well," he continued, "I think your brother and those with him have gone back to Chesterville to take that road. They've determined to their own satisfaction that we're entrapped here on this bridge; and they hope, by going the roundabout way, to head us off—say at the cross-road beyond Dodd's. But we'll fool them,"—chuckling gleefully.—"We'll just let them wait at the cross-road; we'll be on our way to Conesville—and they won't suspect what has become of us. They'll wait for hours, thinking we're still prisoners here."

"And we may be," I remarked pessimistically.

"Not much!"—determinedly.— "We'll be out of this in an hour from now, if I have to swim the horses."

He made his word good, too. Soon the rain had ceased entirely, the clouds were scudding[8] away and the moon was peeping out. The light of the welcome luminary showed us that the flood was rapidly receding. My companion knew the road well; and at last he said:

"I guess we'll risk it, Miss Marjory; there's no danger now. We can't experience any greater mishap than getting our feet wet. And we ought to be on our way; time may be precious to us before we

7 Alacrity - a quick and cheerful readiness to do something
8 Scud - to move or go quickly

reach our destination. What do you say?"

"Let's start," I decided pluckily.

"That's the stuff, Miss Marjie!" the Colonel cried joyfully. "You've got the grit; you'll make your way in the world. So here goes!"

Without serious danger or difficulty we made our way through the falling flood—though the horses snorted and shied and blundered, and I let out a little screech now and then—and gained the foot of the opposite hill in safety. The sky was rapidly clearing; the moon was flooding the wet land with silvery radiance. Up the muddy slope we laboriously climbed and rolled away along the high ridge. But the highway was heavy and our progress was necessarily slow. It was after midnight when we passed Dodd's and took the left-hand road leading to Conesville.

I must have dropped into a doze; for the first thing I realized I was upon my knees in the bottom of the buggy, with my head hanging over the dashboard.

"Whoa!" yelled the Colonel.

The tired horses came to a sudden stop. I scrambled back upon the seat—now tilted at an inconvenient angle.

"What's the matter now?" I demanded crossly.

There was the thick gloom of inevitable doom in my companion's voice, as he answered crustily:

"The front axle has snapped in two!"

Chapter 5

"WELL, now, Colonel Wells, what on earth are you going to do?" I cried, exasperated beyond measure.

"I'll be—be blessed if I know, Miss Marjory!" he muttered helplessly, meekly—letting the lines slip from his nerveless fingers and wearily dropping his head.

A few moments we sat there in sullen silence, watching the reeking horses shifting their positions to ease themselves of the strain of the taut harness. The time seemed long to me; and—tired, sleepy and cross—I whimpered fretfully:

"You're a great cavalier—you are, Colonel Wells! You were going to have everything go just right; and everything's gone just wrong ever since we started. I'm sorry I came with you—so I am; and I wish I—I—"

Emotion—the lump in my throat choked my utterance; but my rash and unreasonable words roused my companion to instant concern and speech.

"Don't say you wish you hadn't come, Miss Marjory," he said plaintively, dejectedly; "don't say you wish you were back home. It hurts me to hear you talk that way, though I know you don't mean it. You don't want to go back home; you're just nervous and out-of-sorts—that's what ails you. And I don't blame you for being a little cross-grained, indeed I don't. You've put up with a good deal to-night—and that's a fact; but I'm in no wise to blame. Am I—eh?"

"Yes, you are," I whined peevishly.

"Eh?"—lifting his head and actually smiling at me, which made me furious.

"Yes, you are to blame, Colonel Wells," I pursued pitilessly.

45

"You tried to act smart by letting Jack know of our—our elopement."

"But that didn't bring the flood, Miss Marjory,"—grinning broadly, vacuously[1].

"And you stopped on the hill back there beyond the bridge, letting our pursuers nearly catch up with us," I continued relentlessly.

"But that didn't cause the axle to break," he chuckled, shrugging his shoulders. Then, earnestly: "No, my dear little girl, you mustn't blame me—your old gray-haired friend—for the night's mishaps. I'm doing for you, Miss Marjie, what I wouldn't undertake or consider for any other bunch of femininity on top of ground; and for the simple reason that—old as I am!—I'm in love with you. Now!"

"Colonel Wells!" was all I could murmur. You could have knocked me over with a powder-puff, Nell Adams.

"There l" he said with infinite gentleness and kindness. "Don't take it to heart; I don't expect you to reciprocate. I'm an old fool; but not quite so big a fool as to expect a sweet young miss like you to care for a battered old wreck like me. All I ask is that you keep in mind that I'm doing my best to serve you, to help you to your heart's desire." —Then, animatedly, cheerfully:—"But pshaw! I must stop talking and go to doing; we're six miles from our destination—and with no time to fritter away. But this has been a night of misadventures, sure. Oh, well! It's all fun if only we look at it that way; and let's so view it. Now, I know there's a farmhouse just beyond the next turn of the road, and we must get to it and obtain another buggy—or other conveyance. But I'm afraid I'll have to ask you to walk that short distance, Miss Marjory. Eh?"

"All right," I consented readily, desperate enough to attempt anything that promised to help us on our way.

The Colonel stiffly descended to the ground and assisted me to alight; and immediately we set out for the farmhouse whose roof glinted in the moonlight, just over a slight eminence. I took the lead along the sloppy highway, holding my skirts high—and catching my breath every few seconds as one or the other of my oxfords threatened to pull off in the sticky mud. After me came the poor old Colonel, literally dragging the horses by the bits and anxiously watching

---

1 Vacuous - marked by lack of ideas or intelligence

the wabbling buggy wheel. And we had a full half-mile of it. Think of that, Sweet Nell!

On reaching the tumble-down old farmhouse our procession halted. I don't know which would have collapsed first, had we had a few more rods[2] to go—the vehicle, the team, the Colonel or your humble servant, Nell. One thing I do know; I thought myself completely gone—entirely exhausted. My shoes were soaked, my feet were wet, my skirts were bedraggled—and my ardor was dampened. I stood in the middle of the road and yawned and shivered, while my cavalier—a depressed but determined cavalier!—holloed and holloed to arouse the inmates of the frowning, uninviting residence facing us.

Not a light twinkled about the premises; not a hint of life became apparent; not a voice responded to my companion's repeated hails.

Once more he bellowed lustily: "Hello! Hello! Hello, I say! Hel-lo-o-o!"

Still all was grim darkness and silence. The Colonel muttered something under his breath; then he turned to me and said:

"Miss Marjie, I'll have to go and pound upon the door. You look after the horses a moment. I don't think they'd try to run away; surely they haven't got snap enough left in them for that. But they might; and—goodness knows!—I don't want to run any risk. You watch them just a minute."

I was too apathetic, too stupid to make reply; but I did as he requested. He shambled to the front entrance of the dismal-looking dwelling and knocked vigorously upon the door; then again—and again.

"I don't believe there's anybody at home," he turned to me and announced—pitiful hopelessness tincturing[3] his tone, in spite of his resolution.

"There's got to be somebody at home," I cried; "we've got to have a conveyance. Try again."

He did so; and immediately an upstairs window flew open, and

---

2 Rod - a unit of length (5.50 yards)
3 Tincture - a slight admixture

a tousled head and bewhiskered face popped out into the moonlight.

"Hello!" called the Colonel, taking a step or two backward and lifting his gaze aloft.

"Hello y'rself!" was the gruff response.

Then something like the following dialogue came to my eager ears:

"Good morning."

"I don't know whether it's mornin' 'r not; I hain't looked at the clock."

I giggled the amusement I felt, in spite of the sad situation in which I found myself.

"We've broken our buggy—"

"Well, what of it?"

"And it's important that we get on to Conesville as soon as possible,—"

"'Tain't important to me."

"And we've stopped to see if we can procure another vehicle."

"No, you can't."

"Haven't you a buggy?"

"No."

"No carriage of any kind?"

"No."

"Nor an express wagon?"

"No, I hain't."

"Nothing of the kind?"

"Nothin'."

"Not even a cart?"

"Nothin' but a big farm-wagon."

"Miss Marjory," yelled the Colonel, "can you—will you ride in a farm-wagon?"

"I'll ride in anything," I shrilled in desperation.

"You won't ride in my wagon, Miss," the man bawled from his place of vantage.

"Why won't she?" the Colonel demanded, bristling.

"'Cause I won't let you have it," the farmer returned coolly.

"And why won't you?" the Colonel persisted.

"'Cause I'm goin' to use it myself, soon as it comes daylight."

"But, my good man," my escort cried wheedlingly, "we'll pay you for the use of it; and—"

"I don't want y'r pay,"—stubbornly; "an' you can't have the wagon."

"How are we to get to Conesville, then?"

"Don't know—an' don't care,"—pitilessly.

"Oh, yes, you do!"—menacingly.

"Oh, no, I don't!"—defiantly.

And down went the window!

"Well, don't that beat the—the devil!" muttered the Colonel; and I tittered outright. I couldn't help it, provoked and perplexed though I was.

The angry Colonel gave a martial jerk to his square shoulders, stalked up to the door and began to kick it savagely. Instantly the upstairs window again flew open; and again the farmer's frowzy head was in evidence.

"Here!" he bawled. "Stop that!"

"Be civil, then," growled the Colonel. "If you don't I'll kick the door down and kick you out of the house."

"Well, what the devil do you want?" the man inquired.

"Want a conveyance to carry us to Conesville."

"Hain't got none I can let you have, I told you."

"Well, have you got any saddles?"

"Yes, got two—a man's saddle an' a woman's saddle. They're both hangin' in the barn out there. Take 'em; an' you can run y'r buggy in the shed at the side of the stable—an' pile y'r harness in it. But, say!"

"Well?"

"Who are you, anyway?"

"Colonel Wells of Georgia."

"Jeeminy! I can't let you take my saddles clear to Georgy with you, mister."

Again I teeheed audibly.

"Nonsense, man!" rasped the Colonel. "We'll take them to Conesville—that's all; and leave them at the hotel or livery barn, with our horses. Then whoever comes here for the buggy and harness will return your saddles. See?"

"Yea. Well, you can take 'em. An' now—goodnight; I'm goin' back to bed."

Once more the window closed, with a crash.

"An infernal chump!" the Colonel muttered as he came out to me. "A regular numbskull, Miss Marjory."

I seated myself upon a sodden bank at the roadside; and my escort took team and vehicle into the barnyard near at hand. After what seemed an interminably long time, he returned with the two horses—stripped of harness and bearing saddles.

"Now, Miss Marjory," he said briskly, with a manly but painful attempt at cheerfulness, "we'll be off again. I just looked at my watch, and it's only two o'clock; so we'll get to Conesville in time for you to catch the early morning train, if nothing else happens to hinder us. And—patience knows!—I hope nothing else will happen,"—grinning facetiously.—"For I've got to confess that, much as I love adventure, I've had about enough for one night. Stand upon the bank there, and I'll assist you into the saddle."

"But I never rode horseback in my life, Colonel," I objected.

"There must be a first time to all things, Miss Marjory."

"I don't believe I can, Colonel Wells."

"You'll never learn younger, Miss Marjie."

"I'm afraid I'll never learn older—never learn at all—is what's bothering me," I explained dully.

"Well,"—impatiently,—"you must try, at any rate. Let me assist you to mount."

"But I tell you I'm afraid, Colonel; I've never been on a horse's back."

"And I tell you that you've got to try—that necessity cares nothing about previous experience, little girl. Here—give me your foot. Up you go."

And up I did go, Nell Adams—and over on the other side, nearly. I clung desperately to the horse's mane and shivered, and plead with my cruel cavalier to help me to the ground—to let me walk to Conesville; but he was inexorable.

"Keep your seat," he cried gaily; "it's all you have to do. I'll lead the horse by the rein. Now! Off we go."

Nell, I was in mortal dread of losing my life then and there. I must have cut a figure; and I've never been able to understand how the old Colonel kept his face straight. I clung to my rolling, jostling perch and let out exclamations and screeches of fright, at regular and frequent intervals. It was like riding an earthquake. I was sea-sick—soul-sick. I was sure I was going to slide off on the one side; I was certain I was going to fall off on the other. I had no riding-habit, of course; and my abbreviated skirts began to work upward—far above my shapely ankles. I made misdirected, frantic and futile efforts to put them down—to restore myself to a semblance of proper maidenly modesty; and almost precipitated my precious anatomy to the earth. I let out a screech of extra length and strength, and implored—humbly implored and beseeched my escort to rescue me from my perilous position. And what do you think? Colonel Wells—the chivalric Southron[4]!—just laughed at me. But looking back at the spectacle I must have presented, I can't find it in my heart to criticise him severely.

But soon I felt a little less like a shipwrecked sailor upon a teetering raft, a little more like a bold mariner upon the deck of his own staunch vessel; and after a mile or two I was rather happy and proud over my new experience. So I requested the Colonel to give me the reins, which he did; and we jogged along quite pleasantly, drowsily talking over our misadventures and speculating as to what had become of our pursuers.

Murky dawn was just coming as we descended the long hill at the foot of which lay the Muskingum valley—and Conesville. Hundreds of birds were singing and thousands of flowers were exhaling their moist fragrance.

The Colonel looked at his watch, and yawned:

"It isn't quite four o'clock; you'll have plenty of time to get a bite of something to eat and catch that five-thirty train. As I told you we would, we've come out all right—triumphant over all difficulties and hindrances."

---

4 Southron – Chiefly Southern : a native or inhabitant of the southern U.S.

There was elation in his voice and manner, but—poor old fellow!—his haggard face and lackluster eyes belied his brave demeanor.

Just as we had got into the village and were moving up the main street, toward the hotel, a thick-set man—with a big, bright badge of office shining upon the lapel of his baggy sack coat—waddled out from a shadowy doorway and threw up his hand, motioning us to stop.

"Whoa!" said the Colonel, reining in—at the same time giving me a swift and meaningful glance.

"Good mornin'," was the man's greeting.

"Good morning," was the Colonel's response.

"I'm the marshal o' this town," the man volunteered—with pardonable pomposity.

"Indeed," replied the Colonel.

"An' 'bout a half-hour ago," the marshal continued, "I got a phone message from Stockton, to be on the lookout fer a runaway couple—an elopin' couple comin' from Chesterville."

He searched our faces, keenly, shrewdly, to note the effect of his words. But I, with remarkable self-control, assumed an air of innocent carelessness; and my companion merely uttered an apathetic "ah?"—and yawned behind his hand.

"What way did you folks come in?" the officer demanded sharply.

"Horseback," the Colonel answered smoothly; and I had difficulty in repressing a giggle, tired and hungry as I was.

"Of course," the marshal snarled; "any fool could see that. But what road did you come? Where'd you come from?"

"We rode in from just beyond Hicksville."

"Did, eh?"—suspiciously.

"Yes."

"Did you see anything of a couple in a two-horse buggy, comin' this way?"

"Yes."

"Where?"

"Just the other side of Hicksville."

"Did you pass 'em?"

"W-e-ll,"—embarrassed for the moment,—"no, we didn't pass them; they turned into a barnyard and stopped."

"You passed 'em, then, didn't you?"

"I suppose you may say we did."

"An' they stopped at a farmhouse, eh?"

"Yes."

"Did you see 'em unhitch—as if they was goin' to stay there?"

"Y-e-s, they—that is, the man unhitched."

"Oh-ho!"—gleefully.—"I have it, then. They've stopped there with relations 'r friends, an' they're goin' to have the Hicksville preacher an' git married. It's all as plain as the nose on y'r face. I'll phone the word right back to the marshal at Stockton. Maybe he can git out there in time to put a stop to the thing."

"Who are the eloping parties?" asked the Colonel, guilelessly, disinterestedly.

"I don't believe the marshal at Stockton mentioned any names; it was him, you know, phoned me. He jest said to keep a lookout fer an elopin' couple; an' hold 'em—if I ketched 'em—an' phone him right away. Said he'd come up with the girl's brother an' settle things. He did say the girl was young an' purty,"—I blushed, Nell, and turned away my face!—"an' the man was an ugly ol' codger with white hair an' mustache an' goatee; an'—"

I tittered; then bit my lips and coughed. Abruptly the marshal stopped speaking and turned his eyes upon me; and from me to the Colonel. Then he blurted out:

"Say!"

"What?" the Colonel returned coolly, though he knew what was coming, I'm positive.

"W'y—w'y," the officer stammered, "you purty near answer to that description."

"Do I?"

"Yes, sir, you do."

"You think I'm ugly?"

"Can't say that you're ugly, exactly; but you ain't a dam bit handsome."—He chuckled asthmatically.—"An' you've got the white hair an' all."

"All men of my age have white hair, do they not?"

"Well, purty nigh all, I s'pect," the fellow admitted, evidently puzzled.

"And," my escort continued, "the parties you were to look for were to come in a buggy, were they not?"

"Y-e-s," the marshal mumbled reflectively, "they was."

'Well, we came horseback."

"That's so."

"And I told you, you remember, of a couple stopping at the farmhouse beyond Hicksville."

"Y-e-s, I remember. Say!"

"Well?"

"Did you notice whether that man had white hair an' so on?"

"He did."

"Sure?"

"Sure."

"An' was the woman young an' purty?"

"Quite young—and very pretty."

It was in order for me to blush again; and I did it—sweetly and naturally. I couldn't help it; the effort I was making to keep from laughing would have brought the red to the cheeks of a stage beauty. But I started and felt instant concern, as I heard the marshal saying:

"But you folks do answer the description mighty well."

"Yes, we do," the Colonel replied placidly, again yawning. "But this young lady's going away on the early up train, and I'm going to stay here; and we're not married—nor thinking of getting married. So we can't be the elopers you're after, eh?"

"No, I guess not. But what's y'r names?"

"Our names?"

"That's what I said."

"I'm Jack Dawes and this young lady is Dorothy Crewe," the Colonel lied glibly.

I gasped with astonishment—then let out a jerky giggle; and coughed distressingly to hide the fact.

"All right," concluded the officer; "I'll phone back to Stockton that you folks has just come in from Hicksville, an' that you seen the runaway couple stop at a farmhouse jest beyond there. That's straight, is it?"

"Perfectly straight; that is, so far as we know."

The marshal turned on his heel and left us; and we continued our way to the village hotel. The modest caravansary[5] had just begun to show signs of waking life. I changed my clothes and made my toilet; and was again presentable—to say the least. We had some trouble in procuring breakfast at so unusual an hour, but an extra dollar neatly did the trick.

As we were leaving the table the Colonel consulted his watch, and said in a cautious undertone:

"If fate will be kind for a half-hour, you'll be on your train and gone, Miss Marjory; and I'll be glad—so glad."

"Glad to have me gone?" I queried, with a fetching pout.

"Now, Miss Marjory," he murmured reproachfully, "you know what I mean."

"Yes, I do, Colonel Wells," I returned, smiling my sweetest; "and you've been very kind to me—very, very kind. But something tells me that dumpy marshal will come waddling in here pretty soon, bent on detaining me."

"I expect him," he said, nodding.

"You, do?" I whispered.

Again he nodded.

"Why? Do you think he suspected us?"

"It's probable. But he'll know who we are as soon as he phones to Stockton; the names I gave will reveal our identity to your brother."

"Yes!" I cried fault-findingly. "I hadn't thought of that. And you're all the time getting us into trouble, Colonel; you're as bad as Leander[6] of the Sunday supplements. What possessed you to do such a silly thing? I admit you were cornered and compelled to prevaricate; but I can't see why you couldn't tell an ordinary lie—give our names as John Jones and Mary Smith, for instance. Why couldn't you—why didn't you, Colonel Wells?"

---

5 Caravansary – any large inn or hotel
6 Leander – Well known character in the early Sunday newspapers

We had reached the stuffy little parlor. I dropped into one of the straight-backed, plush-upholstered chairs, my chin quivering and tears of vexation in my eyes. My companion took a seat at one of the open windows, where he could command a view of the street.

"Miss Marjie," he replied to my outburst, "I just couldn't—and so I just didn't. I wanted to have a little more fun out of the thing. Picture to yourself'—and he chuckled and hugged himself—"the rage of your brother when he got the message from here, that we were masquerading under the names of himself and sweetheart. I can hear him cursing the stupidity of all marshals in general— and the stupidity of the marshal of this burg in particular."

And he laughed till the tears ran down his cheeks.

"But, Colonel Wellsl" I cried. "Think what you've done. I might have escaped; now I'll be held—sure."

"No, you won't,"—stoutly.—"I set out to see you safely through this thing; and I will."

Somewhat mollified and reassured by his courageous words and bearing, I heaved a deep breath of relief. However, I continued:

"But what will Jack and his friends say to you, Colonel—what will they do to you—when you go back to Chesterville?"

"I'm not going back," he smiled.

"You're not going back?"—surprised.

"No. I'm going to take the down train, on my way to Cincinnati and Atlanta. My trunk will come by hack to Stockton, this morning. I arranged everything yesterday afternoon. No, Miss Marjory,"— softly, pathetically—'I've no desire to spend the summer in Chester-ville—with you away."

Nell Adams, I was touched; I couldn't say a word in reply. But I had scant time for tender sentiment, for the Colonel drew my attention by thrusting his head out of the window and hastily jerking it back in again.

"Miss Marjie," he whispered stridently, "here comes the marshal. I've sent your traveling-bag to the station. You slip up the front stairs, down the back stairs and out of the side door; and lose no time in reaching the depot. I'll hold the marshal here, on one pretext or another, till your train's gone."

"Colonel Wells," I began, "I don't know how to thank you; I—I—"

He came up to me, took both my hands in his and murmured thickly:

"Don't thank me, Miss Marjie—don't say a word of the kind. I've enjoyed this elopement more than any other I ever took part in,"—his eyes dancing. "Be a good girl, and take good care of yourself. Probably I sha'n't see you again for months or years, possibly I sha'n't ever see you again; but I won't forget you—Indeed, no. If I were twenty years younger—just twenty years, mind you, little girl!—I'd play this game to the finish; I'd stake everything—win or lose. Goodbye, little sweetheart."

"Goodbye, Colonel Wells," I whispered sadly.

Then, moved by some sudden impulse, I threw my arms around his neck and kissed him; and the next moment I was flying up the stairs—my heart a-flutter, my cheeks a-flame.

Some six months ago, Sweet Nell, I met my dear old cavalier,—I will not say now where or under what circumstances; for that revelation belongs to the concluding pages of this very bulky epistle,—and he told me of his encounter with the marshal, after my departure. That pompous official came in the front door of the little tavern as I went out the side door; and of the Colonel he demanded:

"Where's that young woman?"

"Miss Crewe?" the Colonel countered suavely.

" No, not Miss Crewe!" snorted the marshal. "You two thought you were mighty smart—thought you was foolin' me; but I knowed you all the time—if you did come in here horseback. You bet I did! Your name's Curly Wells an' her name's Marget Dawes"; —Marget! Marget! Just wait till I meet that man, Nell Adams!—"an' you're the 'lopers. Now, where is she?"

"She just went up-stairs," replied the Colonel.

"Well, you go an' call 'er down."

"What are you going to do with us?"

"Ain't goin' to do nothin' with you; her brother says he'll settle with you—if you don't have sense enough, an' shame enough, to skip out fer a healthier climate. But I'm goin' to hold her here till her brother comes after her. Go call 'er down."

Colonel Wells deliberately ascended the stairs, strolled up and down the hall, pottered from one room to another, and finally descended to the parlor and announced:

"She isn't in her room."

The marshal was walking the floor, puffing with excitement and anxiety.

"She ain't?" he gasped.

The Colonel soberly shook his head.

"Well, where is she, then?"

Another negative shake of the handsome white head.

"You don't know?"

Once more my Georgia cavalier silently signalled a negative reply.

"I'll bet she's broke fer the train!" the marshal cried; and with the words he lumbered out of the room.

The Colonel stood at the window and watched the pursy[7] marshal waddling rapidly toward the depot; and laughed—and laughed.

The train was just pulling out. I saw the officer coming, and I went out upon the rear platform of the car and waved him a merry farewell. Then I returned to my seat—and indulged in a good cry.

---

7 Pursy - fat

Chapter 6

THE TRAIN jiggled and bumped along toward Zanesville. Completely worn out by the exciting experiences of the night and my own incongruous emotions, I fell into a doze; and as I dozed I dreamed—dreamed that the train was wrecked, that my neck was broken but that I was alive and keenly observant, that my traveling-bag was burst open and its contents scattered broadcast over the ground, and that I was undergoing a deal of toil and trouble in a fruitless effort to gather up and conceal my skirts and hosiery and shoes soiled by the rain and mud of my rural journey.

When I awoke, as I did with a start occasioned by a sudden stop of the train, I found myself crowded over against the wall and jammed down into a corner and two-thirds of my seat occupied by a fat woman with a squawling baby. My neck was aching excrutiatingly; and I was in an ill-humor, indeed. And that baby kept on crying, Nell—crying because it was puny and wretched; and the fat mother just sat there, unmoved and immovable, squashed down in a half-melted heap, and just let it cry. Oh, I wanted to shake her! At last I could stand it no longer, and I asked her, —with the best grace I could assume,—to let me have the little mite. Without murmur or protest she handed it over to me; and I let it look at my watch and play with my purse till finally the poor little thing closed its eyes and went to sleep. I gave it back to its mother; and she never thanked me, even. But I'd had my reward.

Then I sat up straight and stiff and began to do some thinking about my own affairs. No doubt the marshal at Conesville, I reasoned, had phoned Jack of my escape; and no doubt my stubborn and unyielding brother had telegraphed the authorities at Zanesville to apprehend and hold me—on my arrival in that city. So, to avoid all risk of capture, I decided to get off at Putnam, a suburban station on the west side of the river, and take an electric car into the town.

This I did. It was six-thirty; and the streets were quiet and drowsy-looking. The only other occupants of the car beside myself were two or three laborers with their dinner-pails, a newsboy with a bundle of papers, and a middle-aged, angular and sharp-featured woman with an empty market-basket upon her knees. At the second corner, however, two young women, each bearing a bundle of books and both chattering and tittering merrily, got aboard and seated themselves near me.

The woman with the market-basket nodded to them and smiled a mechanical smile that threatened to crack her hard features.

"Good morning," she said in a vinegary voice.

"Good morning," one of the young women replied amiably.

"It's a nice morning—after the rain," the older woman remarked, with a wry expression of countenance indicative of disapproval.

"Very,"—with a nod and a bright smile. "How's your mother these days, Miss Grimes?"

"Quite well, thank you."

"And your father?"

"He's well."

"And all the rest of the family?"

"All in good health."

The younger woman smiled beatifically, but slyly winked at her companion; and the latter grew red of face and turned her attention to the window and the scenery outside.

The older woman crossed her arms upon the handle of her market-basket, leaned forward and thus continued her interrogatories[1]:

"You're still going to the business school, are you, Miss Grimes?"

"Yes."

"Think you'd rather work in an office than teach school, do you?"

---

1 Interrogatories – set of questions required to be answered by an adversary

"I think I would—yes."

"I see by the papers your sister Sarah has the offer of a position up at Columbus."

"Yes."

"In a real-estate office, isn't it?"

"I believe so."

"Let's see—what's the name of the firm? I saw it in the papers, but I've forgot. What is it?'"

"Durbin and Son."

"That's it; I remember it now. And their offices are in the Branson Building; I remember that, too. What kind of work do they want her to do—keep books?"

"No; they offer her a position as amanuensis[2]."

"Kind of a private secretary, eh?"

"Something like that, I guess."

"It ought to be a pleasant position."

"Yes."

"When does she go?"

"She was to go to-day."

"But she isn't going?"

"No."

"Put it off, has she?"

"She's not going at all."

"Not going at all?"—perfectly astounded.

"No."

"Why isn't she?"

"She thinks she's got a better offer."

"Oh!"—with lifted brows and wide open eyes.

"Yes."

"Thinks she's got a better job, does she?"

"Yes."

"Where?"—quickly, incisively.

"At Parkersburg."

"Oh!"—wonderingly, almost incredulously.

The young woman nodded—and surreptitiously nudged her

2 Amanuensis – a person employed to write what another dictates; secretary

companion.

"In what way does the Parkersburg job suit her better?" the neighborly inquisitor pursued.

"Well,"—sighing resignedly,—"the Columbus people offer to give her two weeks trial, and if she proves satisfactory agree to give her employment at forty dollars a month; but the Parkersburg people offer to take her on trial for a year, at the same price."

"I see. And so she's going to Parkersburg, is she?"

"Yes."

"When?"

'To-day."

"Indeed?"

"Yes."

"Has she written the Columbus people that she's got another place?"

"W-e-ll, no, Mrs. Varley, she didn't write them just that. She sent them a letter yesterday, saying she wasn't very well—which was so, and guessed she couldn't take the place, and they'd better look out for somebody else."

"Oh!"—with a world of obscure meaning.

"Yes."

The car had crossed the bridge spanning the river; and was in the heart of the city. Now it stopped at the comer of Third and Main; and I hurriedly caught up my traveling-bag and got off. I looked at my watch as I reached the curb; the hands marked six-fifty. The Chicago express was due at seven-twenty. I could take it, and change at Newark—for Columbus; and at once I determined to do so, and set off at a lively pace for the depot two blocks away.

And, Nell Adams, I was just jubilant—treading on air. I had set out from Chesterville with no definite destination in mind; I had thought I might go to Columbus—but, then, I might go to Cleveland or Chicago. The fact is I had meant to leave the matter to chance, largely; and for once chance had been kind to me. A situation was open to me—beckoning me, begging me to come; and I was going to accept the welcome offer. I was Marjory Dawes—a poor little waif with no position in view!—no longer; I was Sarah Grimes of

Zanesville, on my way to accept a place with Durbin and Son of Columbus, real-estate dealers in the Branson Building. As Sarah Grimes I had made a rapid and marvelous recovery from my temporary indisposition; and as Sarah Grimes—but the sound of the name set my teeth on edge, Nell, every time I whispered it over to myself!—I was going to follow my hasty and ill-considered letter and reveal myself as bodily proof that I was able and anxious for work.

I know you'll scorn me, Sweet Nell, and condemn me; I scorned and condemned myself—just a little. But the unexpected smile of fortune was too enticing, too seductive, to resist; and I yielded—and didn't feel too bad my weakness. All's fair in love and war, it's said; and all's fair in modern commercialism, also. I wasn't injuring anyone, I argued. The real Sarah Grimes was declining one good position to accept another; I the pretender, was simply taking the rejected place. I'd do my best for Durbin and Son—indeed I would; and no one would be the wiser or sadder. Where was the harm? It was thus I reasoned, Nell; and I was glad—glad—GLAD—that such fair fortune had smiled on me in my hour of need.

I reached the depot and entered the dark and dingy waiting-room; and glanced up at the clock.

"Twenty minutes to wait, if the train's on time—which will be a rarity beyond precedent," I whispered to myself.

The room was crowded; the air was close and ill-smelling. I hustled toward the ticket-window. Several people were ahead of me, and I elbowed for a place—and got it. But just as I was going to call for my ticket I made the startling and demoralizing discovery that my purse was gone!

Nell mine, I don't know how I got out of the jam and to the door; I know I was ready to drop when I reached the open air and sank down upon a truck. My purse was gone! What was I to do? I was faint, nauseated and all of a tremble. The bright sunlight dazzled my eyes; the heat-waves threatened to suffocate me. Apathetically, despairingly, I sat there, thinking—thinking in a circle, thinking to no purpose. Where had I dropped or left my purse? It had hung by a chain to my wrist; and it was gone—with every cent I had in the world, little enough at best. Had I left it on the train? No; I remembered having it on the street-car, when I paid my fare. Had I left it on the streetcar? It was probable, I decided. I scolded myself for my carelessness; I found fault with fate for its unkindness. Then I got mad; and that was the best thing I could have done. For as soon as I got angry I got plucky. I gritted my teeth, gave a vicious little kick at my traveling-bag-and declared under my breath that I'd reach Columbus that day if I had to steal a ride on a freight-train.

But what was I to do? The question would not down; it insisted on presenting itself. I could telegraph Jack to come and take me home, of course. No, I couldn't do that, even; I had no money. Well, I could appeal to the police; and they would send him word. Yes, but I wouldn't; I'd starve, suffer—and die, first! I was going on to Columbus; that was settled. When? On the Chicago express—the next train, due in ten minutes by my watch. But my purse—my money? Well, I'd have to let it go; I had no time to search for it. But how was I to go without a ticket—without cash? Well, I must go; and I would go. And, Nell Adams, I did!

The train rolled in on time—to the second. I joined the crowd; and bravely tripped across the platform, climbed aboard and took a seat—near the rear end of the car. There I sat, stoically awaiting the outcome of my rash venture. Would I be put off? I supposed so. How could I obviate[3] such a mischance? Heaven knew; I didn't! The car quickly filled; but no one sought a seat with me. The train began to move, slowly, rumblingly. Once, moved by instinctive impulse, I half arose with the undefined intent of getting off. But I sank back, and resolutely clenched my hands and set my lips; I'd see the thing through. The train gained in speed, and flew away westward; and there I was doomed by ill-luck and my own rashness to face the tender mercies of a heartless railroad conductor. It was a fearful situation, Nell Adams; and I've often wondered how I braved it.

My grim ogre in blue-and-brass entered the car and commenced to take up the fares. I stiffened myself for the inevitable ordeal; I meant to plead, to wheedle, to do my best to fascinate and win over

---

3 Obviate – to anticipate and prevent or eliminate (difficulties, disadvantages, etc.) by effective measures

that brusque-looking, square-jawed individual in uniform—to gain my way and get free transportation to Newark. Then, like a flash of inspiration from the mischief-maker of the universe, an idea came to me—an idea unconventional, outre[4], outlandish; and I found myself giggling over the mere thought. Would the scheme thus presented to me work? I could not determine, of course. Should I try it? Why not? Failure wouldn't make matters worse—that I could see. But what would be the result of the bold and unmaidenly act I contemplated? I'd make the experiment—and see!

Well up in front sat a big broad-shouldered man wearing a light suit and soft hat. I could see his back only. He had his arms folded upon the seat before him, and was talking to its occupants. His hat set far back upon his head completely hid his features. I could not tell whether he was young or old, handsome or otherwise; but the view of him that chance saw fit to grant me filled me with a belief and confidence that he was elderly, fatherly—and would be impressionable to the pleas of a charming young woman in distress. And so I made up my mind to carry out the plan of procedure that unbidden had come to me.

The conductor reached my side. I was looking out the window. He touched me upon the shoulder; and I turned and stared at him, in assumed surprise and with mute questioning in my eyes.

"Ticket," he said gruffly.

I turned from him and again looked out the window.

"Ticket, ticket," he repeated, twitching the sleeve of my linen traveling-wrap.

Again I squared around and stared at him—this time coolly, insolently.

"I want your ticket," he muttered; "give me your ticket."

"I have no ticket," I replied, lifting my brows in apparent wonderment that he should make such a demand.

"Well, the cash, then," he jerked out. "Where do you want to go?"

"I'm going to Columbus," I returned calmly.

"You change at Newark," he mumbled; "and the fare's

_____
4 Outre – passing the bounds of what is usual or considered proper

one-seventy-five."

"I change at Newark, do I?" I chirped innocently, sweetly, brushing back a little lock of frizzly hair that would persist in getting in my eyes, and smiling most ravishingly at him.

"You do," he answered, unmoved.

"Thank you."—And once more I turned my attention to the scenery flitting past.

"But your fare—give me your fare," he persisted.

"My fare?"—wondering greatly, not a little annoyed, and somewhat incensed.

"Yes, your fare."

"Why—why,"—blushing demurely, but looking him straight in the eyes,—"didn't—didn't my uncle pay my fare?"

"Your uncle?"—starting and sweeping the front of the car with his sharp gaze.

"Yes, sir."

"Which one is your uncle?"

"That big man in the soft black hat and gray suit,"—pointing with white and taper finger, and incidentally displaying my fine opal ring.

"Him?"—also pointing.

"Yes, sir."

"Well, he didn't pay your fare."

"He didn't?"—greatly surprised.

"No; forgot to, I suppose. I'll go back to him. Beg your pardon for bothering you."

He deliberately took up the rest of the fares in the car. Then he retraced his steps to the big man in the gray suit and tapped him upon the shoulder. The man half turned in his seat and looked up into the conductor's face; and, Nell mine, I nearly fainted. My "uncle" was smooth-faced, young, dark and handsome!

I crouched lower in my seat, shivering, panting—but keenly observant. The conductor said something in a low tone; and I heard the young man blurt out:

"What! The devil you say!"

Then he slowly got upon his feet,—my! how big and tall and

fine-looking he was!—and said in a tone of tense restraint:

"Where is she?"

The conductor indicated me with a nod and a jerk of his thumb; and the young man—his square shoulders and jaws set—gave me a penetrating stare. Instantly I was so embarrassed, so ashamed, so distressed that I wanted to die—right then and there. But the young man caught the appealing look in my eyes and cried out cheerily:

"Hello, Bonnie! I forgot all about you."

Then, to the conductor: "See you in a moment."

He strode back to me, smiling broadly, good-naturedly, and, bending close to me, whispered:

"Where to—Columbus?"

"Y-e-s," I managed to murmur, barely able to articulate the monosyllable.

"You got on at Zanesville?"

I nodded.

"All right."

He returned to the conductor, dropped some money into the palm outstretched to receive it, and said—with a heartsome laugh:

"I forgot all about her writing me that she was going to join me at Zanesville. She ought to have come to me and let me know she was aboard; but she wanted to punish me for my forgetfulness, I suppose."

Again he laughed—softly, easily; then he turned and leisurely sauntered back to me.

"Sit over," he commanded, as one having a right.

I was angered by his arrogant and authoritative tone and manner, but I made a place for him; and he dropped into it.

"Now, little girl," he said in a low, confidential but determined voice, "what am I to infer? What's the meaning of it all? Are you just broke or—or—"

I was looking him straight in the eyes, Nell, my anger rapidly rising to the danger point; and he read the warning in my expression, I presume, for he hesitated and stopped. Then, uneasily, he tried to laugh; and made a miserable failure of it, and sat silent—biting his lips.

I took a quick inventory of him, and determined to my own satisfaction the kind of man I had to deal with—the sort of demon I had conjured up. As I have said, he was tall and dark and handsome. His nose was straight and large; his mouth, firm and wide; his eyes, gray and keen. He was a big, virile, forceful fellow—with a good opinion of himself and with a will of his own, but with a saving grace of humor. I read him as sensible but not sensitive; sensuous but not sensual.

He grew more and more uneasy under my close scrutiny; but at last he smiled good-humoredly and remarked:

"You appear to be sizing up your 'uncle'."

"I am,"—smiling back at him.

"Think you'll know me the next time you meet me, eh—Bonnie?"

"I think I shall—yes."

"Well, now won't you tell me why you palmed me off as your uncle and told the conductor I'd pay your fare?"

"I didn't tell the conductor that."

"Didn't tell him what?"

"That you'd pay my fare. I asked him if you hadn't paid it."

"Oh!"

I nodded.

"Well, you told him I was your uncle, didn't you?"

"I—I guess I—I intimated something of the kind to him. He was pestering me; and I wanted to be rid of him. I had no ticket and no money; and didn't know what else to do."

He nodded understandingly.

"I see," he said. "But why did you select me—of all the men in the train? My face look good to you?"

I gazed at him intently, searchingly; but I could not make sure whether he was in earnest or not.

"I didn't see your face," I answered.

"You didn't?"

"No; I saw your back only."

"Is that so?"—chuckling.—"Then you just picked me out by chance. I'm disappointed; I was patting myself on the back—thought maybe you saw something in my face that—that attracted you."—Then, heartily, earnestly:—"No, that isn't what I mean exactly. What I wanted to say is that I hoped you saw something in my face that inspired your confidence."

"Your back inspired my confidence," I explained artlessly.

"What!"

"It did."

"My back?"

"Yes. You looked so big and strong, so much like a man, so—so good and fatherly."

He threw back his handsome head and laughed; then looked at me—and laughed some more. Evidently I was amusing him; evidently he was getting the worth of his money.

"So I looked elderly, fatherly, did I?" he queried when he could command his voice.

"Your back did—yes."

"Well, how about my face?"

"You know your face looks young."

"Do I?"

"Yes, you do."

"How old do you think I am?"

"You're angling for flattery."

"No, I'm not."

"About thirty-nine."

"What!"

"Yes."

"That's your guess?"

"That's my calculation. A back view of you indicates forty-nine, a front view indicates twenty-nine; so I arrived at an average—thirty-nine."

"Well, I'm just twenty-nine—and glad of it. Now, what's your age?"

"Guess."

"Forty."

"You're kind,"—pouting.

"You asked me to guess; and I never could guess."

"I don't care what you think."

"Oh! I don't think you're forty; I just guessed that. I think you're about eighteen. How close am I?"

"You're close—quite close."

"I thought so."

He was silent a moment; then he asked abruptly:

"Are you really without money?"

"Yes, 1 am—of course 1 am," I cried sharply, "or I wouldn't have done what 1 did."

"Of course," he admitted; "I understand that—now. Did you lose your purse?"

"Yes."

"Where?"

"In Zanesville."

"Do you live there?" I shook my head.

"In Columbus, then?"

'No."

"No? Where?"

"No place—at present."

"Oh, You've set out to make your fortune, have you?"

I made no reply.

"Pretty maiden, you're running away from home."

"How do you know?"—pertly.

"I don't know; I guess—and I guess I'm right."

"Well, if you are?"

"You're making a great mistake."

"I don't think so."

"Of course not; they never do."

"They—who?"

"Girls who run away from good homes."

"You're a preacher, aren't you?"—sneeringly.

"I'm anything but a preacher—you ought to be able to see that; but I'm talking good sense—good advice."

"Well, you needn't talk the stuff to me—I didn't ask you for it; and I can take care of myself. I'm very, very grateful for the kindness you've shown me in paying my fare; but I don't want you to lecture me. I never could bear a lecture."

He continued placidly:

'But you admit that you're running away from home—in spite of the wishes of your parents?"

"I have no parents."

"An orphan—true?"

"Yes."

"That changes the aspect of the case somewhat. But whom are you running away from, then?"

"My brother."

"And the cause?"

"He's going to get married."

"I see—I understand,"—the corners of his mouth twitching.— "Where does he live?"

"I think I've answered about enough questions."

"You don't want to tell me where your brother lives, then?"

"No, I don't."

"Nor your name, either, I presume."

"I won't tell you my name."

"Very well. Please forget that I hinted the request. Still I would like to know your name."

"Why do you want to know?"

"I have an interest in your welfare—that's all."

"Have you, indeed?"—sarcastically.

"Haven't I shown it?" he retorted rather sharply.

"Y-e-s," I had to admit.

"And you're going to Columbus?"

I nodded; and wished sincerely he would talk of something more interesting than myself and my affairs—of himself, for instance.

"What have you in view—what do you expect to do?"

"Work in an office."

"Is that so?"

"Certainly,"—severely. "Why are you so surprised?"

"I'm not. Have you secured a place?"

"Yes, I have."

"You're fortunate."

Then he sat silent and thoughtful for some time. At last he remarked, smiling: "No doubt you think me rather—rather inquisitive."

"No doubt I do—rather," I smiled in return.

"And you resent my inquisitiveness—consider it impertinence?"

"I've no right to resent it; I've put myself under obligations to you—unfortunately."

"Come—don't say that!" he muttered, with genuine feeling. "I don't want you to feel that way about it. I simply desire to be your friend; and you're making it hard for me. You refuse to tell me your name or where you came from; and you intimate that I'm making free—indulging in meddlesome interference in your affairs. You're leading me to doubt your sincerity; and I don't want to do that. Won't you answer me just one question?"

"Maybe. What is it?"

"Whose office do you take a position in Columbus?"

"I won't answer."

"All right," he mumbled, and bit his lips and scowled. Then, sourly: "I'm rapidly coming to believe that you're—you're sailing under false colors; that you've got money; that you've been playing me for a sucker."

That hurt, Nell Adams—hurt like a homesick pain. I didn't mind so much what he said as what he didn't say—what he intimated. I knew well what he meant; and I was so shocked and grieved—that a perfect stranger, even, should thus suspect me. In spite of myself my lips began to tremble and tears started to my eyes. I was angry, too—angry that my native resolution had deserted me, that I couldn't conceal my emotion.

"You're very kind," I murmured chokingly; "and you're welcome to your charitable opinion, I'm sure."

Then I turned my back to him and gazed out at the flying landscape, sick at heart.

Presently I heard him saying gruffly—to hide his feelings, it may have been:

"I'm something of a brute, I guess, my girl; and I do beg your pardon. I know you're all right; I know you are. Now, won't you look at me—won't you talk to me?"

I made no reply by word or sign.

"Won't you?" he repeated softly, coaxingly.

Still I remained silent and motionless.

"Won't you—please?"

"What do you want?" I questioned.

"Want you to tum around; I've got something to say to you."

I turned and faced him.

"My dear young woman," he said gravely, "don't you know you did a very foolish thing—a very reckless thing, when you told the conductor I was your uncle and hinted that I would pay your fare—when you put yourself under obligations to me in that way?"

"No, I don't," I replied frankly.

"Well, your answer establishes your innocence—sure,"—with a deprecating, pitying shake of the head,—"your lack of knowledge of the ways of the big brutal world, at any rate."

"It doesn't establish anything of the kind," I cried, piqued that he should consider me a verdant[5] rural school-miss. "I simply took you for a gentleman; and thought you'd be glad to help me out of an embarrassing situation."

"And what do you think of me now?"—coolly.

"I don't know what to think of you."

"Do you still think me a gentleman?"

"I can't say," I replied candidly. "In some ways you've shown that you are; in others you've indicated that you're not. I'm grateful for the service you've rendered me; but I wish you hadn't inquired into my private affairs."

"And you won't tell me where you came from?"—The persistent man!

"No, I won't."

"Nor tell me your name?"—The unexampled audacity!

"Indeed I won't."

"Nor whom you're going to work for?"—The rude and shameless wretch!

"No! No! No!"—with warranted emphasis.

"Why won't you?"

"Why?"—in fine scorn,— "Because you've no right to inquire;

_____
5 Verdant – inexperienced; unsophisticated

and I sincerely wish I'd let the conductor put me off the train."

"No, you don't,"—smiling provokingly.

"I do!"

"You're mistaken; you're rather enjoying holding me at arms' length, as you are. But, say!"

I lifted my brows in answer.

"I'll tell you my name, if you'll tell me yours."

"I don't care to know your name."—I lied there, Sweet Nell— and I knew I lied; I was burning with curiosity to know his name— to know all about him.

"And I'll tell you where my home is, if you'll tell me where you came from."

I shook my head.

"And I'll tell you my business, if you'll tell me whom you're going to work for. There!"

I remained silent.

"You won't do it?"

"No, I won't," I snapped.

"As you like. Now, let me say just a word more—and I'm through. You're going to need friends in Columbus; I'll tell you why in a moment. No, don't interrupt me,"—raising his hand authoritatively.—"I live in the city; I do business there—when I'm not out on the road. I'm going to hunt you up and look after you; you shan't prevent me. Maybe you have friends or relatives there, though—eh?"—lifting his brows inquiringly.

"No, I haven't," I answered coldly. "And now won't you please take another seat? I think we've exhausted the subject."

"We're running into Newark," he laughed carelessly; "so I shan't bother you much longer—and it won't be necessary for me to move to another seat. While I think of it here's the cash-slip for your fare; the conductor objected to receipting farther than Newark, but I fixed it. Now, to conclude briefly what I want to say: you won't be able to hold a position in any office very long at a time, I fear. You're entirely too pretty, too fascinating; and the wives and sweethearts of your employers will get jealous of you promptly."—Was he making sport of me? I couldn't tell; there was laughter in his eyes, but sincerity in his voice.—"I mean what I say,"—evidently reading my thoughts.—"You'll need friends to help you to outride the storm your own sex will raise against you; and—"

"Well, I'll not come to you for a place in your office," I interrupted frigidly.

"It wouldn't be worth your while,"—grinning a maddening grin;—"I wouldn't have you in our office under any circumstances—no indeed. Why, my father—sixty years old and a widower—is one of the most impressionable men; he incontinently falls in love with every pretty face he sees. I've had to discharge three girls in the last year, on account of his frailty. But I've fixed him at last,"—laughing immoderately;—"a week or so ago I engaged a girl as homely as Medusa. If the old man falls in love with her, I'm going to punish him by making him marry her; I can't be devoting half my time to hunting new girls."

Then, rising and standing with a hand on the back of the seat and bending over me:

"Well, here's Newark; and here you leave me. I've got to run up to Mount Vernon and look after a little business. Sorry I can't go on to Columbus with you. But I'll hunt you up; I mean it. And now I'll see you to your train waiting right over there. Come along; give me that grip."

He conducted me to my car and saw me safely aboard. I thanked him and offered him my hand. He grasped it, held it close in his own and said soberly:

"Goodbye. Don't think too unfavorably of me; maybe I'm not as bad as you think. Goodbye—till I see you again."

Then he hurried through the door, sprang down the steps and ran back to his own train. I sat at an open window and silently, thoughtfully let my gaze follow him. I saw him climb aboard and disappear; and unconsciously I heaved a little sigh—of relief or regret, I could not say which.

Then his train began to move; and at the same moment I felt the premonitory[6] jerk that apprised me that my own was starting.

---

6 Premonitory – serving to warn beforehand

One last look I cast in his direction. He had reappeared at a window and was waving his hand at me. I hesitated a moment, Nell—yes, indeed, I did!—then, with my handkerchief, fluttered him a reply.

Chapter 7

AT TEN o'clock I was in the Union depot at Columbus. I followed the crowd out upon High street, and asked a policeman to direct me to the Branson building.

"About six blocks south," he said, "right hand of the street, half way to the Capitol."

I was infinitely relieved that the distance was no greater; for, as I had no money, I must walk and carry my traveling-bag. I set off briskly, gaily; and in due time I reached the frowning front of the building I sought and entered the arched and ornamented portal. "Durbin and Son, real-estate," I said to the elevator boy, as I stepped into the cage.

He gave no sign that he heard me; but, on reaching the eleventh floor, he stopped the car, slid back the door and motioned me to step out.

"Thousand-and-one," he mumbled as I brushed past him.

And right in front of me I saw the number and the firm name upon the frosted glass of a door. Tremulously but resolutely I turned the knob and crossed the threshold—to meet my fate; and found myself in a large carpeted room with desks and chairs ranged about the floor and maps and plats upon the walls. Three or four men were bending industriously over big, open canvas-bound ledgers; and an equal number of women—of middle age and rather unprepossessing, I noted promptly, Nell!—were playing monotonous staccato music upon typewriters.

I stopped just inside the door and, with all the aplomb I could muster, coolly, calmly surveyed the scene. The man at the desk nearest me slowly arose, stretched his arms above his head, yawned, gave a final glance at the pages of his ledger and then advanced and remarked—with a peculiar rising inflection:

"Something for you, Miss?"

"Is Mr. Durbin in?" I asked, my heart in my throat.

"Durbin senior or junior?"—smiling servilely yet impudently and rubbing his hands together.

"Either will do."

"Durbin senior is in; Durbin junior is out of town. What's the name, please?"

Nell Adams, every pen ceased its scratching, every typewriter stopped its clicking, and every ear in that room was cocked to catch my reply. I could see it—I couldn't help seeing it; and I wanted to laugh—oh, I wanted to laugh!

"Marjor—" I began thoughtlessly, in reply to the man's question; then blushed, cleared my throat—and stood embarrassed and silent, like a bashful school-miss.

"Beg your pardon," he murmured, bending toward me and smirking disagreeably, "I didn't catch your name."

"Sarah Grimes," I returned in clear ringing tones, irritated at the man's manner and my own embarrassment.

And, Nell—Sweet Nell, every man turned and frankly stared at me and every woman whirled around and openly and shamelessly rubbered[1]. Then they slyly smiled at one another; and again looked me over, searchingly, critically—and again smiled, and winked and nodded.

What did their pantomimic[2] behavior mean?

I stood wondering—and staring hard into the face of the man who had come forward to learn my mission.

"You want to see Mr. Durbin?" he inquired, his features twitching.

I nodded stiffly.

"The elder Mr. Durbin?"

"Yes," I snapped, mad enough to stamp my foot and scream;

---

1 Rubber – Interpreted to mean gawk, as in rubbernecking
2 Pantomimic - Communication by means of gestures and facial expressions

and one of the unattractive females tittered.

"Have a chair," suggested the man, pushing one toward me.

I dropped into the proffered seat; and the fellow shuffled to the rear of the long room and through a door, and closed it after him.

Then such actions on the part of those people, Nell Adams! They winked and leered and giggled; and made sly remarks—loud enough for me to hear.

"What did I tell you, old boy?" said one man to another. "Hey?"

The "old boy" chuckled, and shrugged his shoulders.

"You were right," he said. "And now the orchestra 'll commence to play."

"Uh-huh!" laughed a third. "Regular slide-trombone solo with bass-drum accompaniment as a feature, too."

"Old Cock-a-doodle 'll be right in his element," snickered the first.

"And Neddy-boy, steady-boy, will go right up in the air again,"—from the second.

"Say!"—from the third.

"Huh?"—from both the others.

"Wonder what ever made him do it—hey? Neddy-boy, I mean. Don't he know a good thing when he runs on to it? He must have strange notions of—of—female unattractiveness, for instance, eh?"

"Well, I should say!"

"Isn't that the truth!"

Then all three laughed.

The women at the typewriters said nothing aloud; they just kept stealing glances at me and giggling and whispering among themselves. I began to grow uneasy, alarmed. What was the meaning of such unusual and rude conduct? My advent had occasioned it—that was patent[3]; and my presence had inspired their remarks. But what was the meaning of it all? I couldn't determine; and I grew more and more fidgetty as the moments passed. Then an awful, awful thought presented itself. Was it possible they knew the real bona-fide Sarah Grimes—and knew I was an impostor? Horrors! I had an arctic chill and then went into a torrid fever—all in a few seconds. Sarah

3 Patent - obvious

Grimes! At that moment I sincerely regretted that I had ever heard the name. Mercy! What a fool I had been—what a fool I was! No doubt the genuine sterling-brand Sarah had applied for the place in person; and of course they knew her. Oh, cruel fate! Why hadn't I thought of that possibility sooner? What a pesky fix I was in! And, old chum, I was gravely considering the advisability of ignomini-ous[4] flight, when the man who had delegated himself a reception committee of one returned to me and said:

"Mr. Durbin will see you in the private office."

I resolutely pulled myself together and arose to my feet. Then I coolly gave a few shakes and pats to my skirts, collectedly administered a few deft touches to my hair—and calmly caught up my traveling-bag and followed my guide, scornfully ignoring the glances that were following me.

A half-minute later I stood in the august presence of the senior member of the firm of Durbin and Son, real-estate dealers. And what a surprise—what a relief his revealed personality was to me, in a way, Nell! I had expected to face a grim, gruff ogre; instead, I looked upon a dumpy, rotund little man, bald-headed, bulbous-nosed, ruddy-cheeked. A narrow fringe of fuzzy, frizzly gray hair semi-circled the back of his head; and two little bunches of the same texture and color did duty as side-whiskers. He wore dark coat and trousers, white waistcoat and drab spats. Chum mine, he looked for all the world like Foxy Grandpa! His round pale-blue eyes flew open at my entrance—wide, very wide; and he arose and bowed.

"Have a chair—have a chair, young lady," was his greeting; and he continued to bob and smile. "Perhaps you'd better remove your wrap; it's warm—quite warm to-day."

I followed his suggestion.

"So you're Miss—Miss Grimes—Miss Sarah Grimes."

"Yes, sir," I murmured, barely above a whisper.

"And you're here."

That fact was so evident that I did not see fit to comment upon it; so I kept silent. But Mr. Durbin was not satisfied with my silence; and he repeated:

---

4 Ignominious - humiliating

"And you're here, I say."

"Yes, sir."

"In spite of your letter saying you would not come."

"I—I got better so I thought I'd—I'd come."

"Of course; I see. You made a quick recovery."

Again I kept discreetly silent.

"I say you made a quick recovery."

"Y-e-s," I replied.

What was he aiming at? I wondered—I wondered!

"My son engaged you as our private amanuensis—private secretary, I understand."

Well, I didn't understand, Sweet Nell; and I was in a fearful quandary at once. What was I to say? What was the straight of the matter? Had his son engaged me—Miss Sarah Grimes? I didn't know; and I was scared silly.

"He did engage you, didn't he?"—rather sharply, I fancied.

"Y-e-s,—yes, sir,"—in reckless indecision.

"When was it?"

Now I was scared sick!

"I—I think it was a week or so ago," I murmured thickly.

"Ah?"

"Yes, sir."

"About a week ago?"

"Y-e-s."

"You're sure?"

"Why, yes—that is—yes, I guess it was just about a week or so ago."

"Uh-huh! And he told you all about—about me?"

"All about me!" Heavens! What did he mean? And what was "all about me?" Now I was scared insane! I didn't have sense enough left to do anything but swallow and blink.

"Did he?"

"Y-e-s," I gulped.

The old gentleman began to quiver and shake all over—his mouth tight shut, his eyes squinted. I just gazed and marveled. Was he threatened with an epileptic spasm or an apoplectic[5] seizure; or was he just struggling with a desire to laugh—or cry? I couldn't tell—to save me; and I was duly worried. However, he recovered—controlled his working features and went on:

"Did he—Edward, my son—talk with you?"

Not knowing what else to do, I nodded—ever so slightly.

"Over the phone; or did he call—call to see you?"

I was recovering my equanimity[6]. I couldn't gather what the old fellow was hinting at; but I made up my mind to brave the thing through. So I answered:

"He phoned me first; then called upon me at my home."

"He did, eh?"—gleefully rubbing his hands.

"Yes, sir,"—firmly:—"he did."

"And—and he saw you?"

"Why, of course."

I was so completely mystified with his strange questions and peculiar manner, that I felt like flying from the room.

"Was it by daylight he saw you, or—or in the dark?"

"Sir!"

"Now—now!"—with raised finger and quick concern.—"Don't misunderstand me, my dear young woman. What I mean to say is, did he see you by daylight or just by lamplight?"

"He saw me by daylight, sir. But why—what's the difference?"

"Nothing much; nothing much. I was just wondering. And you were looking as—as well then as you do now, were you?"

"Sir? Looking as well? I was as well; yes, sir."

"You were looking as winsome and pretty, eh?"

I could do nothing but blush demurely.

"And he engaged you, did he, and told you to report here for work?"

"He did,"—frigidly.

"Well, that boy of mine's a precious fool—if there ever was one."

Again he commenced to quake and quaver—like an inverted

---

5 Apoplectic - overcome with anger; extremely indignant
6 Equanimity - mental calmness, composure

mold of blanc-mange[7]; and his ruddy features commenced to undergo all sorts of antic twitchings and tricksy spasms. I grew alarmed about him. Waa he subject to such attacks; and were they of a serious nature? Then, of a sudden, he sprang to his feet, slapped his thigh, and opened his mouth and let out a whoop of laughter. And I was indignant as an insulted queen; and wanted to fly at him and scratch him. What kind of a place had I got into, anyhow? Were the people in that office all crazy; and was the head of the firm the maddest of the lot? I wanted to know!

Up and down the room he paced, chuckling, chortling, gurgling—and exploding.

"Mr. Durbin," I cried, exasperated.

He stopped laughing, looked at me vacantly; then began to laugh harder than ever—literally stamping the floor and flagellating[8] his body with his arms.

" Mr. Durbin!"—more sharply.

"Miss Grimes," he answered, instantly sobering and returning to his chair.

"You insult me," I said severely.

"No-no!" he protested. "I intend no discourtesy. You understand the cause of my merriment, undoubtedly, don't you?"

"You're laughing at me."

"No—Indeed, no!"—hastily.—'I'm not laughing at you; I'm laughing about you."

"What's the difference?"—testily.

"Why, you understand why I'm laughing, don't you?"

"I do not."

"I thought you said Ned—my son, you know—told you all about me."

"He—he mentioned you," I stammered; "I think that was about all."

"Oh! Was that all? I misunderstood you; and I don't wonder you misunderstood my merriment, I don't wonder you took it amiss.

---

7 Blanc-mange - a usually sweetened and flavored dessert made from gelatinous or starchy ingredients and milk
8 Flagellate – whip or scourge

I humbly apologize, Miss Grimes. And now a question or two, to avoid embarrassing explanation. My son said nothing to you about my—my weakness, as he is pleased to term it?"

I shook my head, deeply puzzled. Nothing about my being overly impressionable—overly susceptible to the charms of the fair sex?"

Nell Adams! A great light broke in upon me! What had I done— what had I done! I had recklessly assumed the name and character of Sarah Grimes and had taken her place with Durbin and Son; and Ned Durbin, the junior member of the firm, was the young man I had met on the train; and the elder Durbin was the impressionable father of whom the son had spoken. I sat gazing fixedly, stonily, at the old gentleman's rubicund[9] features; and I felt myself falling, sinking— down, down, down. As one in a dream I saw my companion rise from his chair and hasten to the water-filter in the comer of the room. On returning to my side he said:

"Here—have a drink, Miss Grimes; you're looking pale and sick. Your journey and the heat have been too much for you."

With trembling hand I took the proffered glass and drained it. Then I murmured:

"Thank you. I turned suddenly ill."

" Feeling better?" he inquired with real solicitude.

"Yes, a little."

"You look strong. Isn't your health good usually?"

"Very good," I hastened to say; "but I've not been feeling well for a few days. You know I mentioned my indisposition in the letter I sent you."—Then as a quick afterthought:—"I had my sister write it for me."

Sweet Nell of old Oberlin, I was both surprised and delighted with the readiness and celerity[10] with which I was learning to play my part—was learning to deceive and lie. The old gentleman replied to my implied interrogatory:

"Yes, I got your letter yesterday, saying you were sick and couldn't accept the place; and it was the first intimation I had that

---

9 Rubicund – ruddy, rosey
10 Celerity - rapidity of motion or action

Ned had engaged you to come. You see he left the city over a week ago, to look after some coal lands over in the eastern part of the state ; and I didn't know he had you or anyone else under consideration—and inspection."—He smiled radiantly, benignly; and I kept repeating over and over, under my breath: "Inspection, inspection! In the name of common sense what does he mean?"—He continued: "So, when I got your letter I didn't know hardly what to make of it. But I'm awfully pleased that you got able to come, for we've been having a devil of a time here."—He slapped his thigh and laughed wheezingly; and I straightened up and began to pay more attention to what he was saying.—"To make the true condition of affairs here plain to you, I'll just say that my son Edward's a very peculiar young man. He's a big handsome fellow,"—our opinions coincided, Nell!—"like his mother's people and not like his sawed-off old dad,"—grinning good-humoredly,—"and he ought to be a regular ladies' man; but he's anything but that. He's all business—that's what he is; has nothing of tender sentiment about him—has no taste nor admiration for the fair sex at all. He thinks a woman was made to bake and brew—or to do office work, like any other piece of machinery; that's a fact—and that's all. I'm telling you all this so you'll know how to take him. He isn't much like me,"—nodding, smiling—and winking ever so slyly,—"so we've had some differences of opinion and not a little mild trouble about the running of our business. I'd like, for purely aesthetic reasons, to have the office full of pretty young women—I enjoy their pleasure and society; but he won't hear to anything of the kind. He says I'm a foolish old beau, that I'm all the time making love to every good-looking girl I meet, that I ought to have a guardian or be in an imbecile asylum, and that my admiration for the girls spoils them and unfits them for business; and I think him a practical, materialistic, unsentimental wretch,"—smiling sweetly, blandly. "So, to patch up a sort of truce, to maintain a kind of armed peace and neutrality, for the last year I've let him have his way in regard to things; and I've tried to be very circumspect in my behavior. But Ned's unreasonable. Why, he's turned off every comely girl we've had, every young woman that was good to look upon, and has installed three or four things with faces and forms that would make an automobile shy off the highway. Did you notice them as you came in, Miss Grimes?"

"I believe I—I did," I said hesitatingly.

"And what did you think of them?" bending eagerly toward me.—"Now, give me your honest opinion."

"Well, I hardly think—think," I stammered, "they'd take first prize in—a beauty show."

"First prize—in a beauty show! I guess not! Why, it sets my teeth on edge just to look at 'em. Now, I claim I'm a connoisseur when it comes to female beauty; and I admit that I'm attracted and fascinated by a fair face or lovely form, and at times I may make myself just a little ridiculous—considering my age—by bowing too frequently and too profoundly at the shrine of some sweet divinity. But it's just the artistic temperament, the love of the beautiful implanted in me; and I've always been so. And Ned has gone too far in his heartless and heathenish iconoclasm[11]—too devilish far, Miss Grimes. Within the last year we've had two or three girls in the private office here that I could look at without having an attack of St. Vitus' dance; and the minute that degenerate son of mine found me paying the slightest attention to them, according them the slightest courtesy—like presenting them with a bunch of flowers, a box of candy or a bag of fruit, or offering them a lunch ticket or theater ticket—he has incontinently[12] discharged them. I told him when he dismissed the last one, a month or so ago, to select one to suit his own depraved taste; I'd got tired of his fault-finding. He said he'd take me at my word and would find a woman with a face like that of a Chinese idol; and that if I fell in love with her and began to make myself ridiculous and obnoxious, he'd appeal to the courts to make me marry her. And now he's gone and picked you out. Oh, Lord! Oh, Lord!"

He lay back in his chair and rolled and laughed, and kicked his heels together and roared.

"I can't understand it—I just can't!" he gasped, his face purple, tears rolling down his cheeks.

11 Iconoclasm – attitude of a person who attacks settled beliefs or institutions
12 Incontinently - without due or reasonable consideration

"Can't understand what, Mr. Durbin?" I questioned.

"Can't understand your coming," he panted.

"Why can't you understand my coming?" I asked artlessly.

"Oh! I guess I can understand your coming all right," eyeing me admiringly; —"it's Ned engaging you to come that puzzles me."

"Why?"—smiling ravishingly at him.

"Why! You know why, Miss Grimes. You're about the prettiest girl I've seen in years,"—inclining his head and smirking ridiculously;—"and how that chump of a Ned ever came to pick out you as a sure cure for sentimentality, after seeing you, is more than I can fathom or comprehend. He must have thought you ugly, repulsive—of course. The dolt! For if he had a glimmering idea of how blissfully and dangerously attractive you are,"—the old simpleton, Nell!—"he wouldn't have you in the office for anything—under any circumstances."

I had the hardest work to keep from saying—"that's what he told me"; but I bit my lips and kept quiet. The garrulous[13] old fellow went on:

"But he's made his bed, and now he's got to lie in it; he's hired you—and here you are. And I'm mighty glad you're here. The bargain between him and me was that he was to make his choice and both of us were to be satisfied—for a year, at least. I'm satisfied—and likely to remain so; but I doubt if he'll be—very long. But, according to the contract, he can't discharge you; I won't allow him to—I'll hold him right to the agreement. And won't he kick up a shindy[14]—when he begins to realize what he's done! Oh, my!"

He laughed heartily, wheezingly, pounding his knees and wriggling.

"Mr. Durbin," I said timidly, regretfully, "I think I'd better not stay."

"Huh?" he jerked out, sitting up very straight and looking hard at me. "What?"

"I think I'd better not stay," I repeated.

"Better not stay? Why, of course you'd better stay; and of

---

13 Garrulous - pointlessly or annoyingly talkative
14 Shindy – fracus, uproar

course you will stay. Do you suppose I'm going to let you go—the only really good-looking girl we've had in the office in a year? Not much! I won't hear of your leaving—not at all. I wouldn't dare to let you leave, at any rate—when my son has chosen you and sent you here. No, indeed!"

And he grinned and winked—openly, shamelessly.

"But I'm not very well, you know," I weakly objected, and—"

"Oh, that's all right," he interrupted cheerily; "and you'll be all right. You're strong—I can see that; you're just suffering from a temporary indisposition. If you don't feel like going to work to-day, you can wait till to-morrow; we've waited so long, we can wait a little longer. Then, you'll want to secure you a room. There's a pleasant place out on East Gay; I'll give you the address and a recommendation to the landlady, and you can run out there on the car. Several of our girls have roomed there. You'll find a good restaurant in the near neighborhood, where you can take your meals if you like. By the way, it's about lunch time now. Won't you go out with me?"

"No, I—I thank you," I replied in a half-whisper, my brows knit thoughtfully. Then, with quick decision: "And I think I won't—won't accept the place, Mr. Durbin."

"Won't accept the place!"—incredulity and consternation in voice and expression of countenance.—"Oh, come now! You don't mean that. Say that you don't—please say that you don't."

"But I do mean it."

"No, you don't—no, you don't! Why, what leads you to say such a thing?"

"I'm a—afraid I'll make trouble between you and your son," I faltered.

"No danger—not a bit—not the least," he exclaimed excitedly. "Why, I tell you I wouldn't dare to let you go, since he's selected you and had you come on here; that would make trouble."—And once more he grinned and winked, slyly, facetiously.—"And I won't hear of your going, for my own sake; a maid of beauty is a joy forever, to me. No—no! You stay; we'll have great fun—great times. Listen!"— impressively leaning toward me, his finger upon his lips.—"I'll be good—very good, and very discreet; I won't be a bit familiar or offensive. I'll just pay enough attention to you to keep Ned in a stew, to exasperate him to madness."—"He was bubbling and fizzling with half-suppressed merriment.—"I want to teach him a lesson; and I want you to help me to do it. We'll have great times—lots of fun. Won't you stay—won't you help me?"—coaxingly, wheedlingly.

"I don't—don't know" I murmured moodily. "Won't your son discharge me, as he has the others, when he learns—discovers that I'm—I'm not—not unattractive?"

And I blushed as prettily as I knew how, Nell mine; and it would have done your soul good to see the look of worshipful admiration that dear old gay-boy gave me!

"Discharge you?"—bristling valiantly. "I rather guess not; you say you'll stay—and you'll stay. I'm a part of the firm; I'm the head and front of it. I let him run things largely; but my word goes—when I set my foot down and say it goes. He won't try to cut up any didoes[15], though seeing he's engaged you himself; and it'll be great sport to see him squirm. Oh! it'll be a good lesson to him—just what he's been needing. I've wanted him to think about marrying—he's old enough; but he's snubbed me every time I've suggested such a thing. We'll teach him a lesson—you and I. Say you'll stay."

"I've—I've a notion to stay," I replied, irresistibly attracted by the idea of getting even with Mr. Edward Durbin, for his smartness on the train.

"That's it; of course you'll stay."

"But he may claim he—he never hired me—never engaged me," I suggested as the possibility presented itself to me.

"Huh?" the old chap ejaculated.

I repeated my words.

"Oh, he couldn't make any such ridiculous claim as that!"—smiling reassuringly, confidently.—"Why, here's your letter to prove he engaged you—and here you are. No, you stay—and have no fear. Ned'll be home to-morrow, probably; and then the fun'll begin."

And, Nell Adams, it did!

---

15 Didoes - a mischievous or capricious act

Chapter 8

I ENTERED upon my duties with Durbin and Son, the morning following my arrival in the city. Mr. Durbin greeted me smilingly, effusively; but made no further mention of the subject of our conversation of the day before. However, he placed a fine bouquet of roses upon my desk; and, from time to time, as we worked, he fixed his eyes upon me admiringly, worshipfully, and heaved a sigh that seemed to come from the soles of his patent-leathers. It was nice, Nell—ever so nice! He was so respectful, so reverential. At such times a little quiver of gratification and delight played up and down my spine, and a little tinkling tune of bliss sang in my soul. I've learned one thing—if no more, Nell Adams. It's nice to be admired of men—little matter who the man is or what he is like, so long as he doesn't become bothersome. Admiration is more satisfactory than love in this respect: one can enjoy it without reciprocating.

Mr. Durbin took me out and introduced me to the men and women in the outer office; and the men mumbled "Miss Grimes" and shook my hand heartily, and the women looked me over and sized me up and gave me the tips of their fingers. And then all of them opened up a stock-exchange of sly winks and glances and gestures; and the parade was over and the wild girl from Chesterville was led back to her cage.

All the forenoon Mr. Durbin and I worked quietly and busily, seldom exchanging remarks except about the business engrossing our attention; but as the noon hour drew near my employer's manner underwent a change. He grew fidgety, apparently absent-minded; and frequently consulted his watch. I could read him, Nell; I knew what was in his mind—what was coming. At last he hemmed and hummed, and said—haltingly, lamely:

"It's—it's about my lunch-time, Miss Grimes; so I—I guess we'll stop right here and go out and have something to eat."

"We?" I murmured sweetly and demurely, lifting my brows.

"Why—why, yes,"—and he coughed and squirmed.—"Won't you go along with me—won't you accept my hospitality?"

I shook my head, smiling my sweetest.

"You're hungry, aren't you?"—in kind and genuine concern.

"Not very,"—with the faintest accent on the very.

"Oh, yes, you are!"—persuasively, wheedlingly.—"And you can't do anything here in my absence."

"I can rest, Mr. Durbin."

"True, Miss Grimes. But you'd better come out and have something to eat."

"Maybe I will—after a while."

"But come now; it will save time, you know."

"Save time?"—with a hint of frigidity in my voice and manner.

"Well, that is—isn't—that isn't exactly what I mean,"—stammering and getting red in the face.—"I—I mean simply that you can't do anything till I return, and I can't do—do much in your—your absence; and, then, I think it would be—be pleasant for us to lunch together, especially as you re a stranger in the city—hem! Don't you, Miss Grimes?"

"I guess I'd better stay here, Mr. Durbin; I'll write a letter, maybe, and be ready for work on your return."

He was not satisfied,—I had not expected him to be, Nell!—on the contrary, he was sorely disappointed. I could see that; and I giggled a little inward giggle. I was having great fun, Nell mine!

"You can't stand it to do office work unless you eat regularly," he argued. Then, with a courtly bow: "And the bloom will fade from your damask cheeks and the light from your lustrous eyes, if you neglect your meals."

The old dunce! I got up and went with him. What was the use of wasting time and breath—when I knew I meant to go all the time!

The outer office was empty except for the man who had his desk near the door. He looked up, then ducked his head and grinned—amusedly, knowingly.

As we stood waiting at the elevator shaft, I remarked slyly:

"We're not beginning our first day together very well, are we, Mr. Durbin—do you think?"

"I think we are," he chuckled boyishly, quaking and shaking all over and making the fuzzy bunches of hair about his ears quiver like thistledown, "first rate—just right."

"But your son will be home to-day, you say."

"Probably—this afternoon."

"Well, he'll object—make trouble, won't he?"

"About what?"

"About our going out to lunch together."

"Why, he won't know anything about it,"—beaming seraphically[1].

"He won't?"

"Why, no. How will he?"

"The man in the office, who saw us come out, will tell him."

"Think so?"

"Of course he will."

"Jones?"

"I guess that's his name—yes; the man at the desk near the door."

"That's Jones," he nodded, smiling broadly. Then, chuckling asthmatically: "You think that he'll tell Ned?"

"To be sure."

"What makes you think so?"

"I—I saw him look at us—in a funny way."

"You did?"

"Yes."

"Was he grinning?"

"Yes, he was."

He laughed, and coughed, and sputtered.

"I saw him, too," he wheezed huskily "and he'll tell Ned—I know it. That's what tickles me; that's where the fun comes in. But

---

1 Seraphically – angelically

you needn't be afraid; Ned won't dare to say a word—I've got him this time!"

I didn't feel so much assurance, Nell; but I said no more.

But we did have a great lunch, old chum. Mr. Durbin laid himself—and his money—out to do the handsome, and he succeeded; and I showed my appreciation by eating heartily and by favoring him with my most fascinating smiles. The old youngster was in a heaven of glory and delight; and his fat round face beamed like a stage moon. He was so well pleased with my gracious behavior and so vainglorious[2] over our mild escapade—that I could see he considered quite a wild adventure, under the circumstances!—that be proposed rashly that we play truant and go to the matinee, instead of returning to our work. I felt the danger, Nell; and I had to call him back to a sense of duty. He was clear out on the daisy-fringed border of gentle dalliance[3] and undying love; if he had got me to that matinee, I'm confident he would have proposed to me right off.

On our way back to the office, he began:

"Now, as we've broken the ice, as it were, Miss—Miss—"

"Grimes," I prompted, wondering what was coming.

"Oh, I recall your name well enough!" he teeheed gleefully. "But I was just thinking whether I might—mightn't—might—"

"Well?" I murmured softly, snuggling a little closer to his side. I saw he was going to unbosom and unburden himself in some way, Nell; and I wanted to encourage him all I could—for his soul's sake!

"Why, the—the fact is," he went on, squaring his shoulders and strutting, "I was thinking—wondering whether I mightn't—mightn't—"

Again he came to a stop, smiling an unctious, inane smile at me.

"Go on," I murmured, my eyes downcast.

"Well,"—in evident desperation,—"'Miss Grimes' seems so formal, so—so distant, I was wondering whether I mightn't call you 'Sadie.'"

Nell Adams! I wanted to kill him right there! "Sadie!" Did you ever! I always did despise that name. The old dunce!

---

2 Vainglorious - boastful
3 Dalliance - casual romantic relationship

"No, you may not!" I answered promptly and firmly.

"No?"—grinning vacuously.

"No!"

"Well," he persisted, 'Sarah,' then—just for the sake of infor-mality; I always did think 'Sarah' a sweet old-fashioned name."

'Well, I don't!" I said icily.

"No?"

"No, I don't!"

"What shall I call you, then?"

"Mr. Durbin, you can call me 'Miss Grimes,'"—frigidly.

"Not even 'Miss Sarah' or 'Miss Sadie' eh?"

"No; 'Miss Grimes' will please me best, Mr. Durbin—thank you,"—very frigidly.

"All right—all right," he hastened to say. " I hope you haven't taken my little suggestion amiss. I only wanted to be friendly—to make you feel more at home in our employ, in my company. All right Miss—Grimes."

And I think the old codger meant what he said, Nell—just that and nothing more; or, rather, that he thought he meant that. You un-derstand? But I was mad—vixenish! The old pest! "Sadie!" A snub-nosed kitchen-miss's name! "Sarah!" A freckle-faced nurse-maid's cognomen[4]! Bah! It was awful! I had a notion to pull the old gay-boy's fuzzy side whiskers—I did, honestly!

Well, that afternoon Mr. Ned Durbin returned to the city. I heard him when he came into the outer office—the communicating door was ajar; and I recognized his voice at once. And the queerest little shiver—of delightful dread and dreadful delight!—rustled the hair on the nape of my neck; and I braced myself and got ready to face the inevitable. How would he act? What would he say? What would he do?

I saw Mr. Durbin cock an ear and listen. Then he said:

"Why, that's Ned."

I just nodded, my heart fluttering and buzzing like a humming-bird.

"Miss Grimes is here," I heard Jones say.

---

4 Cognomen - nickname

"That so?" Mr. Ned replied. "All right; glad of it."

His footsteps approached the door; and I felt all stuffy—like he was walking up and down my chest. Then the door swung open—and he stood within the room. I could not lift my eyes from the work before me.

"Hello, father!" he cried cheerily.

"Hello, Ned—my boy!" Mr. Durbin returned. "Glad to see you back."

Then all was silent as death. I knew very well what was going on—that Mr. Ned had discovered me, was staring straight at me. What would he say? What would he do? Oh, it was terrible, Sweet Nell! Yet I was full of laughter, and wanted to screech hysterically. At last, after what seemed minutes, I managed to look up; and—

There he stood stiff as a statue, boring me through with his keen eyes; and his father was looking at him, in questioning wonder.

"How do you do," I chirped prettily—a little plaintively, I presume.

Surprise, incredulity, anger—were written upon his handsome features.

"Why—why," he jerked out, "what the dev—you—you?"

"Why, you recognize Miss Grimes, don't you, Ned?" Mr. Durbin interposed, his apple face spread in an amused grin.

"Miss Grimes?"—with a start.

"To be sure."

"Oh!"—slowly, drawlingly, the light of a great understanding illuminating his dark countenance, "Miss Grimes, you're—you're here, I see."

"Yes," I murmured.

Nell, he showed himself a thoroughbred. He began to smile and talk, apologize for not recognizing me at once,—think of the absurdity of it!—asked me when I got in; and completely bamboozled his dear old dad. Then he hung up his hat in the closet and withdrew to the outer office.

When we were again alone, Mr. Durbin whispered lispingly:

"What do you think, Miss Grimes?"

"About what?" I asked innocently.

"About Ned's not recognizing you?"

"I—I don't know, I—I guess. Why?"—suspiciously.

"I believe he did recognize you all the time."

I gave a guilty start. It was so hard to feel myself Miss Sarah Grimes and yet know myself Miss Marjory Dawes. Did Mr. Durbin suspect that I was masquerading?

"Y—e—s ," I whispered questioningly, with dry lips.

"Yes," my companion went on glibly, "I think he recognized you; but I think he just came to a realization of how—how pretty you are—and it sort of upset him."

"Think so?"—tittering, greatly relieved.

"Yes, I do."

"Perhaps."

And I calmly resumed my work.

A half hour later Mr. Ned again came in, and said briskly—rather brusquely: "Father, I'm knocked out; I wish you'd take these rent bills up to the Falstaff building, and collect. A turn in the open air will do you good—eh?"

"I s'pose so," Mr. Durbin grunted somewhat ungraciously.

It was plain he did not desire to go—did not want to leave his son and me there alone, for some obscure reason of his own, I fancied; but he took his hat and his departure.

Mr. Ned cooly closed the door, seated himself and began to look over some legal papers. I worked away, Nell—silently, rapidly; but I was full of laugh—in spite of my fear and trembling. At last he tossed the papers upon the desk between us and, leaning forward and smiling a cold and nasty smile, said slowly and distinctly:

"Now, my little girl, we'll thresh this thing out—right here, and this minute."

I folded my hands in my lap—they were cold as ice, Nell!—and looked him full in the face, bravely yet not defiantly.

"What're you doing here?" he pursued.

"Working,"—ever so innocently and sweetly.

"Indeed!"—angrily.

"Yes."

"Well, don't get funny now; this is no funny matter. You are palming yourself off for Miss Grimes?"

"I am Miss Grimes," I answered calmly.

"Oh!"—with a sneer.

"Yes, sir."

"Not much—not to me."

"To your father—and all the rest, I am."

"Well, where is Miss Grimes?"

"How should I know?" I countered.

"You do know."

"Do I?"—smilingly, provokingly.

"Yes. Where is she?"

"In Parkersburg."

"What? Take care, now!"

"She is."

"How do you know?"

"Well, I know."

"Why didn't she come—why did she go to Parkersburg?"

"She got a better job, she thought."

"Oh!"

I nodded, still searching his face.

"Did she send you in her stead?" I shook my head.

"No?"

"No."

"How did you learn about this place, then, and that I had engaged her---and that she wasn't coming?"

I kept silent.

"Tell me,"—sternly.

"I won't,"—firmly.

"You won't?"—gruffly, his brows knitted.

"No."

A few moments he glared at me, nervously drumming the desk, with his clenched hand. "You say she didn't tell you about this place?

"I didn't say."

"Well, did she?"

"She did not."

"Is she a friend of yours?"

"No."

"An acquaintance?"

"No."

"Have you ever met her?"

"I have not."

Clearly he was puzzled. He frowned and pursed his lips.

"And you won't enlighten me—won't tell me anything more?" he said.

"No, I won't."

"Answer me this one question: did you have this place in mind when we met on the train?"

"Yes."

"You did!"—with a start.

I nodded.

"And you knew me to be a member of the firm?"

"No."

"Now!"

"Indeed I did not,"—on my dignity,—"and you have no right to question my word."

The merest suggestion of a smile relaxed his stem mouth, Nell; and he said quickly:

"I beg your pardon, Miss—Miss—"

"Miss Grimes," I prompted, giggling.

"I don't know what to call you," he muttered irritably.

"Miss Grimes," I repeated.

"Nor what to think you," he went on, again fixing his eyes upon me, sternly—but admiringly, I imagined.

"Think me just what I appear to be," I suggested.

"An arch little adventuress?"—his eyes twinkling.

"You're—you're mean, Mr.—Mr. Ned," I pouted.

"Mr. Ned—eh?" he smiled.

" Oh!" I cried in confusion—partly real, Nell!—"I didn't mean to call you that; I've just been thinking of you by that name, to distinguish you, in my mind, from your father, Mr. Durbin."

"Well, 'Mr. Ned' is all right, I suppose; at any rate, I've no radical objection to it. You may continue to think of me as 'Mr.

Ned,' if it pleases you. But what am I to call you?"

"Miss Grimes, I told you."

"But you're not Miss Grimes," he objected.

"I'm filling her place, performing her duties, and—"

"But you won't be long," he interrupted, the stern look coming back to his face.

"I won't?" I queried faintly.

"No, you won't."

"You mean to discharge me?"

"I never engaged you."

"Well, what do you intend, then—to send me about my business, or—or hand me over to the police?"

And I feigned a fear that I partly felt.

"Neither," he smiled indulgently; "I mean to find you another position."

"Another position?"

"Sure."

"You needn't trouble yourself," I snapped, really quite angry; "I found this one for myself, and I can find another."

"It may not prove so easy, little girl."

His voice was soft with genuine kindness, I thought.

"I don't care," I murmured, tears of distress in my eyes; "I don't desire your help. A pretty figure you'd cut—sending me to somebody else, when you won't have me yourself."

"Yes," he admitted, nodding gravely, "there is a difficulty I hadn't thought of. It would look rather peculiar—and prove rather embarrassing, no doubt. But you can't stay here."

"Why can't I—Mr. Ned?"

"Why can't you!"—crossly.—"You know why, Miss—Miss— oh, the devil! I can't call you Miss Grimes, when I know you're not Miss Grimes. But you know why I can't have you here. My father would be neglecting business and making a fool of himself, inside of a week; he'd carry flowers to you, want you to go out to lunch with him, try to carry you off to every matinee and—"

I giggled outright.

"What amuses you?" he demanded sharply.

"You," I replied.

"What's so amusing about me?"—peevishly.

"Your marvelous knowledge of your father's frailties."

"What do you mean? Explain."

"He has already carried me flowers, had me out to lunch and insisted on taking me to a matinee."

Oh, Nell Adams! I wanted to scream with laughter. If you could have seen the look on that young man's face!

"Well I'll—I'll be—be" he muttered and then he sat silent, biting his lips and scowling.

After a few moments, however, he resumed in a cold business-like tone:

"Miss—Miss Grimes,"—I could see that it cost him an effort to thus address me!—"it's not necessary for us to discuss the matter farther. You can't stay here; you must go. My father, according to your own testimony, has already been making a fool of himself; and shortly he'd become a consummate nuisance to you, to me—and everybody concerned. He's old—in his dotage, I sometimes think, judging from his foolishness; but he's my father—and I'm in duty bound to respect him and keep him, as far as possible, from making himself ridiculous and, at the same time, keep him from making me and our business the laughing-stock of the town. I'd really like to have you remain; I think you'd prove satisfactory, if it wasn't for your good looks. But it's out of the question; I can't risk keeping you—it won't do."

"But your father won't want me to leave," I objected.

"Of course not!"—gritting his teeth.

"And he's the senior member of the firm," I suggested softly.

A moment he searched my face; then:

"Well, what of it?"

"He ought to have a say in the matter."

"Is that so!"—and again he stared hard at me.

I nodded.

"Well, he—he didn't hire you."

" Neither did you."

"And, for that very reason, you've no place here."

"True, probably. But what will you say to Mr. Durbin? How will you explain?"

"Explain what?"

"Explain why you've broken your word—the bargain you made."

"The bargain?"—plainly puzzled.

Once more I nodded, smiling, my eyes half-closed.

"I don't understand you, I guess. What bargain?"

"You know," I said placidly; "the bargain you made with your father: that you were to select a girl for the place, that she was to stay a year—if she proved satisfactory, and that he was to marry her—if he indulged in any gallantries."

His face went blank; and I laughed—a little tinkling, silvery laugh, Sweet Nell.

"Who told you all that?" he cried, smiling a sickly smile.

"You did,"—triumphantly.

"I did? On the train?"

"Of course."

"Not all of it, did I?"

"Your father told me a part."

Again I had to laugh at his rueful expression of countenance.

"And we're a pair of precious idiots," he growled; "I'm getting to be as bad as he is."

"Well," I pursued, coquettishly cocking my head and lifting my brows, "what're you going to say to your father? He thinks me Miss Grimes, thinks that you engaged me, thinks that you consider me safely unattractive. Are you going to admit your—your mistake, and own up that I am—am dangerous; or are you going to reveal my duplicity—confess that fate has outwitted you?"

"I'm not outwitted."

"No?"

"No, indeed."

"Well, if you betray my duplicity, how will you explain that you did not denounce me as soon as you discovered me in the office?"

"I'm not going to explain anything, my dear child."

"Oh!"

"No, I'm not going to do any of the things you mention,"—quite decidedly.—"My father wouldn't—simply couldn't—keep his mouth shut; I know him. The reporters would get hold of the thing, and the papers would be full of it; and I shouldn't hear the last of it for a year. No,"—shaking his head and smiling rather wearily,—"I know a better way out of the muddle. I'll let you stay here a week or two; then you must tell father that you don't like the job—and resign."

"I must?"—indignantly.

"I see no other way."

"Well, I won't do it."

"Why?"

"Why? What a question! Places are not so easy to secure—you say so yourself; and I'm not going to throw up a situation without cause. I know I shall like the place—I know I shall; and I'm not going to lie—just to throw myself out of a job. No, indeed I'm not! You can discharge me—by telling your father I'm not Miss Grimes; but I'm not going to resign. So there!"

He looked—and looked—and looked—at me, Nell. At last he muttered:

"You're a perverse child—a regular spoiled girl, you are."

"I don't think it's nice to call people names," I pouted, bewitchingly as I knew how, "just because they don't agree with you."

He lay back and laughed. Then he consulted his watch, and said:

"You're irresistible, little girl. You win: I lose. You can stay till you find another place. Is that fair—is that a bargain, that you're to stay on as Miss Grimes till you secure another situation, and then resign?"

"Yes," I agreed.

"All right."

And I stayed.

Chapter 9

THE next morning when Mr. Ned came into the office, he stopped short and glared at the bouquet his father had just placed upon my desk—his lips drawn into a tense straight line, his nostrils dilated. Mr. Durbin silently noted his big son's attitude and expression of countenance; then he silently but shamelessly winked and grinned at me. And I had all I could manage, Sweet Nell, to keep my tricksy[1] face straight.

Mr. Ned turned and gave his father a look, in which reproach and disgust were mingled and blended; then he turned his attention to me.

"Miss Grimes," he began abruptly, drawing a morning paper from his pocket, "I see they've been having rather a strange elopement down in your corner of the state—down in the Muskingum valley."

Nell, that brief and seemingly insignificant statement threatened to send me in a heap to the floor. I knew in a moment just what it meant—thought I knew just what was coming; and I never felt so much like giving a scream and fainting dead away, in my life. Things in the room began to turn all yellow and green and black; my fingers and toes got all tingly; and awful sounds began to crack and roar in my ears. But my native common sense—the little I have, Nell! did not entirely desert me, and I managed to get mad at my foolish self; and then I was all right again—all in a jiffy. What difference did it make, anyhow, what Mr. Ned suspected or learned? I asked myself the question. Already he knew I was not Miss Grimes. What matter if he discovered who I really was? So I lifted my eyes—and coolly,

1 Tricksy – difficult to handle

fearlessly met his look.

"Y-e-s?" I murmured. softly, indolently, questioningly, in answer to his remark.

"Yes," he went on, with a queer, puckery smile, "an old graybeard of sixty or more eloped with a pretty miss in her tender teens. Which was remarkable enough in itself, but not half so remarkable as the fact that the bit of romantic folly ended in an unromantic fiasco. It appears from the report in the Journal here,"—tapping the paper with his fore finger and almost leering into my face, "that the precious pair of young and inexperienced nestlings began their flight from the little inland town of Chesterville, and—you know where that is, Miss Grimes?"

This question with startling suddenness.

"Yes, indeed," I replied promptly and placidly; "I've been there."

"Oh!"—with a world of sly and obscure meaning.

"Uh-huh,"—smirking ravishingly.

"W-e-ll, as I say, the pair set out from Chesterville—in the dead and dark of night, in the midst of a mad storm, and in a two-horse buggy—to make their way to the nearest railway station some miles away; and—in spite of muddy roads, and accidents by flood and field, and the hot pursuit of a hotter brother—they reached their destination, just in time to catch the early morning train up the valley. But here comes the strange, the unromantic, the sad part of the story. Apparently the two sweet childish things had grown tired of each other in so short a time. Undying love had died—and all that. What true-lover's quarrel they had in the murk and the mud of the night will never be known—alas! But this fact stands out like a week-old beard on a tramp's face: at the station they parted; the young lady went north and her bold and rheumatic cavalier went south. And now the sweet and misguided young miss's brother is keeping the wires hot, telegraphing the police of Zanesville and Columbus—and sundry other cities, to be on the watch for her and apprehend her and have and hold her, till his arrival. He describes her as young and inexperienced in the ways of the naughty world, but beautiful beyond compare—enchantingly, seductively beautiful. The description of her—as given by the veracious reporter for the voracious public—is calculated to make an impressionable man's mouth water."

"Your rather inadequate account of that description does make my mouth water," chuckled Mr. Durbin, hugging himself and rolling his eyes ecstatically. "Oh, I wish I were on the police force this minute!"

The son turned and glowered at the father, Nell; and the father promptly and undignifiedly kicked up his heels and went into a convulsion of merriment—and laughed, and laughed, till his fat face was a quivering mass of purple, fringed with fuzzy, silvery hair and studded with teardrops. The son scowled darkly and bit his lips. Oh, Nell—Nell Adams! I did so want to let loose and screech; but instead I controlled myself—how I did I haven't the faintest idea!—and cried excitedly, clapping my hands:

"Oh, Mr.—Mr. Ned!"—And immediately Mr. Durbin ceased to laugh and was all attention, and somewhat displeased over something, I could plainly see.—"But what're their names—of the eloping couple? Maybe I know them. What're their names?"

Mr. Ned looked me straight in the eyes, the corners of his wide mouth twitching.

"Well, now, maybe you do," he said. "Let me see,"—consulting the paper;—"why their names 're Colonel Wells and Marjory Dawes. Do you know them, Miss—Miss Grimes?"

His eyes were sparkling; the corners of his mouth were still twitching.

"No, I don't know them," I replied, reflectively shaking my head,—and I was telling the truth, Sweet Nell of old Oberlin; for who does know anyone, even himself?—"but I've met them."

"Indeed?"—smiling.

"Yes, Mr. Ned."

Did I see Mr. Durbin the elder wince? And what would cause him to wince? Ah, I had called his son "Mr. Ned!" Did he think I was getting too familiar? Was the old beau getting jealous? I wondered—oh, I wondered!—and tittered a little, under my breath.

"And is Miss Dawes as—as beautiful as the credible reporter would have the credulous public credit her with being?" Mr. Ned was saying.

I paused a moment before making answer, to admire his skillful juggling with words—and to consider what my reply should be. Then I returned modestly, but glibly:

"You oughtn't to ask me such a question, Mr. Ned; you know one woman never admires another—really and truly."

"Oh!" he laughed. "I see. Well, did those people live in Chesterville—both of them?"

"Miss Dawes did," I returned frankly; "Colonel Wells lived in the South somewhere, I think."

"Uh-huh. Well, the paper says it's now the opinion of the young lady's friends that she did not really elope with the gay and festive Colonel, at all; but just used him as a convenient crutch upon which to limp out of reach of her brother, at whom she was angry on account of his approaching marriage. Do you know anything about that?"

And once more he was boring me through with his keen gray eyes.

"How should I know, Mr. Ned?" I parried neatly.

"True enough," he muttered slowly and thoughtfully; "how should you?"—Then, with a quick change of manner:—"But perhaps you'd like to look over the account yourself, eh?"

"No, thank you," I replied, beautiful candor beaming from my countenance, I'm certain; "I'm not much interested."

"All right,"—briskly,—"we'll get down to work, then."

And I sat and worked and wondered, and wondered and worked. Did he know—did he suspect—did he guess? I couldn't decide. I had met my match, chum mine; and I couldn't read him.

At lunch-time Mr. Ned was absent from the office; and again I went out with Mr. Durbin.

"Miss Grimes," he remarked as we were returning, "I noticed you calling my son 'Mr. Ned.'"

"Yes?" I replied tentatively.

"Yes; and I wouldn't do it, if I were you."

"No?—stiffly, but sniffing fun in the air.

"No, I don't believe I would."

"Why, Mr. Durbin?"

"Well, my reason for cautioning you is this: I want you to continue in our employ—want you to, awfully bad; and I'm afraid Ned—he's so devilish peculiar!—will think you entirely too familiar in thus addressing him, will misunderstand you and take it amiss. I'm afraid he will—that's all."

"Do you—you think he will, Mr. Durbin?"—with assumed fear and trembling.

"No—no! Don't misunderstand me, Miss Grimes. I don't know that I think he will; as I just said, I simply have a fear that he will—that he may, at any rate. Understand?"

"Y-e-s, I—I guess so. And if he should, Mr. Durbin?"

"Huh?"—alertly.

"Why, if he should think me too unconventional—if he should get affronted, what of it?"

"What of it?"

"Yes."

"Oh, nothing—nothing! Only—only he might make your unconventionality an—an excuse to discharge you."

"To discharge me?"—In well-feigned dismay.

He nodded—very gravely.

"Well," I murmured caressingly, trustfully, "you wouldn't—wouldn't let him, would you?"

"Not much I wouldn't—not much!"—and, Nell, you should have beheld the pomposity of his strut!—"No, indeed, I wouldn't let him discharge you. But"—confidentially, "I want everything to go along smoothly and pleasantly, you know—you understand. As I said to you, Ned's a mighty peculiar chap; as near as I can understand him and his whims and prejudices, he has no fancy for women at all. He dislikes the whole sex—pretty ones in particular, I guess. I must admit, though,"—beaming worshipful admiration upon me! "that he talked more to you this morning, than I ever knew him to talk to a woman before in his life—on any subject outside of business."

Poor old fellow! I really felt sorry for him, Nell. How the big virile son had pulled the wool over his little aesthetic dad's eyes!

"Still you fear he might object to my addressing him so—so

informally?"

The dear old chap nodded, bestowing upon me a look of due and impressive gravity. And then I exploded a bomb under him, Nell—a bomb that shattered his complacency, and broke him all up.

"Why," I chirped artlessly, "he told me this morning he didn't care if I called him 'Mr. Ned.'"

The bomb had gone off; and he was up in the air—out of sight. When he finally alighted upon terra firma, tattered and torn and blank of countenance and bankrupt of breath, he gasped:

"He—Ned told you that, Miss Grimes?"

"He did, Mr. Durbin."

"Said that to you?"

"Yes."

"Well, I'll—be—blowed!"

I thought he had already been blowed, Nell; but I didn't say so.

We had reached the foyer of our office building. Mr. Durbin began to gurgle and sputter, and wheeze and chuckle; and all the way up in the elevator he went out of one spasm into another.

When we were again seated in the office, he looked at me—a dazed, all-gone expression upon his fat round face—and muttered in awe-struck tones:

"Miss Grimes, you're a wonder, a witch—that's what you are. Yes, you're more than that; you're an enchantress, a—a—what is it you call it?—a siren. Why, you've had more influence over Ned in twenty-four hours than all the other women he has ever come in contact with have had in twenty-four years. Yes, you have; I'm telling you the truth."—I knew the dear enthusiastic old fellow wasn't telling the truth, chum mine; knew the son wasn't half the woman-hater the fond father imagined; but it was sweet to hear such an encomium[2] upon my prowess as an enchantress pronounced, just the same.—"But I don't know whether to be delighted· or concerned about what you've told me; don't know whether Ned is just coming to his senses—or just losing 'em. I'm a little suspicious he isn't just right, a little fearful something ails him. Does he—he appear all

2 Encomium – A speech or piece of writing that praises someone or something highly

right to you, Miss Grimes?"

"Yes, indeed," I murmured in a tone of deep sincerity. And I wasn't prevaricating a little bit, Nell—as you will readily guess; Mr. Ned did appear all right—did look good to me!

"You can't realize how glad I am to hear you say that," Mr. Durbin pursued. "And you think, then, Miss Grimes, that Ned is just—just unbending, as it were, just yielding to the fascination of your beauty of person and character, just coming under the influence of your witcheries?"

I dropped my eyes and blushed prettily and properly.

"Really, Mr. Durbin," I made answer, "I—I haven't thought much—much about it." What a monstrous fib, Nell Adams! I hadn't been thinking—hadn't been able to think—of anything else.

"Well," my companion concluded, preparing to resume work, "I only hope my dreams and desires may come true. I'd like to see that boy—as a fit punishment for his past contempt for the female sex, and for the scorn and abuse he has heaped upon me—smitten with an absolutely hopeless passion. There!"

The cruel and wicked old wretch! 1 didn't want to see Mr. Ned punished like that, Nell—smitten with a hopeless passion. No, indeed!

Well, several days passed without material change in the status of our affairs. Mr. Ned said no more about my leaving; and I made no effort to secure another position. I was content to let things drift, to let time and fate decide for me what I couldn't decide for myself. I've said no material change took place in our affairs; but a few things I noted. Among others, every time I passed through the outer office especially when unaccompanied—those men and women out there had a deal of nudging and winking, and gawking and giggling, to do; and it became more and more nearly unbearable. Jones, the hollow-cheeked, red-haired man at the desk near the door, was particularly offensive. I couldn't pass him without being conscious of his disrespectful smirks and insinuating leers. Also, I noted that Mr. Durbin donned a new panama hat and lavender tie and sported a new fob chain, and that Mr . Ned arrayed his fine figure in a new summer suit. Then, I noted—with growing concern, and amusement closely akin to pleasure!—that every time Mr. Durbin placed a fresh bouquet upon my desk, Mr. Ned promptly had a spell of the sulks, and every time Mr. Ned drew near me to dictate a letter Mr. Durbin had an attack of the fidgets. And the thought came to me: Marjory Dawes, your presence in this office is going to make serious trouble; you're arraying[3] father against son and son against father. And I was worried—really and truly worried, my Nell!—and didn't know just what to do.

One evening about closing time, a week after my arrival in the city, Mr. Ned sauntered into the private office, an afternoon paper in his hand. He gave me an odd, quizzical look as he drew near my desk; and I started, wondering what was coming. Having indented a place upon the paper with his thumb nail, he threw the sheet upon my desk; then he turned and walked over to a window and stood staring out moodily, his hands thrust deep into his pockets, his square shoulders sagged.

I glanced at the paper in front of me, and read:

"Mr. Jack Dawes of Chesterville, of whose sister's elopement with a man old enough to be her grandfather mention was made some days ago, is in Columbus, looking for the recreant miss. The brother has traced the misguided sister to this place and has evoked the aid of the city police to aid him in the search. Thus far no trace of the young woman has been discovered. However, the brother has determined to a certainty that his sister came here alone and that the gallant old beau in whose company she left home has made tracks for the South. Evidently he was in haste to seek a more congenial clime, and to escape the wrath of a justly incensed brother."

I was mad at once—mad all through and all over! Wouldn't the silly newspapers ever get through publishing lying stuff about me? Me! And Jack was making a prime nuisance of himself! Why didn't he go back home and behave himself? Oh, but I was good and mad, Nell! Mr. Ned left the window and, dropping into a chair, remarked carelessly:

"What do you think about that, Miss Grimes?"

I glanced up at him. The mean thing! He was laughing at me—

---

3 Array – To place in desired order

with his eyes!

"I—I suppose it's all so," I stammered.

"What're you two talking about?" Mr. Durbin interjected testily.

"Talking about a little article in the paper here, father," Mr. Ned returned quietly—but actually winking at me; "it's something that wouldn't interest you, I think. By the way, won't you step out and see if Clawson has those deeds ready?"

The father withdrew, frowning pettishly; and then the son hastened to say—in a low, confidential tone:

"What do you think about that, Miss Grimes—honestly, you know?"

"I've told you," I said coldly.

"No doubt Mr. Dawes is greatly worried over the mysterious disappearance of his sister, "don't you think so, Miss—Miss Grimes?"—provokingly drawling the name.

"Perhaps," I murmured curtly and noncommittally.

"If I knew anything of the whereabouts of his sister," he continued deliberately, "I think I'd go to him and tell him—just to set his mind at rest." He was eyeing me sharply.

"Would you?" was all I could say.

"I think I would. What would you do, under similar circumstances, Miss—Miss Grimes?"—again drawling the name.

"I think I should attend to my own business."

"Should?"

"Yes—and would."

"Oh!"

"Yes."

"But, as I say," he persisted, "no doubt Mr. Dawes is worrying; and it's a worrisome thing to worry."—Then, after a moment's seeming reflection: "I think I'll see Mr. Dawes and have a talk with him; maybe I can help him out in his search." He sat looking at me, waiting for me to say something in reply; but I kept still. And then Mr. Durbin returned; and the three of us together left the office.

I was "next," of course; I was positive Mr. Ned Durbin had spotted me as Marjory Dawes. But I didn't much care; I was becoming a sinful and hardened little baggage, I guess, old chum.

The next morning, contrary to his custom, Mr. Ned was in the office on my arrival; and his father was absent.

"Good morning," I twittered cheerily.

"Good moming," he croaked moodily.

Then I discovered the morning Journal upon my desk; and I knew he had put it there—knew there was something in it about me and my affairs, and I began to run down the column of locals as I drew the pins from my hat. Yes, there it was—impudently staring me in the face.

"Mr. Jack Dawes of Chesterville," it ran, "left for Zanesville over the eleven-forty B. and O. last night, on his way home. To a Journal reporter he gave the information that he had not found his sister, but that he had received positive assurance from a reliable source that she is in the city, in the employ of a reputable firm. He expressed himself as greatly relieved, if not wholly satisfied, and said he would pursue his quest no further at present. He left full of admiration for the Capital City, its growth and prosperity. Mr. Dawes is a well-to-do merchant in a flourishing town."

I finished reading the rather important paragraph, gave a little sigh and went and hung up my hat.

"Well?" Mr. Ned ventured, in a tone of pique and impatience mingled.

"Well?" I countered coolly.

"What have you to say?"

"Nothing. Why should I?"

"Are you pleased or displeased—Miss Dawes?"

I knew it was coming, Nell; but I could not keep from giving a slight start, nevertheless. And I felt the color flaming up in my cheeks.

"Neither, Mr. Edward Durbin," I answered smoothly and firmly; "I'm absolutely unconcerned."

"That so?"—tantalizingly, smiling broadly.

"Yes, sir."

"Well, I presume you know who it was went to your brother and gave his assurance of your well-being—eh?"

"I presume I do. Why did you do it?"

"To ease his mind."

"How kind, how considerate of you!" I cried sneeringly.

"Don't you think I did right?"

"I think you meddled—unwarrantably."

His dark face flushed; and, for the moment, I feared I had gone too far.

"You think that, Miss Dawes?"—very slowly and soberly.

"W-e-ll, haven't I room—haven't I reason to think it?" I faltered.

"I think not, Miss Dawes."

I was silent a moment; then I queried:

"What did you tell him—Jack?"

"Told him you had a place in my office and were all right."

"Is that all?"

"That's all."

"You didn't tell—tell him I—I sent you to him?"

"I certainly did not."

"Did he ask if I sent you?"

"He did."

"And did he appear hurt that I had not sent you?"

"Yes, he did."

"Poor old Jack!" I murmured, almost forgetting the presence of my companion. "He treated me shabbily, shamefully; but I don't want him to worry about me. But now he'll be pestering me with letters, be begging me to come home."

"No, I think not," Mr. Ned said, shaking his head.

"Why won't he, then?"

"I arranged everything in a satisfactory way; I'm to look after you."

"You are?"

"Yes."

"You are?"

He nodded, smiling coolly, provokingly.

I was red-hot inside and ice-cold outside, Nell.

"Just what arrangement did you make with my brother?" I asked, with a fine show of scorn that was lost upon my companion.

"A very simple one," he grinned in reply. "He's to let you alone till you get ready to return to Chesterville, of your own accord; and—"

"Which time will never come," I interjected.

"I'm to stand sponsor for your good behavior—"

"What a beautiful arrangement!" I cried snappishly.

"Look after your welfare,—"

"How very kind of you!"

"And report to him occasionally how you are coming on."

"A transfer of guardianship!" I sneered. And then the big—big brute, Nell Adams, lay back and laughed—laughed loud and long!

I got up and walked over to the window, my lips trembling, my sight blurred by tears. He followed me, laid a hand kindly on my shoulder and said gently:

"Look here, Miss Dawes; don't feel hurt about this thing. I've tried to do you a kindness. Your brother was here in the city, resolved to make a fool of himself. He meant to search for you, have the police on your track as if you were a common criminal, have the papers full of you and your affairs—and all that. And it would have made it very unpleasant for you, given you an unsavory notoriety, done violence to your reputation forever, perhaps. I had a hard time of dissuading him from his purpose; and I had to promise him all I've told you, before he'd consent to act sensible and turn his face toward home. No, you oughtn't to feel hard toward me; really you ought to thank me—though I'm far from wanting you to do so." He made a move to leave my side.

"But I don't like to have a guardian, Mr. Ned," I pouted tearfully; "I don't like to be bossed. That's one reason I ran away from my brother. And think of your sending a report of my behavior to Jack—just like a teacher reports an unruly child to its parent! Oh, dear—dear! I just can't stand it—I can't!"

He put his hand upon my shoulder—and let it slip down almost to the level of my waist. Oo-h! You can imagine how I was frightened, Nell!

"There—there, little girl!" he said softly. "I'll—I'll—"

I don't know what else nice and comforting he might have said, Sweet Nell of old Oberlin, but just then we heard his father coming through the outer office; so we got into our chairs and got down to work. Pshaw!

Chapter 10

SEVERAL weeks passed; and it's truly surprising how many unimportant and trivial things can happen in several times seven days. Perhaps, Nell, you'll charge me with culling out the least important and most uninteresting events to write about, and maybe you'll be right; but here goes, anyway.

I liked my place, and got along with my work as slick as you please; but I was in a state of delightful uncertainty all the time, as to Mr. Ned's moods—and his father's tenses. At one time the former was formal and distant, at another time familiar and near—sometimes quite near; and on occasion the latter was fidgety and peevish, and again he was bland and chummy—sometimes almost too chummy. If I favored the father with a smile, the son favored me with a frown; if I looked unutterable things at the son, the father muttered unutterable things under his breath—and got up and paced the room and walled his eyes like a dying tragedian[1].

It was a new and rare experience, Nell; and, in spite of some drawbacks and inconveniences connected with it, I think I rather enjoyed it.

One afternoon Mr. Ned covertly told me a funny story as he sat dictating to me, and we both laughed heartily. You've noticed, haven't you, old chum, how one's enjoyment of a story depends much more upon who tells it, than upon the story itself and how it is told? Well, Mr. Durbin became aware of our merriment, of course; and he got up and stalked over to us and said brusquely:

"Are you two young addle-pates[2] laughing at me?"

1   Tragedian – An actor who performs in a tragedy
2   Addle-pate – one who is unable to think clearly in his head

116

Mr. Ned froze stiff in his chair and silently sat and stared at his audacious parent. Mr. Durbin stared as hard at his son, his face very sober; but I thought I detected a funny little twinkle in his round pale-blue eyes.

I precipitated myself into the breach, as peacemaker, with:

"No, indeed, we weren't laughing at you, Mr. Durbin; Mr. Ned was just telling me a funny story."

"O-h!"—with an indescribable expression of voice and countenance,—"O-h! All right, then."

And forthwith he whirled and returned to his desk and took his seat. I looked after him, concerned, and noted that his shoulders and back were quivering and shaking in a strange manner; but I couldn't tell whether he was convulsed with rage or remorse.

"The egotistical and supersensitive old dunce!" Mr. Ned muttered; but he had to grin.

Lunch-time arrived; and Mr. Durbin came up to me,—right in the presence of his son!—and said boldly:

"Miss Grimes, will you—that is, have you any objections to going out to lunch with me?"

"Why—why," I stammered in genuine confusion, "I—no, I've no objections, Mr. Durbin."

"Very well; come on, then."

I cast a glance—a sort of appealing one, at Mr. Ned as I left the room. His face was stern; his wide mouth was set.

As we passed through the outer office, Jones gave me the meanest look I ever got in my life—a kind of insolent, menacing leer that made me shiver.

On our way back from lunch, Mr. Durbin stopped to talk with an acquaintance; and I hurried on. The outer office was empty but for Jones. He gave me another of his mean looks; and I skurried past him, shuddering at thought that I was alone with him. My heart began to beat wildly, sickeningly, and my limbs began to tremble. Judge of my relief, Nell—my unexpected and infinite relief!—to find Mr. Ned in the private room. He had been sulking, and had not gone out to lunch at all.

As soon as he caught sight of my face, however, his attitude, demeanor, and expression of countenance underwent a sudden and electrical change. Springing to his feet, he cried sharply:

"What's the matter, Miss Dawes? What's the matter?"

I burst into tears, Nell; I just couldn't help it.

"What's the matter?" he repeated. "Tell me at once."

His voice was kind enough, but it revealed inflexible purpose of mind.

"Oh, nothing—nothing, Mr. Ned!" I sobbed.

"Yes, there is. Out with it."

"Oh, I'm just foolish—that's all!"—bravely striving to smile—"I was just hurt—and—and scared—a little."

"Who hurt you—who scared you?"

"I don't want to tell you, Mr. Ned."

"But you must."

And I looked up at him—and believed him.

"It was Jones," I said.

"Jones?"

"Yes."

"Jones!"—oh, so fiercely, so awfully!

I couldn't do anything but give a wee little nod.

"What did he do to you?"

"He didn't do anything; he—"

"What did he say to you?"

"He didn't say anything," I explained; "he just—just looked."

"Is that all he did?"

"Y—e—s."

"I understand. Well, I'll 'tend to Jones; I'll settle his hash[3]!"

"Oh don't, Mr. Ned! Please—"

But he was out the door, and had banged it shut. And, oh, I was frightened—in good earnest, Nell mine! Mr. Ned was so big and so strong, and so gloriously angry; and Jones was so small and stoop-shouldered and scrawny, and pusillanimously[4] insignificant. But, in spite of my concern, I didn't clap my hands over my ears and screech, nor did I give a few gasps and faint. Instead, I opened the

---

3   Hash – a mess
4   Pusillanimous – Showing a lack of courage or determination

door—just a wee crack!—and peeped out. If Mr. Ned meant to kill Jones, I wanted to be ready to hollo for help—just before the last breath left the puppy's body!

My champion strode up to his victim and gave him a slap between the shoulders, that almost jolted him from his stool.

"Jones" he cried, "what have you been doing to Miss—Miss Grimes, I mean? What have you been doing to her, I say?"

"No—no—nothing, Mr. Ned," the puny little man stammered, struggling to his feet; "nothing at all."

"Yes, you did!" Mr. Ned growled savagely. "Don't you lie to me!"

"I—I just looked at her," the vile fellow whined.

"That's it; that's what she said—that's it! Well, don't you do it any more. Understand?"—menacingly.

"Y—yes, sir."

"And don't you speak to her."

"I won't, sir."

"And don't you talk about her."

"All right, Mr. Ned,"—very, very meekly.

"All right it is. But if you forget your promise, I'll take you by the neck and fling you down the elevator shaft. And we may as well have a complete understanding right now; and you can bear the word to your associates. If there's any more nudges or winks, or hints or flings, in this office, about Miss Grimes, or about my father, or about me and my business, I'll fire the last one of you. Understand that?"

"Yes, sir."

"Pass it along, then; and remember that it goes. I've got tired and disgusted; and I won't tolerate any more of your scandalous behavior—from man or woman. And as for you, Jones—you miserable blackguard[5]!—I've a notion to discharge you this minute."

"Oh, don't do that, Mr. Ned—don't say that!" the poor poltroon[6] pleaded. "I don't know where I can get another job; and you know I have a wife and four children. Please don't discharge me!"

---

5 Blackguard – A person, particularly a man, who behaves in a dishonorable or contemptible way
6 Poltroon – An utter coward

I thought it about time for me to interfere—to intercede in the fellow's behalf. So I walked out and said timidly—for I was desperately afraid I might make matters worse, the humor Mr. Ned was in:

"Don't discharge Mr. Jones—for my sake, Mr. Ned. Don't heap hardship upon his innocent wife and little children, in an effort to punish him."—Then, looking at the crest-fallen wretch and realizing how he was suffering:—"And I think you've punished him about enough, Mr. Ned; I think he understands you, and I don't think he'll repeat his offense. Will you, Mr. Jones?"

"Of course I won't, Miss Grimes," he mumbled thickly, humbly. "But indeed I didn't mean anything; I just wanted to be sociable and—"

"Stop that," Mr. Ned muttered threateningly; "cut that out Jones. Miss Grimes isn't asking you for apologies or excuses; she's just interceding for you—and you ought to be too ashamed to try to wag your tongue. That's all, now; I'm done. You can get to work."

At quitting time that evening, the junior member of the firm remarked to the senior:

"I've got a little private matter I desire to talk over with you, father; wait a few minutes, please."—Then, to me:—"You may go at any time, Miss Grimes."

Of course I withdrew; but not before I had noticed a worried expression dispel the wonted jollity[7] of Mr. Durbin's ruddy countenance, and a look of fixed and stern resolve settle upon Mr. Ned's dark features. As I stood waiting at the elevator shaft I discovered that I had forgotten to bring with me a small parcel from my desk, a trifling purchase that I had made at the noon hour; and, thoughtless of the private interview in progress, I retraced my steps to get it. But as I re-entered the outer room, I caught the sound of my employers' voices in spirited conversation; and I paused, irresolute[8]. However, the first words I heard fixed my attention and held me to the spot. I was the subject of the conversation; and Mr. Ned was saying:

"It isn't you I'm thinking about, father. You're old enough to take care of yourself, to attend to your own business—yes; old enough to

---

7 Jollity – Lively and cheerful activity or celebration
8 Irresolute – Showing or feeling hesitancy; uncertain

know better, too. But I'm thinking about Miss Grimes; I'm trying to protect her, to save her from being sneered at and talked about. I've read the riot act to Jones—"

"And now you think you'll read it to me, your father—eh?" Mr. Durbin shrilled angrily. But I thought there was a half-smothered minor tone of amusement in his voice.

Mr. Ned pursued evenly but indignantly, decidedly:

"And I've issued orders to the rest of the force, through him, that there's to be no more of their cursed nonsense; and given warning that I'll discharge the last one of them, if I see or hear of another wink or word reflecting upon Miss Grimes. And now I give you the same warning."

"The same warning—to me?" queried the father.

"Yes, the same warning—and to you."

"Why, what do you mean, Ned? Explain."

"You're the cause of all the trouble, father; you know it. You've been the cause of all similar trouble in the past; you know that, too. Well, it's got to stop; your nonsensical actions have got to cease; you've got to stop forcing your attentions upon Miss Grimes—that's all."

"I don't force my attentions upon her."

"You do."

"I don't! Has she ever complained to you, that I force my attentions upon her—hey?"

"N—o,"—rather reluctantly.

"Well!"—triumphantly.

Despise me, if you will, for a conscienceless little eavesdropper, Nell; I despised myself. I should have slipped away, I know; but I didn't—I just couldn't. I sha'n't try to excuse myself on the ground though,—which shows I still have a faint spark of honor left!—that I was afraid the two men might engage in mortal combat. No—no, I've not fallen so low as all that! I knew very well the son wouldn't harm the father; and I knew equally well the father couldn't harm the son. No, I just desired to hear what they were saying; and I stayed to gratify my curiosity. Honest confession precipitates me into downright confusion, Nell; but I trust it'll be good for my soul.

"Well," Mr. Ned resumed, after a slight pause, "you've got to quit your foolishness."

"My foolishness!"—wrathfully.

"Yes."

"As you're pleased to term it. And if I don't?"

"Then, I'll discharge you."

"Oh, you will!"—sneeringly.

"Yes, I will."

"Ho, ho!"—laughing scornfully.—"Ned, you're talking through your hat; and the most silly thing about it is you know you're vociferating[9] through—through your head-covering. Discharge me! You know you couldn't discharge me,—me, the senior member of the firm!—if you would; and you wouldn't if you could. If you want to dissolve partnership, though—why, say so."

Nell, I was getting stirred up—agitated. Was I—innocent little Marjory Dawes of sleepy old Chesterville!—fated to disrupt and dissolve the great and prosperous real-estate firm of Durbin and Son? Heaven forbid! That wouldn't do—wouldn't do at all! I'd have to take a sneak—just have to. However, Mr. Ned's next words greatly relieved me.

"I don't want to dissolve our partnership," he replied to his father's testy challenge; "you know I don't. But things can't go on this way; you've got to behave."

"Oh, stuff!" the old gentleman cried inelegantly. "I am behaving myself; and I'm living up to our contract. You're the one that's trying to kick over the traces, Ned, my boy. You know very well what our agreement was; and I'm going to hold you to it, rigidly. You've hired Miss Grimes, and she's doing the work all right; and she's got to stay a year—that's all. You said you'd bring a girl here, with a face that would stop a clock. Well, I s'pose you think you've done it; you had the whole country to choose from, anyhow, and Miss Grimes was your choice,"—Oh, Nell—Nell! I was all puffed up with laughter; and hardly able to breathe!—"Now you've got to be satisfied; I'm not going to give you any more chances. And I'm not going to act the boor with Miss Grimes, just to please you, either; I'm going to

---

9 Vociferate – Shout, complain, or argue loudly or vehemently

treat her courteously, kindly, generously, and if you don't like it—well, you can do what you threatened. There!"

"What can I do?" Mr. Ned demanded.

"What you threatened, I said."

"Well what?"

I listened breathlessly for Mr. Durbin's reply.

"You can go to the probate judge and get a license, and make me marry the girl—that's what."

I let out a little giggle—and clapped a hand over my mouth; then listened eagerly for Mr. Ned's response.

"I can, can I?" he growled.

"Sure!" chuckled the father. "I'm ready to marry her at any time."

"And no doubt you're egotist enough to think she's ready to marry you—eh?"

"I don't know,"—gurgling and sputtering;—"she doesn't act averse to my company, my attentions, as you may have noticed."—The vain old coxcomb[10]! I felt like rushing in and slapping his face!—"At any rate, as I said, I'm quite ready to marry her."

"You're too damn—entirely too ready to marry her!" Mr. Ned muttered wrathfully.

Mr. Durbin could no longer restrain his merriment; he whooped right out loud, and stamped the floor and coughed. I had to stuff my handkerchief in my mouth to keep from giving vocal utterance to the glee that was effervescing and bubbling within me. I heard Mr. Ned get upon his feet, and say with grave and proper dignity:

"It appears there's little use in talking to you, father; you're hopeless. I—"

I realized that the curtain was about to fall upon the little one-act farce-comedy that I had been witnessing—with my ears alone; and I made a quick and noiseless retreat. You'll think me awful, Nell mine—I know you will; but you'll have to admit that I still possess the virtue of candor—when I'm permitted to choose the subject, occasion and confidant!—and that courage still abides with me, or I couldn't make the confession I have.

---

10 Coxcomb – a vain and conceited man

Both my employers were a little glum the next forenoon. However, in the temporary absence of the junior member, the senior remarked to me:

"Madame Schumann-Heink sings at the Great Southern to-morrow night. Of course you're going to hear her, Miss Grimes—eh?"

"I don't know whether I'll go or not," I returned carelessly but candidly; "I know so little about music."

You remember I've got Quaker blood in me, Nell; and, in consequence, don't care for music as I should.

"Oh, you must go, Miss Grimes!" Mr. Durbin cried, in astonishment not unmixed with dismay. "Indeed you must go. Why, it'll be great, grand, sublime, a perfect artistic triumph and treat. You mustn't think of missing it; it's the opportunity of a lifetime—the chance to hear Madame Schumann-Heink is. You'll enjoy it—never fear; I know you've the artistic temperament, even if you don't know much of music. And I happen to recall right now I have two tickets; and I'd be delighted to have you go with me—if you will."

"Why, I—I don't hardly know, Mr. Durbin," I said hesitatingly; "I—I—"

"Of course you will," he interrupted cheerily. "Say you will."

"Well, then, I will—since you already have two tickets."

The old fellow was flattered. He thought his native eloquence, his persuasive powers, had brought me round; and he sat and plumed himself in great complacency.

That very evening I descended in the elevator—how paradoxical it sounds, Nell, to say "descended in the elevator!"—with Mr. Ned; and he remarked:

"Madame Schumann-Heink and her company are to be at the Great Southern tomorrow night, Miss Grimes."

"Yes," I answered—a little quaver in my voice and a little quiver in my heart. I felt certain I knew what further he was going to say.

"Yes," he went on nodding· "and won't you grant me the pleasure of taking you to hear her, Miss Grimes-Miss Dawes?"

There it was—as I had expected; and I was just sick! And I had promised Mr. Durbin! Pshaw! I wanted to stamp; I wanted to cry. I was so upset! Why was the father so previous and precipitate;

and why was the son so dilatory[11] and deliberate? Pshaw! And again—pshaw!

Mr. Ned noticed the perplexed and puckered frown upon my face, and said:

"Wouldn't you like to go, Marj—Miss Dawes? Wouldn't you like to hear the great Schumann-Heink?"

Then the humor of the dilemma irresistibly appealed to my sense of the nonsensical—and the thought came to me that Mr. Ned deserved to be punished just a mite for his inexcusable delay in making his request; and I smiled brightly, sweetly, and replied:

"I am going to hear Madame Schumann-Heink, Mr. Ned."

"Does that mean that you consent to go with me?" he inquired, eagerly, I fancied.

"N—o," I drawled coquettishly, "I'd like to go with you, ever so much but—but I can't."

"Can't?"—sharply, explosively.—"Why?"

"I've—I've promised to go with somebody else."

"Oh!"—a mere angry grunt.

"Yes,"—very, very sweetly.

Then, following a momentary hesitation, he said:

"I meant to ask you yesterday, but forgot."

Forgot! Well, Nell Adams, I was furious! Forgot! I'd rather be scorned than forgotten, any day in the week—wouldn't you? So I turned my face from him, pouting.

We were just stepping out upon the street; and I heard my companion saying, in a tone of real or well-assumed disappointment:

"I'm very sorry, really greatly disappointed, that you're to have other company. May I inquire the name of—of the lucky fellow?"

"Your father," I answered, without looking at him.

"Humph!" he snorted angrily, contemptuously.

Then,—the big ungallant, ill-tempered bear!—he whirled and walked away, leaving me standing there, waiting for my car.

And I was disappointed, vexed, hurt, chum mine—I couldn't hardly tell why; and when I got to my room I had a good cry.

Of course I went to hear the great Schumann-Heink; but I didn't

---

11 Dilatory – Slow to act

enjoy the performance a bit—not a bit. I was out of sorts, someway; and I wasn't nice at all to Mr. Durbin—the poor old fellow! In fact I was really quite rude with him, I fear; but he pretended not to notice, and was all suavity and graciousness. I ought to have been ashamed; and I was ashamed later that night—and took another good cry.

Then Mr. Ned had a spell of the sulks that lasted several days; and I was miserable. I don't know why I should have been, exactly—now that I think the thing over; but I was. I guess I must have been sorry Mr. Ned was so sad.

But at the end of about three days something happened that brought bloom to my cheeks and balm to my heart. Mr. Ned, bending over my desk and examining some work I had done, looked up suddenly and asked me a question; and, absent-mindedly, he called me "Marjory." I fairly jumped; and so did he—for his father was in the room. Then I blushed and smiled, and he smiled and got red of face; and both of us looked anxiously toward Mr. Durbin. But that dear and accommodating old man was intent about his business. A half-minute later I was making my typewriter fairly dance, and Mr. Ned had gone to the outer office—whistling happily.

"W—e—ll," drawled Mr. Durbin, whirling about in his chair and eyeing me—suspiciously, I feared and fancied.

Then he got upon his feet and tiptoed across the floor and closed the door, and came and leaned on my desk.

"What do you think?" he whispered mysteriously.

"Think?"—and I stared hard at him, trying to read his face—striving to learn what he had in mind.—"Think about what, Mr. Durbin?"

"About Ned's quick recovery?"

"His recovery?"

"Yes; recovery from his attack of dumps."

"Oh!"

"Uh-huh. What do you think about it—about what cured him?"

I was nervous, concerned. Had the sharp-eared old fellow overheard his son call me Marjory?"

"I—I don't know what to think, I—I guess," I faltered in reply to his reiterated question.

"I think you cured him," my companion chuckled.

"Yes?"—I didn't know what else to say.

"Y-e-s,"—teeheeing and cackling,—"you must have said something awfully nice to him; he came in moping and mooning, and he went out whisking and whistling."

He paused to get his breath; then he continued, bobbing his head and gurgling down deep in his throat, till the bunches of funny fuzzy hair around his ears quivered and danced in rhythmic sympathy:

"Yes, you cured him; case of similia similibus curantur[12], I guess—eh?"

"I don't know what you mean, Mr. Durbin,"—which was quite true.

"Oh, yes, you do!"—grinning cherubically.—"You threw him into an attack of the dumps, by going to the opera with me; and then you cured him by smiling upon him."

"Why, Mr. Durbin!" I exclaimed in genuine astonishment and confusion. His ready discernment was surprising.

"I mean what I say," he went on, sobering. "He's jealous of me; and he couldn't and wouldn't be jealous of me, if he wasn't in love with you. Now!"—triumphantly.

I couldn't say a word, my dear Nell; I could only sit and stare, dumbfounded. And my speechless embarrassment so tickled the old pest, that he immediately went into a spasm—no, a series of spasms!—of hilarity. When he saw that I was recovering and about to say something—something caustic, I can tell you Nell!—he instantly controlled himself and, holding up a warning finger, said impressively:

"Wait a moment, Miss Grimes; I'm not quite through. Ned don't know he's in love with you, but I do; I know the symptoms of the malady—you bet! And you're in love with him."—The impudent old wretch! I bridled instantly.—"There, there! Maybe you don't realize it, but you are. Young folks seldom do recognize the insidious complaint, till their cases are hopeless. But,"—shaking his head and grinning like a mesmerized gargoyle,—"what you've done to that boy of mine is simply wonderful, marvelous. He's never been

12 similia similibus curantur – "likes are cured by likes"

in love with a bundle of femininity before in his life,"—I wished I could believe his positive statement as very truth, Nell; but I lacked the faith!—"but he's a goner now; I can see it. And all you'll have to do to keep him in love with you, Miss Grimes—you do want to keep him in love with you, don't you?"

"Why—why, Mr. Durbin!" I gasped, startled. "Such a question!"

"Well, it is rather a silly question," he teeheed. "Of course you want to keep him in love with you—whether you care for him or not; you wouldn't be a woman, if you didn't want to. But I know you do care for Ned—no—no! Don't say a word in contradiction of my statement; I know you do. And now listen to me; listen!"— very impressively, very gravely.—"I'm an old man—old enough to be your father; and nothing would please me more than to be your father. No—no, don't say a word! I admire you, I like you, enjoy your company and love to have you near me, and all that; but I'm not quite such a fool as to expect—or desire, really—you to feel that way toward me. I'm not quite such a fool as that, Miss Grimes; but I rub the mark. Wait—wait! I'm almost through. I've been wanting Ned to fall in love; and I'm tickled to death that he's fallen in love with you. Just a moment—just a moment! I want him to marry; and I want him to marry you. My plans and schemes are working out all right, But here's a bit of advice in the shape of a bit of wisdom: the thing a man always wants and is determined to have is the thing he thinks he can't get. Understand? Catch on? Well, all right, then."—I must have nodded, Nell; but I wasn't aware of it.—"Now, we must keep Ned hot on the trail—you and I; and the very way to do it is to keep him uneasy, anxious, in a stew. See? Yes—all right, then. And our plan'll be to go on just as we're going, only—only—we'll pay just a little more attention to each other. Can I depend upon you; will you join me in the scheme? Good! All right!"—Nell Adams, I know I hadn't nodded a nod or winked a wink!—"That's settled, then. And don't weaken; don't get softhearted—and begin to pity the big dolt. If you do, you may lose him. 1 know men. Besides Ned's been so uppish, so scornful and cantankerous, that he deserves a taste of a purgatory of pain before he enters into a paradise of bliss—with such a girl as you."—The dear poetical old chap!—"There—that's all. Now, Miss Grimes, will you shake?"

And we shook!

Chapter 11

FROM that time on, Nell darling, there was something doing daily in and about the real estate offices of Durbin and Son. The more chummy and chuckly Mr. Durbin became, the more giddy and giggly I made myself; and the more frantic and furious Mr. Ned grew. Poor boy! It was cruel; he must have suffered dreadfully. I pitied him at times, but I held firm. However, I think his suffering was as nothing compared with that of the flock of carrion crows in the outer office. Oh, how they did want to flap their wings and peck and caw—and didn't dare to! Not a croak did they utter. If they talked about their employers and me, they must have hired a hall somewhere to do it in; at any rate, they didn't do it about the office.

Occasionally I went to a play or other entertainment with the junior member of the firm; and then he was delighted, apparently—and so was I, undoubtedly. But more frequently by far,—to the junior's chagrin and my disappointment!—the senior anticipated the junior's good intentions. Heighho! But things were at sixes and sevens in that hive of industry; and all on account of the advent of a little tousle-haired, gray-eyed queen! Now, grin, you dear old chum!

Summer went and autumn came; and the hours were rosy—like the changing foliage. Sometimes my hopes soared aloft with the airy thistledown; and again they sank to earth with the falling leaves—to be trampled under foot. Part of the time I tripped over the hills of delight, and part of the time I trudged through the valleys of despair; but Mr. Durbin stood tiptoe upon the mountain-tops of ecstasy and glory all the time—and flapped his arms and crew.

One day Mr. Ned said to me—very, very soberly:

"Marjory,"—he was calling me by my christian name, by that time, when he wasn't too huffy with me to call me anything!—"will you answer me a question?"

Oo—h! Was he going to propose—in such a sudden and off-hand way? My heart flitter-fluttered so tumultuously, so deliciously, that I could barely murmur—my eyes demurely dropped:

"If—if I can, Ned,—Mr. Ned."

"You can,"—solemnly, almost funereally[1]. Oo—h! It was coming!

"I will, then," I breathed softly.

"Why do you persist in carrying on with father, as you do?"

Stuff! I was so disappointed I was almost ready to cry. Such a silly question—and when I thought him on the point of proposing! Surely men are the dumbest things, Nell Adams—especially young men who are in love and aren't fully conscious of their condition or their opportunities! Such reflections made me wrothy[2]!

"Why do I persist in carrying on with your father?" I snapped.

He nodded, his eyes half-shut.

"I don't," I fibbed.

"But you do."

"What do you mean by 'carrying on?'" I demanded haughtily.

"You know, Marjory."

"I don't !" I cried. "I don't!"

"I mean just what I said."

"Well?"

"I mean you persist in flirting with father."

"Oh!" I laughed mirthlessly. "But maybe I don't flirt with him."

He gave me a searching look; then he muttered thickly:

"Maybe you don't—that's so";—and, oh, Nell, I began to tremble with fear that the thick-pated fellow was going to take my rash hint in earnest!—"but I think you do."—Again I could get a full breath!—"Yes, you flirt with him, Marjory; and you permit him—no, you encourage him—to make a spectacle of himself, an old fool of himself. And you don't care for him—not a mite."

---

1 Funereal – somber, gloomy, mournful
2 Wrothy - wrathful

"Think not?"—teasingly.

"I know you don't."

Well, then, why was he always stewing so over the matter? I couldn't understand.

"Maybe I do, though," I persisted perversely.

"All right—maybe you do, then; have your way."

And he got up and flung himself out of the room.

I saw that I had gone too far, old chum; and I was properly worried—and properly punished. All that week he gave me scant attention and scanter courtesy, speaking to me only when he couldn't avoid it; and I lost all faith in Mr. Durbin and his silly schemes and plans for subduing and winning his savage son—and was so cross to the old chap I must have made his fleeting days miserable. Life wasn't a grand sweet song all the time, Nell—not by an appreciable per cent. Part of the time it was antic, frantic ragtime; and the rest of the time it was a dolesome, unwholesome funeral march.

One day, near the end of that memorable week, Mr. Durbin sprung a surprise on me that was a surprise. On returning from lunch I found him alone in the inner room, teetering back and forth in his pivot chair, swinging his feet, twiddling his thumbs—and grinning like a Sozodont[3] girl.

"Hoho!" he cried, laughingly, explosively, as I came in the door.

"What's the matter now?" I demanded, pettishly stamping.

"Nothing at all, Miss Marjory Dawes!"

What? Had I heard aright—or was my inner consciousness playing tricks with me? Had my skirts become unfastened and fallen about my feet, I could not have been more disconcerted. Marjory Dawes! Was I awake or dreaming; sane or silly? I stood staring vacantly at my grinning companion, till he aroused me with:

"It surprises you that I know your real name, doesn't it, Miss Dawes?"

"A little," I admitted faintly. Then, in measure recovering my equanimity: "Who told you?"

"Guess,"—manifesting infinite enjoyment.

---

3   Sozodont – Popular brand of oral hygiene product from the mid-nineteenth century to the early twentieth century

"Mr. Ned."

"Y-e-s, he did and he didn't."

"Explain, Mr. Durbin."

I had removed my hat and my wrap and was rearranging things upon my desk.

"W-e-l-l,"-gleefully, childishly,—"I suspected your real name that day Ned brought in the paper telling about your eloping with the old colonel";—who would have thought it, Nell mine—that old Foxy Grandpa could be so shrewd, so secretive?—"but I became satisfied of the truth of my guess just a few minutes ago."

"Indeed?"

"Yes."

"How?"

"Go over and look at the blotter on Ned's desk."

And then he went into the worst spell of the hysterical risibilities I ever saw him have. Wondering what I was to see, I walked over to Mr. Ned's desk. My eyes fell upon his blotter—and horror of horrors! He had scribbled all over it, in pencil—absent-mindedly, of course:

"Marjory Dawes, Miss Marjory Dawes, Marjie, Marjory, Marjory Dawes."

And down in an obscure corner—but standing out as if emblazoned in letters of blood and flame, Nell—"Marjory Dawes Durbin!"

I fairly gasped at the unexampled audacity, the unmitigated juvenility, of the thing; and Mr. Durbin watched me—and squirmed and twisted, and wheezed and whooped.

"So you see Ned did tell me," he cried, clapping his hands and knocking his heels together; "and you see, too, that he's a goner."

"A goner?" I queried, dropping into my chair.

"Yes; he's dead gone on you."

"Why, Mr. Durbin, how inelegant!" I exclaimed.

"But how expressive—and how true," he teeheed.

"I'm afraid he's gone from me," I said gloomily.

"What makes you say that?"

"Because I think it."

"And what makes you think it?"

"The way he acts toward me; he's so cold, so distant—doesn't pay any attention to me, hardly."

"Nonsense!"—snapping his fingers superiorly, contemptuously. "That's just a man's way; he's just pouting. No—no! He'll come around all right. Has he asked you to go to the play with him to-night?"

1 thought he asked this question a little anxiously.

"No, he hasn't," I replied.

"Well, I'll ask you to go with me, then. But if he does ask you, you'd better go with him, I—I guess; yes, I think you had. Maybe we'd better not push him too far—right now, anyhow."—Then, abruptly:

"Say!"

"What?" I queried.

"Ned knew you weren't Miss Grimes the first day he saw you in the office, of course, didn't he?"

"Yes, of course."

"Well, why didn't he say something—expose you, eh? And what brought you here—to palm yourself off as Miss Grimes? Tell me all about it."

I complied with his request, told him everything; and his delight was unbounded—was a revelation in the way of giggling gymnastics and chuckling calisthenics.

Mr. Ned was in the office just once that day; and he didn't ask me to go to the play with him. And when the father and I took our seats in the dress circle that night, there sat the son,—directly in front of us!—with a beautiful young woman at his side. She was beautiful, I admit it, Nell mine;—and that's a great condescension for me!—and I was so blinded by the kaleidoscopic and devilish antics of the green god of jealousy, and so deafened by the taunts and flings and gibes and jeers the little verdant imp shrilled into my ears, that I couldn't see the actors or hear a word they said. I looked at Mr. Durbin—the old bungler!—and he looked at me, wagging his head like an imbecile paralytic.

"Who is she?" I murmured cautiously.

"Miss Frances Garland," my companion whispered in reply,

"daughter of John Garland of the Capital City Electric Supply Company; her father's very wealthy."

'Twas then the iron entered my soul, Nell Adams of other days! She was the daughter of a wealthy man; I was an orphan and a beggar. She was beautiful, and tall and willowy; I was just pretty, and short and graceless. She was elegantly and faultlessly gowned; I was dowdy—just dowdy!—compared with her. Oh, the comparison hurt, I can tell you! And I wanted to die; and I resolved to die—just as soon as I could determine on a nice easy way of doing the thing! But, no—I wouldn't die for a little while! I must settle accounts with Foxy Grandpa first! Of course I'd kill him! But how? What sort of death would be fit punishment for his crime—his many crimes? And I sat the play out, in unseeing, unhearing, unspeaking silence—in the blue-black gloom of despair and hate and revenge!

When the curtain had fallen upon the last act of the miserable and monstrous melodrama, my escort and I gloomily arose to make our way out. Then it was Mr. Ned first became aware of our presence, apparently. I believe he knew we were there all the time, Nell, for I caught him slyly squinting over his shoulder more than once— I'm sure I did, almost; but he pretended to be so absorbed in the princess-like Miss Garland and her fascinating talk, that he couldn't see or hear anybody or anything else. The mean thing!

But just as we arose he slowly turned around, gave a well-feigned start and said:

"Why, Miss Daw—hem!—Miss Grimes, you here—and father, too? You two must have been completely absorbed in the play—or in each other's company";—oh, but I wanted to scream and scratch, Nell Adams!—"you kept so still. Miss Grimes, permit me to present Miss Garland; father, you know Miss Garland, of course."

Miss Garland smiled and murmured my name and gracefully inclined her tall and willowy form; and I smirked a frozen smirk and muttered her name and bobbed stiffly. I couldn't help being rude; and Mr. Ned looked on amused—I just know he was amused, Nell!—the corners of his big mouth twitching.

"Did you enjoy the play?" he asked heartlessly.

I didn't answer him, I didn't dare to try to answer him. I believe

I should have burst out weeping and wailing right there. But Mr. Durbin—he thought he was coming to my rescue, the dear kind-hearted old briggler!—tittered in mock gleefulness:

"Oh, yes! Yes, indeed; we enjoyed it immensely."

"Well," Mr. Ned went on forcing the conversation, Miss Garland and I are going down to Paff's to have supper. Won't you go along with us—you two?"

Again I remained silent.

"Yes, do come with us," Miss Garland murmured.

"Will we go with them, Miss Daw—ahem! Miss Grimes?" Mr. Durbin said pityingly, caressingly, bending toward me.

I saw Mr. Ned give a start and glare at his father; and, sad as I was, Nell, I came near letting out a little giggle.

"Will we go?" Mr. Durbin repeated.

"No!" I replied snappishly. "I've got a headache,"—and I did have one; and a heartache, too!—"and I don't care to stay out any longer."

"All right," Mr. Ned smiled, giving Miss Garland a meaningful glance which she was quick to return, "we'll sup together some other time, then. Good night."

Out on the street, in the frosty air and the dappled shadow and sheen of the arc lights, I hurried along like mad, almost forcing my escort to break into a trot to keep up with me.

"Why such a rush, Miss Dawes?" he panted. "Hadn't we better take a car—eh?"

"No," was my monosyllabic and crusty response.

"Well, why—why are you—you hurrying so?" he puffed.

"Because I want to get to my room, that's why."

Oh!"—as much a groan as a reply.

"Yes. And you needn't accompany me; I can go alone."

"Oh, I wouldn't think of permitting you to do that!" he gasped, "No, indeed!"

Then I relented—just a little!—and slowed down.

"You're out of sorts to-night, Miss Dawes," he wheezed.

"Am I?"

"Aren't you?"

"Yes I am."

"Have—have I done anything to—to displease you?"—anxiously, meekly.

"Yes, you have."

"What—why—what, may I ask, Miss Dawes?"

"Everything!" I burst forth. "You've bungled everything—that's what you've done; and I'm disgusted with you and all your idiotic plans and schemes. You assured me that Ned—Mr. Ned—liked me; and told me the way to win him was to—to—well, to flirt with you—that's what you did. And now he doesn't care for me at all—and I don't think he ever did care for me; and he's taken up with Miss Garland, and she's beautiful and rich, and I'm homely and poor, and—and—oh, dear—dear!"

I broke down and began to boohoo,—in a soft and seemly manner, of course!—and Mr. Durbin laid a fatherly hand upon my shoulder and pleaded soothingly:

"There—there, little girl, don't cry!"—I had to smile through my tears, to hear him unconsciously quoting Riley!—"Everything will come out all right; don't get discouraged. Just remember the blotter you saw on his desk to-day; keep your eye and your mind on that—and you won't lose heart. Now, listen; let me tell you something."—And I dried my tears and did listen, warm hope gradually returning to my chilled heart!—"Ned's trying the same game you've been working; he's trying to bring you round, just as you've been trying to bring him round. And you're as big a dunce as he is,"—chucking me under the chin,—"to let him see that you care. Now the time's come for us to change our game a mite. He's come to the conclusion that I'm not dangerous to his prospects. See? And now he thinks he'll punish you a little bit, by paying his attention a to Miss Garland. Understand?"—I nodded, and gently pressed his arm.—"Well, here's the thing to do now—and the only thing: you must catch another fellow. Do you follow me?"

"I-I guess so," I cooed, a half-sob in my voice. "But what good will that do?"

"It'll bring Ned back to you—in a hurry."

"Do you really think it will?"

"Of course it will."

My own intuition told me it would, Nell; but I could not refrain from saying:

"Sure, Mr. Durbin?"

"Dead sure,"—with all the unction[4] and assurance imaginable.

"But maybe he likes Miss Garland," I objected.

"No, he doesn't," the old gentleman replied quickly, "I know he doesn't. The only thing that puzzles me about the whole thing is that Ned should pay any attention to any woman; I know he never has before. He's got at it all at once; but he seems to be making up for lost time and opportunities, I must say."

I had to cough to smother a giggle.

"And you think if I get another—another beau, it will—will"

"It'll fix everything," he interrupted.

"Then," I said resolutely, "I'll have another young man enamored of me before the week ends."

I spoke so confidently, sweet Nell, because I knew just what I was going to do—and how I was going to do it. My landlady had a nephew, a Mr. Morse who worked in the offices of the Mondarun Coal Company,—a most despisable, cigarette-smoking little dude!—and he had shown a decided desire to make himself agreeable to me. Hitherto I had snubbed him unmercifully; but now I meant to smile on him divinely. I needed him in my business, Nell!

Well, to be brief for just once in my life, things worked out as I planned; that is, they worked out to an extent, as I planned. The next Sunday evening found Mr. Morse and me at the Congregational church on East Broad street. I had ascertained in advance, by the help of Mr. Durbin, that Mr. Ned and Miss Garland would worship on that particular evening at that particular church. So I was not at all surprised to see them as soon as my escort and I entered the edifice, threading the aisle just ahead of us; and, by wasting a little cajolery upon the impressionable usher, I managed to be seated near them—in direct line of their vision. Then, when I saw that Mr. Ned and Miss Garland were aware of our presence, I was satisfied—and, for the moment, very, very happy!

4 Unction – exaggerated earnestness

I don't know what kind of a sermon Mr. Gladstone preached, Nell—except it was a good one, of course, for he never fails to preach acceptably, I understand; I was too busy wondering what Mr. Ned was getting out of the discourse—and the situation!—to get much out of it myself. Yes, call me an impious little wretch; I shan't care. I'm laying my soul bare at the confessional; and I'm going to tell the truth, the whole truth, and nothing but the truth. So now—and there!

The next day Mr. Ned was all smiles and affability; and I flattered myself that I had already won out—on the first deal. But on the Wednesday night following he took Miss Garland to a concert; and I wasn't quite so cocksure of my good fortune. And so things went for another week or two, Mr. Ned paying court to Miss Garland and Mr. Morse paying court to me; and all the time I was playing cross purposes with my desires; and Mr. Ned—well, I couldn't tell what he was doing, except that he was—was hurting me! One thing I was sure of, however; while Mr. Ned was kindness itself and geniality personified, as far as I was concerned, he seemed to be edging farther and farther away from that tender intimacy I so fondly desired. I got nervous, cross, and I snapped him off whenever he spoke to me; but he—the great big admirable but provoking dolt!—just grinned blandly, maddeningly, and wouldn't get out of humor—simply wouldn't. And I got to hating him—I knew I did; mind, I don't say I know I did.

One day Mr. Durbin inquired:

"How're things coming on, Marj—Miss Dawes?"

"They're not coming on at all," I replied peevishly.

"No?"

"No, they're not."

"What seems to be the trouble, Marj—Marjory?"

"Nothing—only Mr. Ned's in love with Miss Garland."

"No, he isn't,—shaking his head and grinning broadly, exasperatingly.

"But he is."

"No; he's in love with you, Marjory—dear. I'll tell you what I think's the the trouble—the reason he doesn't pay more attention to you; you've let him know you worry over his apparent devotion to

Miss Garland, and—"

"But I haven't let him know," I protested.

"But you have."

"Why, I've never said a word—"

"True," he interrupted, "but you've let him see that you're worried; and, man-like, he's gloating over the fact and pluming himself upon his irresistible prowess as a lady-killer, and is bent on amusing himself to the utmost—watching you make a wry face at the bitter medicine he's giving you. Now, you listen to me; take my advice, and—"

"I have taken your advice, Mr. Durbin, all the way along; and it's only made matters worse."

"Not at all—not at all!"—sanguinely, complacently.— "Things're all right; if you'd only think so—and act accordingly."

"Act? How shall I act?"

"Act as if you didn't care a snap for Ned, as if you were perfectly satisfied with Mr. Morse and the world in general, as if every hour were an open flower and you were a butterfly sipping it sweets— that's how to act. Act cheerful and—and saucy, and a little devilish; in other words, just be your sweet, natural, fascinating self—as of old. Then Ned 'll drop that self-satisfied and self-righteous smirk of his—and begin to see things of nights, and sit up and take notice, and inquire where he's at. I know; you'll see!"—chuckling in anticipatory glee.—"It won't be two days till he'll begin to scratch his head and wonder about the change in you; and he'll end up by trying to find out the cause—by trying to pick the truth out of you. And then, when he does come to you with his sly questions and his blarney, just you hold him at arm's length—just you pretend you're too happy and contented to give him a moment's time or thought. That'll fetch him. You'll win out that way, Marjory—dear; yes, you will."

And, as usual, I believed all he said, Nell; and I felt so much better, so relieved, so lighthearted, that I hummed a little tune as I resumed my work. Well, the result of my following Mr. Durbin's suggestion proved the old fellow a sage and a prophet. The very next day Mr. Ned noticed my changed demeanor and remarked upon the new shirt-waist I had donned; the following day he mentioned how well I was looking—and gave me a quizzical look, and sighed; and the next he was plainly puzzled, amorously anxious, and dolefully down in the dumps.

As soon as opportunity offered he said to me:

"You appear to be in a merry mood to-day—for several days, in fact—Marjory."

"Yes?"—smiling a new coquettish smile I had been practicing.

"Yes; and you're looking well, too."

"Thank you, Mr. Ned."

"Oh, the devil!"—irritably.—"Drop that mister business. I call you Marjory; you call me Ned—just plain Ned."

"All right, Mr. Ned—I mean plain Ned."

Then both of us laughed.

"Say!" he cried suddenly. "I believe you're getting prettier every day."

"Thank you again—Ned."

I looked up into his face, to find his keen eyes fixed upon me—admiringly, devouringly.

"Hem!" he coughed behind his hand. "Do you think of going to see DeWolfe Hopper play 'Wang' day after tomorrow night?"

"I think of going—yes."

"Will you go with me?"

"I can't."

"Can't?"—sharply.—"Why?"

"I've promised to go with Mr. Morse."

"Oh, I see!"—biting his lips.

"Yes."

"Well, turn him down—and let me take you."

"No, indeed—Ned."

"Why won't you?"

"Why? You know why I won't."

"Would you rather go with him—that mealy-faced little dude?"

I kept silent.

"Say!" he insisted.

"Well, I—I suppose I would"—hesitatingly, prettily,—under

the circumstances, anyhow."

"Maybe you'd rather go with him, under any circumstances—eh?"—plainly piqued.

"Oh, I—I don't know! I don't want to say that—I guess; I don't want to hurt your feelings."

He glared at me like he'd like to catch hold of me and crush me.

"Besides," I went on smoothly and sweetly, "Miss Garland will be expecting you to take her, won't she?"

"Humph!" he snorted. "Miss Garland has no mortgage on me, my time or my attentions. But if you don't want to go with me—why that settles it."

And he whirled around and left me,—the overgrown selfish boy!—his very back looking sulky.

And, oh, I was in such ecstasy, dear old chum! Ned had come back to me, and humbled himself; and I had had the pleasure of throwing him down—throwing him down good and hard. But still—still I was just a wee bit dissatisfied, just a wee bit sad; for I did so desire to go to that play with him!

And then came the deluge, Sweet Nell of Oberlin—the end of all things!

Chapter 12

IT WAS the first day of November, Thursday. I arrived at the office a few minutes ahead of time; and found Mr. Ned already there and in earnest conversation with a portly man of middle age, with a pug-like face and yellowish-green eyes. I was surprised that my junior employer should be so early at his place of business; more surprised that he had brought his traveling-bag and light overcoat with him; and most surprised that a stranger should be there on business, at so unusual an hour.

As I entered the inner room, Mr. Ned was saying:

"Yes, I know my option expires at two o'clock this afternoon; and, of course, I can't ask you to extend it—"

"I wouldn't do it if you did ask me to," the man interrupted in a stubborn, matter-of-fact tone and manner.

Unheeding my advent, they went on talking. Mr. Ned replied to the stranger's surly interruption:

"Of course you wouldn't, Klein—I know that; but I'm not asking you to, remember."

"I know you're not. But what I came here for is to find out what you're going to do. Are you going to take the property—or not?"

"You'll learn that at two o'clock this afternoon."

"But I'd like to learn it now,"—persistently, doggedly.

"Well, I can't tell you."

"Won't, you mean."

"I mean what I say, Klein—I can't."

"Don't you know?"

"No; I wish I did. Have you another offer?"

"I've given a second option on it; and the parties are anxious to close the bargain."

"I see. Who are they?"

"I can't tell you that, Durbin."

"All right. I'm not overly anxious to know, I guess."

"And you won't say now whether you'll take the property?"

"I can't, I told you,"—impatiently.

"Well,"—leaning back and yawning cavernous,—"your last minute of grace is up when the clock strikes two; remember that."

"I'll remember."

"If you don't close by that time—to the fraction of a second, you don't close at all."

Mr. Ned made no reply; and Klein continued:

"I don't believe you want the property at all, Durbin. And, if you don't, why the devil don't you say so—and let me dicker with somebody else?"

Again Mr. Ned said nothing; he simply sat and smiled. Mr. Klein suddenly sat up straight and, knowingly squinting his small yellowish-green eyes, he grunted:

"I know what you're holding off for, Durbin; you can't fool me. I'm on."

"Well?"

"You're waiting to hear from the East—hear whether the Transylvania Company decides to enlarge its freight yards; you think you can sell to them—if they do decide they want more room."

"Think so?"—smiling blandly.

"I know so, I tell you";—puckering his smug face in a scowl,— "I'm on. You've got an option on a bunch of lots and old shacks, at—about twice what the bunch is worth on an open market. If you find out you can treble or quadruple your money—by selling to somebody that has to have the property, just has to have it—you'll close with me; if you find out you can't, you won't. And you're holding off to the last minute, hoping you'll get a straight tip—learn something certain. You're a sly fox, Durbin; but I'm on—you see."

"I see you are; you're very astute, Klein. And what do you think the Transylvania company will do, eh?"

Mr. Klein surlily shook his head. "Don't know," he muttered.

"Sure you don't," Mr. Ned smiled; "but what do you think?"

"I'm not going to say. I was a fool to give you an option on the property; and a double fool to give a second option to the other fellows. I might have had the chance with the Transylvania myself."

"Maybe they won't decide to enlarge their yards, though," Mr. Ned suggested.

"Well," growled Klein, "if they don't enlarge 'em, neither of you parties will take the property; and there I am—left with it on my hands just the same as if I'd never given an option on it. While if the railroad does enlarge its yards, you fellows are likely to be on to it—and close the bargain with me. And I've locked the door between myself and a big pile of money. I've only got one consolation, though."

"What's that?"

"I don't really think the Transylvania people 're going to improve."

"No? You said a moment ago you didn't mean to give me your opinion."

"Well, I have done it," Klein growled.

"Anyhow, the thing'll be decided to-night."

"Yes. I wish my option ran till to-morrow at two o'clock."

"But it doesn't,"—grinning like a snarling pug dog.

" No; but the other fellows' does, doesn't it? How long does theirs run?"

"Till four o'clock this evening."

"That all? You didn't give them much of an extension of time over mine."

"No,"—a mere grunt.

"How was that, Klein?"

"I got suspicious something was up—so many of you fellows wanting option on that piece of real-estate—though I didn't find out what was up till yesterday; and so I just gave the new parties two hours over you, to make up their minds in."

"I see. And you think they're playing the same game I am, do you?"

"Yes—of course."

"I'd like to know who they are, Klein."

"You'll never know from me."

"All right,"—laughing lightly.—"Well, I'm going out of the city to-day, on business; and I won't be back till this evening—late. Now, I'll tell you what I'll do: I'll wire or phone the girl here—Miss Grimes, my decision, just after noon; and she can call you up and inform you. That do?"

Klein obstinately and emphatically shook his big fat head.

"What's the matter?" demanded Mr. Ned, jerking out his watch and consulting it. "Don't the arrangement suit you?"

"No," mumbled Klein.

"Well?"

"It's too uncertain, too much latitude for mistakes and misunderstandings—under the circumstances."

"What do you suggest, then?"

"That you draw up a little paper, agreeing to take the property and stating that your father is to act for you—"

"Father's in bed with a cold."

"Well, the young lady, then."

"Go on."

"Stating that the young lady is to act for you in the deal, as you will be absent; and if she adds her signature to yours on the agreement, the sale is closed and the property is yours. Then you can wire or phone her your instructions—whether she is to sign it or not."

"W-e-l-l," Mr. Ned replied slowly and thoughtfully, "I see nothing wrong about that; but we'll draw up the document in duplicate and—"

"What's the use of doing that?" Mr. Klein interrupted hastily, wrinkling his face in a scowl.

"No use, maybe—but we'll do it; and we'll make the agreement on my part an acceptance on yours—that is, that I agree to take the property and you agree to the arrangement and the terms."

"All right," mumbled Mr. Klein; "but I don't see any use of having the thing in duplicate."

"Well, it won't do any harm, at any rate," Mr. Ned said smoothly. "Miss Grimes, write what I dictate, please."

I sat down to the typewriter; and soon had the paper prepared. It was a provisional agreement on the part of Edward Durbin, to purchase a piece of real-estate owned by Horace Klein, designated as the Klein coal-yards tract, at the named price of seventy-five thousand dollars; also, it stipulated that Horace Klein accepted the above price for the property named; and provided that the agreement was null and void unless signed by Edward Durbin, Horace Klein, and Sarah Grimes—amanuensis for the firm of Durbin and Son.

"That's all right," Mr. Ned said briskly when I read what I had written. "Here, Klein—let's sign it."

Rather reluctantly, I thought, Mr. Klein put his scrawling signature to the two papers; and Mr. Ned hurriedly added his. Then the former thrust one of the folded documents into his pocket, and grunted:

"Now, I'll come in here at one o'clock—unless something keeps me away—and wait till two. Then if Miss Grimes doesn't sign up these papers, the deal's off. Is that straight?"

"That's straight," Mr. Ned answered. "And if she does sign 'em, the deal's closed. Is that straight?"

"Straight as a string," laughed my employer.

"All right," growled the morose Mr. Klein—and waddled from the office.

"Now," Mr. Ned cried energetically, again consulting his watch, "let's have a distinct and definite understanding of this matter, Marjory; and then I must be off to catch my car. Listen, now. I've signed a provisional agreement to purchase a piece of real estate from Klein; your signature to that agreement makes it binding upon me to take the property and pay for it. The property's worth about twenty-five thousand dollars, on the market—not a cent more. I've agreed to take it at the price of seventy-five thousand—fifty thousand more than it's worth. You've learned my reason for desiring to purchase it at three times its real value. If the Transylvania company decides to enlarge its yards, I want the property by all means. The railroad company'll have to have it, they can't do without it; and I can get any price for it I have the conscience—no, the gall—to ask. But if the Transylvania company determines not to enlarge its yards,—and the decision will be made to-night,—I don't want the property at all; I would be sinking just fifty thousand for nothing. See?"

I nodded very gravely. Such stupendous figures, when applied to money, almost took my breath away, Nell Adams.

Mr. Ned continued rapidly: "All right. I've had an option on that piece of property for the last six months; I caught a rumor of what the railroad had in mind—and tied onto the thing. Now, I'm going to try to determine by noon whether I desire to close the deal that makes it mine. That's what I'm leaving town for. I'm going to run down to Newark, to meet a friend from New York, who'll be on the B. and O. train for Chicago. He's in a position to know what the Transylvania means to do—will do to-night. I wrote him two weeks ago; and day before yesterday I got a letter from him, saying for me to meet him at Newark to-day—that he would have positive information for me."

He got upon his feet and began to put on his overcoat, continuing:

"Now, here's your instructions—a final word: If I wire or phone you to sign that agreement, do so; if I send you word not to sign it, or you don't hear from me at all, don't sign it—that's all. Everything clear?"

"Yes," I murmured faintly, appalled at the responsibility that was to rest upon poor little insignificant me. Then, as an afterthought, I said: "What time will I get word from you, Mr. Ned—Ned?"

And I couldn't help but blush a little, Nell!

The big, virile, handsome fellow smiled down upon me, as he made answer:

"Some time between one and two. You be sure and be here."

"But something might be wrong with the phone, Ned, or the telegram might not reach me in time," I objected.

"Well, we'll have to take the risk; it's the best we can do."

"And another thing."

"Yes?"

"How about my signing my name as Sarah Grimes?"

"No harm will come of that," he laughed lightly; "this deal isn't likely to become a case in court."

"Who is this man Klein, Ned—Mr. Ned—Ned?"—again blushing.

"He's president of the Mondarun coal company."

"Well, what am I to do if you send me instructions to sign those papers and he fails to come around?"

"You must find him—dead sure."

Then he came up to me, and playfully yet soberly put his hand under my chin and turned my face up toward his.

"Little girl," he said, "I'm going to depend upon you to carry this affair through all straight, even if I can't depend upon you in some things."

"Why, Ned," I murmured, "can't you depend upon me in—in everything?"

"I wish I could," he muttered earnestly;—then, looking through my eyes and down deep into my soul:—"and—and I guess I can."

With that, he bent and kissed me. Then he sprang away from me, waved his hand and cried cheerily, laughingly:

"So long!"

And I stood stock still, listening to his receding footsteps; and my heart was echoing his laughter, Nell Adams!

The forenoon passed pleasantly, quickly; I was glad to be alone—happy to have no company but my thoughts.

I went to lunch at eleven-thirty; and, as I was in a hurry to return to the office, I went to the Busy Bee—a restaurant near at hand. Barely had my order been filled, when two men came in and took a table near me, just behind me.

"It's all right, I tell you," I heard one of them say; "no chance for a mistake."

The voice was the voice of my little cigarette fiend, Mr. Morse; and I was about to turn and recognize him, when I heard him continue—in excited, incautious tones:

"No, Walsh, it's a dead sure thing. If Ned Durbin doesn't take the property by two o'clock—and I don't believe he will, for he doesn't know what I do,—we want to close our option, tie right onto it. What do you say, Walsh?"

"Don't know," the other man muttered. I was alert, interested, concerned—at once; and determined to glean the full import of that conversation, if possible. So I neglected my lunch and devoted my energies to an attempt to hear all that was said. The clatter and confusion of the big room was terrific; but, as I sat almost as close to Mr. Morse and his companion as each sat close to the other, I succeeded in catching nearly every word they uttered.

My little dude pleadingly continued:

"Why, Walsh, we don't want to let a good thing like that get away; it's the chance of a lifetime. We don't stand to lose a cent—"

"You mean you don't," Walsh interrupted; "but I stand to lose fifty or sixty thousand—maybe."

"I tell you you don't stand to lose a cent," Mr. Morse cried, almost frantically; "it's a dead sure thing. The Transylvania's going to enlarge their yards—that's all. And we'll stand to win a hundred thousand, at the smallest figure; and fifty thousand of that'll be yours. That gives you an even chance for your money, even if we didn't know anything about what the Transylvania means to do— which we do know."

"I don't know anything," Walsh objected.

"Yes, you do; I've told you."

"Well, you'll have to show me, Morse; I'm from Missouri, when it comes to a deal as big—as this—and my good money backed only by another fellow's wind."

"Why, what do you mean, Walsh?" almost whimpering, the little insignificant putty-face!—"You and I have this option—your money against what I know; and surely you're not going to—to—"

"Yes, I'm going to back right square out of the thing—right this minute, unless you show me,"—firmly, inexorably.—"You're urging me to close the deal; but you haven't got a cent in it. If we win, you get half; if we lose, you lose nothing. I say you've got to show me."

"But, Walsh,"—really whining lugubriously[1],—"I can't tell you when and where and how I got my tip—I can't!"

"Well, you can—and you will, or the game's off. There!"

_____
1 Lugubrious – mournful, gloomy, sad

"Well," Morse cried in desperation, "if I must, I must—that's all; for I can't lose the only chance I've ever had to get on my feet. But, Walsh, you must promise me to keep mum; it would play the devil with me, if you'd ever tell on me. You must promise not to tell."

"Oh, I promise that!" Walsh laughed disagreeably.

How I despised that little dope fiend! I felt, rather than saw, him sweep a glance in my direction; and I feared he might recognize me, though my back was toward him. I was greatly relieved when he again turned leaning far over the table and speaking so low I could not catch all he said. However, this is what drifted to me—in shreds and tatters:

" Well, here's . . . I got next. Klein . . . cousin in employ . . . . sylvania comp . . . . . . ; . . . he's high muckamuck . . . . . he wrote Klein . . . . . . going to enlarge . . . . yards, sure. I stole . . . . . . Klein's desk. See? "

"Got that letter with you?" I heard Walsh say distinctly.

"Yes,"—almost a whisper.

"Let me see it."

A momentary pause in the conversation; the crumpling crackle of stiff paper; then, from Walsh, exultantly:

"Say! That's all right; that reads good—to me. But, hello!"— shrewdly, sarcastically.

"What?"—from Mr. Morse, sharply.

"I see now why Klein was so anxious to have me sign a provisional contract—a contract to be void unless signed by you before four o'clock to-day. I wondered why he wanted that; now I know. The infernal scoundrel!"

"What do you mean, Walsh?"—anxiously, fearsomely.

"Why, don't you catch on? Klein doesn't want us to close the deal, he wants to sell the property to the Transylvania himself; and he doesn't mean to give you a chance to sign that contract—that's what."

"Doesn't—mean—to—give—me—a—chance—to—sign—it?"—slowly, thickly.

"That's what I said. Of course he doesn't mean to give you a chance to sign it; he means, to avoid you—to be in hiding."

"Good heavens!" Mr. Morse gasped. "Do you think that?"

All at once, Nell Adams, I caught on, too; and I sprang to my feet, nearly upsetting my chair as I did so. Klein had played the same trick upon Mr. Ned! He didn't mean to give me a chance to sign the agreement he and my employer had signed—the one he had in his own possession; he didn't mean to come back to the office at all.

I don't know how I got out of the restaurant; I don't know whether Mr. Morse saw and recognized me or not. I do know I hurried back to the office as fast as I could go—thinking, thinking, wildly, erratically, irrationally. What could I do? I must get to sign that paper; I must—I must! It was half-past twelve; I mustn't wait. What should I do—what could I do? The thought that I mustn't sign the paper till I had heard from Mr. Ned never entered my noddle[2]; that part of the arrangement was out of my reckoning. All I could think was that my employer—my dear young employer!—was about to be defrauded; and that I must prevent it. I must get the tricky president of the Mondarun coal company back to our office; but how—but how? Ah, I had it—I had it! And my feet fairly flew! No doubt Klein was already in hiding—with no intention of turning up till after four o'clock, after the options had expired; but no doubt, I argued, somebody at his office was cognizant of his whereabouts. And I thought I knew how to entice him from his hiding-place.

On reaching my place of employment I went to the phone and called up the office of the Mondarun coal company.

"Hello!" I said. "This the Mondarun coal company? You say it is? All right. Is Mr. Klein there? He isn't?"—I felt sure that he wouldn't be.—"Well, where will I find him? Oh! you don't know, you say?"—My suspicions were already confirmed.—"Yes, it's important—very important. Yes. Well, it doesn't make any difference who I am; but I'm down at the Neil, and I want to talk business to him. Yes—very important, I said. You think you might find him? All right. Oh! just say that a man down at the Neil wants to talk Transylvania to him. Yes, Transylvania; I think he'll catch on. Does he know me? No; but it's to his interest to get acquainted with me. Say

2 Noddle – a person's head

that to him. Yes; yes, that's it. I'll be waiting at the clerk's desk. Oh! well, I'll know him; and I'll be on the watch for him. Yes, indeed— right away. Uh-huh, Transylvania. All right. Goodbye."

I had spoken in as coarse and rough a voice as I could command; and you know I'm something of a mimic when I try, Nell. Still I thought the man at the other end of the line was somewhat suspicious, and I feared he might call up central to confirm or deny the truth of my statement that I was talking from the Neil. But I had played my first card, and could not recall it. I hoped it would win the trick; hoped Klein would think some representative of the Transylvania company was at the Neil, anxious to talk to him about the purchase of the piece of property on which my employer had first option.

I was trembling all over with undue and unusual excitement; and I could hardly hold the pen as I sat down to write:

"Mr. Horace Klein:
    "Come to Durbin and Son's office at once. I am ready to sign the agreement signed by Edward Durbin and your- self this morning.   Truly,
                "Sarah Grimes."

Then I called Jones in from the outer office and said to him:

"Jones,"—I called him just Jones, Nell; I was wasting no titles of respect upon his like just then! "do you know Mr. Klein of the Mondarun coal company?"

"Yes, Miss Grimes,"—very respectfully, "I know him when I see him."

"Well, make yourself acquainted with the contents of this note— that you may be able to recall what it's about, if necessity arises."

Jones read the brief missive; then silently looked at me for further orders,

"Now," I commanded loftily, "take it up to the Neil and give it to Mr. Klein; and see that he reads it and accompanies you back here."

" All right, Miss Grimes. Will he be awaiting me there?"

"I don't know. But if he isn't there, wait for him; and if he doesn't come in—let me see—in a half-hour, you phone me. And, Jones, listen!"—with all impressiveness.

"Yes, Miss Grimes."

"You can't imagine how important your mission is; how important that Mr. Klein should get that note and be here before two o'clock. If he fails to come, we'll both lose our jobs."

"Oh, dear!" he ejaculated in genuine consternation.

"Now, be off," I cried. Then, as an afterthought: "And don't let Mr. Klein strike you."

It was an unfortunate remark. The fellow's jaw dropped; my innocent warning had greatly alarmed him. For the moment I feared I had spoiled everything—feared Jones would refuse to serve as my messenger.

"Go!" I commanded sternly. "Go at once!"

"But—but—" he stammered, "what do you mean by saying Klein may strike me?"

"The note will make him mad—that's all," I hastily explained. "But you be off; and remember you'll lose your job if you don't have him here before two o'clock."

"But maybe he'll refuse to come," was the fellow's natural objection.

"If he says he won't come, tell him we're on to his game—and will carry the case into court. Now, skidoo!"

And he went—like he had an invitation to dine somewhere, Nell!

I sat and waited and worried, and worried and waited; and fidgeted and consulted my watch, and then fidgeted some more and again looked at my timepiece. One o'clock passed, one-thirty came and went; and no Mr. Klein put in an appearance, no Jones phoned me. It was like having a spell of nightmare upon a bed of sickles, Nell! Oo-h! I don't want to think of it any more!

At one-forty-five the door opened and—in the two men came. Both were puffing; and Klein was red-of-face and perspiring, though the day was raw. I motioned the latter to a chair and signalled Jones to leave the room. Then I said quietly:

"Hand me the paper you have, Mr. Klein; I'm ready to sign it."

"Did you phone to my office for me?" he countered brusquely.

"I did," I replied coolly.

"Saying a man wanted to see me on business, at the Nell?"

"Yes."

"What made you do that?"

"You know."

"Well, don't you know you're likely to get into trouble for such a thing as that?" blusteringly.

"I think not,"—smiling sweetly.

"There wasn't any man at the Neil, wanting to see me; and—"

"Jones was there."

"Y-e-s"—sullenly;—"but—"

"Hand over the paper, Mr. Klein."

"You're ready to sign 'em, are you?"

"Certainly."

"Have you heard from Durbin—saying for you to sign 'em?"

"No; but I'm ready to sign them."

"W-e-ll,"—opening his small yellowish-green eyes wide and pouting his full lips, "don't you know that would be illegal?"

"Give me the paper," I insisted.

"It won't do any good for you to sign 'em—when Durbin hasn't ordered you to; it won't stand in law."

I said no more for a moment. Instead I deliberately took out my watch and looked at it. It wanted but five minutes of two.

"Mr. Klein," I said slowly, returning my timepiece to its fob, "do you refuse to let me sign that paper?"

I knew he was playing for time. "Why—why," he stammered; and came to a stop.

"Shall I call in the office force and inform them you refuse to let me sign that paper, Mr. Klein?"

He got purple in the face and the cords of his short neck swelled; but he silently pulled out the paper and handed it to me.

"Jones," I called triumphantly. The fellow came in.

"Jones, I want you to see me sign this. Read it over."

When it was all over, Nell Adams, the starch was all out of me; I was a rag! I went home, miserable with a nervous headache; but happy—so happy! And I went to bed without any supper; and fell asleep murmuring:

"Oh, I did it—I did it! I did it for Ned—my Ned!"

But, oh, the blackest of black disappointments fate had in store for me!

Chapter 13

I DID not wake till late the next morning; and the first thought that came to me—wasn't it strange, Nell!—wasn't of Mr. Ned and what he had done to me the day before, but was of what he had said to me: "If you don't hear from me, don't sign the papers!"

And the disquieting question immediately presented itself: "Did I do right in not heeding his positive order—or not?"

I arose and began to dress—hurriedly, feverishly. My head had quit aching, but it felt numb and dumb and dizzy; and my fingers shook so that I could hardly fasten my clothes. Had I done right—or had I done wrong? Pshaw! Why hadn't I thought of that before? If—if I had made a mistake,—oh, I wouldn't think of such a thing!—what, then? It was too awful! Of course I hadn't committed a blunder, I tried to assure myself—of course I hadn't! Mr. Ned's message had failed to reach me, or he had not met his friend at Newark, or the friend had misinformed him; to be sure that was the way of it! And I had picked up reliable information; I had done what anyone of common sense would have done—had done what Mr. Ned would have had me do, could I have communicated with him at the time. Of course I had done right—of course I had!

My brain began to clear; my spirits began to rise. My train of reasoning allayed my fears, quieted my nerves; and the crowd of blue-devils that had beset me whisked themselves out of sight, and there stood Cupid—dimpled, rosy, smiling! At once I was happy, jubilant! Everything would be all right—more than all right! Mr. Ned would be pleased with what I had done—delighted; he would praise my devotion to his interests and compliment me upon my shrewdness and keen business sense. I knew he would! And—and—

157

well, there was no telling what he might do, in a moment of gratitude and joy!

I hurried down to the street, treading upon air. The sun was shining bright; the sparrows were flitting here and there and chirping merrily. What a good world it was to be in—to be sure! I stopped at my usual place and ate a hearty breakfast, all the while smiling, dreaming—dreaming day dreams the most delightful. Maybe Mr. Ned would—would—well, maybe he would! And maybe we'd go abroad; and—oo-h!—but that would be great! And we'd have a lot of money; and—just to think!—I could feel that I had helped to make it! Oh, bliss and glory!

I was an hour behind time, but I didn't care for that; and I knew Mr. Ned wouldn't care—when he learned what I had done for him. Oh, wouldn't it be great—just simply great!—to tell him? I could hardly wait till I reached the office; and I didn't walk from my car to the curb—I flew. Oh, how pokey the old elevator was! And I flirted my skirts through the outer office, unheeding the stares bent upon me, entered the inner room and stood in the presence of—Mr . Ned.

He sat slouched down in his arm chair, in true American style— his hands thrust deep into his trousers' pockets, his chin upon his breast. Apathetically he glanced up as I closed the door behind me, and gave a slight start—of surprise, I thought; and I wondered why. But he merely nodded, and sank back into his listless attitude. Not only was he sunk in the depths of his chair, but he was sunk in the depths of despair—that I could plainly see; and I giggled inwardly, thinking how I'd boost him out of both with the giant-cracker of good news which I had concealed on my person and which I meant to touch off. I knew what ailed him—of course I did! He was griev-ing over his ill luck—that was it. No doubt the Transylvania compa-ny had decided to enlarge their freight yards—no doubt they had!— and this morning the news was current and Mr. Ned had heard it; and now—not knowing what I had done, teehee!—he was blue over his fancied loss of the property. Oh, hadn't I a pleasant surprise in store for him—and wouldn't he be delighted!

"Good morning," I said brightly.

He looked up at me, gropingly, questioningly; but no smile

lighted the depths of his sombre features.

"Good morning, Miss Dawes," he mumbled huskily.

Miss Dawes! And at such a time—right when I was about to treat him to a pleasurable surprise! The day before it was—Marjory; and now it was—Miss Dawes! What could it mean? It was mean, anyhow! Never mind! I'd punish him for that—by withholding my news and teasing him about his spell of the blues.

"You don't seem in a very good humor this morning, Mr. Ned—Ned," I pouted prettily, dwelling fondly, lingeringly, upon the italicised word.

He gave me another of those strange, inquiring looks; then he muttered glumly:

"Not very, I guess."

"What's the matter?"—hanging up my things.—"Sick?"

"No,"—curtly.

"Are you worrying about your father? Is he worse?"

He shook his head.

"How is he this morning?"

"Better."

"I'm glad to hear it," I murmured. "But what's the matter with you—Ned?"

He made no answer; simply accorded me another of those searching, wondering stares.

"Well," I said softly—striving to force a little pathos[1] into my voice and squeeze a little moisture into my eyes, "you don't have to tell me, if you don't want to—of course."

Still he made no answer; just continued to look at me in that peculiar, interrogative way. It made me all prickly—all fidgety. How odd he acted! Was he just down in the dumps over his fancied loss? Or was—was it something else? Seeing he didn't mean to speak—didn't mean to enlighten me, I went on, at a venture:

"You didn't phone me yesterday."

He kept silent.

"Did you?—"impatiently, insistently.

"No."

---

1 Pathos - an emotion of sympathetic pity

"Nor telegraph me?"

"Of course not,"—gruffly.

"Well, you needn't be so—so cross about it," I quavered; "I didn't know—know but you might have done so, and failed to—to—"

I choked up and stopped; but he gave no heed to my emotion, had no concern, apparently, for the hurt he had given me. He just kept his eyes fixed upon me—that expression of mute, mysterious inquiry upon his dark face. Exasperated, I cried—triumphantly, dramatically:

"Well, Mr. Edward Durbin, I signed the papers, anyhow!"

I expected him to be surprised—greatly surprised—joyfully surprised; expected him to spring to his feet, to exclaim, to—well, to catch me in his arms, maybe, and—and! But judge of my surprise, my disappointment, my dismay, Nell Adams, when he did nothing but nod surlily and say:

"Yes, I know you did."

I fairly jumped.

"You know I did?" I cried.

He nodded.

"How—how—who told you?"

"Jones."

Jones! I had forgotten all about Jones and his knowledge of what I had done. Jones! The meddler—to tell Mr. Ned what I wanted to tell him! But if Jones had told Mr. Ned of my signing the papers, what was the matter with my dear young employer? The question immediately presented itself, and was disturbing, disconcerting; and it would not down—and I out with it.

"Well, if Jones has—has told you," I murmured tremulously, "why—why are you so—so dejected?"

"Yes, sure enough—why!"—a sarcastic growl.

"Yes, why?" I insisted, undefined fear nagging me. " Why?"

"Well,"—a sneer lifting one comer of his wide mouth,—"I suppose it is unpardonable in me to be feeling bum; I ought to be feeling as frisky as a yearling colt—as skittish as a skeeter. Of course most fellows when they lose forty or fifty thousand dollars feel real gay; but somehow I don't. I'm not appreciative of the good things of life, I suppose."

"Lose forty or fifty thousand dollars!" I exclaimed. "Why you're not going to lose that amount—you're not going to lose anything."

"No?"—in wide-eyed incredulity.

"No, you're not,"—with great assurance, more than I fully felt, perhaps.

"I'm glad to hear that I'm not to lose anything, I'm sure,"—the merest semblance of a smile twitching his lips;—"for the prospect has been worrying me a bit, I admit. Still I haven't as much faith in your statement as I would like to have."

"Why, do you think you're going to lose money on that property—that Klein property?" I cried.

"I do—of course 1 do."

"You can't Ned· you can't—I tell you!"

"That's what you say—Marjory; I hear you. But why can't I?"

"Why? Haven't you heard, Ned?"

"Heard? Yes, I've heard—heard more than enough, such as it is."

"But haven't you heard about the Transylvania?"

He looked at me—and looked at me, as if he thought me crazy.

"Yes, I've—heard—about—the—Transylvania," he said very slowly and soberly.

"Well?" I cried triumphantly.

"Well?" he demanded—almost rudely.

"Why, the Transylvania has decided to enlarge its yards."

"Indeed?"—his brows lifted.

"Yes."

"Is that so?"—in apparent amazement.

"Yes, that's so,"—a little nettled.

"You know that to be a fact, Marjory?"

"Yes, I do."

"W-e-ll, I'll not inquire where you got your information; but it differs very materially from this."

With the words he picked up the morning Journal from his desk, indicated a paragraph on the railroad page and handed the paper to me. I took it and read:

"Latest dispatches from New York confirm the report that was current on the streets at ten-thirty last night, that the Transylvania had decided not to enlarge its freight yards at this place. This is sorry news for Columbus; and sorry we are to have to give it out. But—"

I read no more, Nell Adams! I let the paper drop to the floor, and sank into a chair and covered my face with my hands. Everything turned bluish-black and yellowish-green; and I thought I was going to faint—and wanted to! Oh, what had I done? What had I done—done—done—done! And "done" was the word that kept snapping and cracking in my ears: and "done" were my dreams and my prospects; and dun looked the future! Surely I had went and gone and done it! I wanted to cry, but I couldn't; I wanted to swear—but I wouldn't!

The enormity of my blunder appalled me, for the moment, paralyzed my faculties. Then, little by little, I began to recover—began to collect my wits and really think. Why, the thing couldn't be so—it just couldn't at all; and it just shouldn't! I had tried so hard to do something right; and it had gone right wrong! But it hadn't, I wouldn't believe it—and I didn't believe it!

I peeked through my fingers at Mr. Ned. He was looking at me steadily, gloomily—but pityingly, I thought. The discovery made me sorrowful—made me glad; and the tears began to come. Then a little sob shook my shoulders.

"Marjory," my companion said hoarsely but kindly.

"W-what, N-Ned?" I articulated with difficulty.

"Don't worry; the thing's done—and can't be undone now."

A flame of anger flared up within me and flashed into my eyes. I jerked my hands away from my face, crying:

"It's done, and can't be helped, Ned—Indeed! There's nothing done that can't be helped; there's nothing done that needs to be helped. That paper lies—so it does!"

"Does it?"—amusedly.

"Yes, it does. I heard Mr. Morse say—"

"Ah, Mr. Morse!" he interrupted, sitting up very straight and stiff. "I thought it would all come out, if I only waited long enough;

I thought Morse had something to do with the thing. Now, tell me all about it, Marjory."

"About what, Ned?"

"About what Morse had to do with your signing those papers, of course."

"Why, he hadn't anything, only—"

"Well?"—impatiently.

"Only I overheard him say something to another man."

"Oh!"

"Yes."

"That's all, eh?"

"Yes, that's all."

"Who was the other man?"

"Morse called him Walsh."

" I know Walsh. Now, where did you overhear them talking?"

"At the Busy Bee."

"When you went to lunch?"

"Yes."

"You took a seat near them, or they took a seat near you—which?"

"They took a seat near me."

"I see. Well, what did you hear them say? Tell me everything."

I did so; and, at the conclusion of my recital, he remarked— shaking his head pityingly and smiling tenderly:

"I don't blame you for being fooled, Marjory."

"Fooled, Ned?"—puzzled.

He nodded, still smiling commiseratingly.

"I don't understand what you mean."

"They tricked you, Marjie."

"They? Who?"

"Why,"—half irritably,—"Klein and Morse and Walsh—that's who."

"You mean that they just—just—"

"Yes; they just put up a job on you."

I sank back in my chair, nerveless, helpless.

"They—put—up—a—job—on—me!" I murmured thickly.

"Yes, they did—damn 'em!" Mr. Ned muttered.

"But, Ned," I objected weakly, "Mr. Klein wasn't at the restaurant."

"That made no difference."

"It didn't?"

"Why, no,"—impatiently.—"Can't you understand?"

"I—I guess not," I had to admit.

"Well, listen," he cried; "I'll explain. Klein wanted to sell the property to me, at the exorbitant price of my option—which I was a fool ever to take. So, with the aid of Morse and Walsh, he hatched up a scheme to load it on to me. He came here yesterday morning, thinking his pretense that he didn't want to sell would make me anxious to close the bargain; but I fooled him—disappointed him. Then, when I told him I was going out of the city, he saw his chance to load it on to me by tricking you; and, with the aid of Morse and Walsh, he brought the thing about. He had them follow you to the restaurant and play the little farce-comedy they did. You thought they were there by accident; but they weren't. They took you in; but, as I said, I don't wonder. It was slickly done."

"Oh, Mr. Ned—Ned!" was all I could whisper.

Then, as a quick afterthought:

"But Mr. Morse and Mr. Walsh had an option on the property, too."

"Simply a part of the play," he replied, sadly shaking his head.

"And," I persisted, "Mr. Klein hid from me—and didn't mean to come to the office at all."

"All a pretense, Marjory—to make you eager to put your signature to the papers."

I straightened up in my chair and said tersely, flatly:

"I don't believe it."

"It's true—too true."

"I don't believe it, I say."

"Nevertheless, it's true, Marjory."

"Then,"—my anger rising, from pique and nervousness, I suppose,—"you think I've been fooled, do you?"

"Of course,"—quite calmly.

"And that I'm a fool!"

"I didn't say that."

"Well, you hinted it; people can't be fooled unless they're more or less fools."

"Now!"

"You might as well call me a fool—and be done with it."

"Now, Marjory!"

"Oh, you might!"

"Marjory, you're unjust, unreasonable."

"Most fools are," I snapped.

He just shook his head and smiled—protestingly, provokingly.

And then I broke loose:

"And I'm not such a fool as you think me, Ned Durbin. Those men weren't shamming; it was all real. Mr. Klein had had word from the East; and he didn't want to sell the property; and he did hide from Mr. Morse and Mr. Walsh and me; and those two did have a second option on the property. There! I'll never believe anything else, either. And that paper there is mistaken; the Transylvania hasn't decided not to enlarge their yards. Now!"

And I settled back and looked him square in the face, coolly, defiantly. His own countenance brightened a little—whether from belief in my very decided declaration or from admiration of my spirit of self-assertiveness, I couldn't make sure, Nell; and he muttered:

"What makes you say all that so positively, Marjory?"

"Just because—because—"

I was earnestly and busily searching for my reason.

"Well?" he cried.

"Because I feel it. There!"

"I wish I could feel it," he grinned dejectedly.

"I just know it," I insisted.

"A case of woman's intuition, eh?"

"I suppose so—yes; but I do know it—just the same."

"W-e-ll," he said slowly, reflectively, "maybe you do, but I don't; and that's what worries me. The thing looks crooked enough to me. Why, Marjory,"—argumentatively, "the idea of Morse and Walsh having a second option on that property is absurd, preposterous. Morse is just a clerk in Klein's employ, and he hasn't a dollar; and—"

"But Mr. Walsh has," I interrupted valiantly.

"Yes," he admitted "Walsh may have money—lots of it; I don't know. He's a politician, a hanger-on of the city administration. But here are the objections—to me: Why should Klein give an option to his own employee, Morse? And why should Walsh go in with Morse—the latter having no money? And how did they happen into the restaurant at the opportune time—and happen to take seats right where you could overhear what they said? And, above all, why were they so incautious—in so important a matter? It all looks bad—to me."—Then, shaking his head and sighing heavily:—"And the Journal can't be mistaken; it's not guesswork with them. No, my fifty thousand has gone glimmering, little girl; but,"—brightening, with a too evident effort,—"I'm not going to worry—not going to worry like I was just before you came in, anyhow."·

And he gave me the oddest, shame-faced side glance.

"What do you mean?" I inquired unconcernedly.

He squirmed uneasily, Nell, and his handsome face flushed a dull red; and I wondered what was coming.

"Marjory," he said huskily, "I've got a confession to make; and I won't feel right till I've made it. Listen, now; and don't interrupt—let me get through with it as soon as possible."—What on earth was coming, Nell Adams?—"I went down to Newark yesterday and met Jim Golden, my friend from New York. It took him but a few minutes to convince me that the Transylvania company wouldn't decide upon the contemplated enlargement of their yards, and that I didn't want the Klein property; so I dismissed the whole thing from my mind and gave my attention to some other business. It was late when I got back to the city last night; and I didn't learn a thing about the final action of the Transylvania and what you had done, till I came to the office this morning. Jones informed me of your—your rather indiscreet act, as soon as I came in; and I was amazed, thunderstruck. I didn't know what to think; I couldn't think for a while. I just slouched in here and lopped[2] down in my chair—completely knocked out. I tried to brace up and grapple with the problem of why you had done such a thing; but I only partially succeeded—and

---

2 Lopped - to hang downward : droop

I couldn't find a loose end to begin on. Then you didn't come, and it was time for you to be here; and an hour passed and still you didn't come, and—and—"

He paused, shook his head in a grave and embarrassed manner, and restlessly drummed the arm of his chair with his strong, lean fingers.

"And?" I queried, interested, but little suspecting what was coming.

"And then," he resumed resolutely, "I—I got to thinking— here's the confession, the hard part, Marjie!—you hadn't committed an unwitting blunder, but had willfully proven false to the trust I had reposed in you; got to thinking you had joined Klein and Morse in a scheme, to swindle me, and—"

"Mr. Edward Durbin!" I exclaimed, sitting primly and sancti-moniously erect.

"Don't say a word!" he muttered, gritting his firm, white teeth. "You can't say what ought to be said of me; you can't swear! I'll just say this one thing in extenuation of my unexampled assininity, though: I guess my jealousy led me to think as I did."—His jealousy, eh? Nell, I began to feel right good, for the moment!—"I thought of your intimacy with Morse, and of Morse being in the employ of Klein, and of Klein's peculiar actions here at the office, and of your delay in putting in an appearance—till I got to thinking you weren't coming back at all; got to thinking Klein had divided up with Morse and you, and that you two had skipped; got to thinking—oh, the devil!—got to thinking all sorts of insane things. And I was sur-prised when you came; I was honestly. Now!"

I just sat and looked at him, Sweet Nell of old Oberlin; and never said a word in reply. What should I say—what could I say? What was there for me to say—me who had lost him fifty thousand dollars? But how should I feel toward him? That question was more pertinent; but no more easily met and solved, I found. Should I feel hurt—and hate him, feel outraged—and despise him? Or should I accept his plea that his unpardonably poor opinion of me and his want of trust in me were due to temporary aberration of mind oc-casioned by mad and unreasoning jealousy? In one sense that was flattering to me, Nell; in another it wasn't so flattering. Maybe Ned's mean thoughts were due to jealousy, though, I argued with myself; for men will do and think such silly things, when jealous! So I sat thinking and staring, and staring and thinking.

"Don't look at me like that, Marjory!" he cried, hitching his chair closer in front of me and bending forward and seizing both my hands. "I've been fair, I've told you just what I thought; maybe I shouldn't have told you at all, though. But I couldn't keep from it; I felt so good to find out it wasn't so, to find out you just blundered—and in trying to do me a good turn. Say you forgive me; say you do!"

He drew me toward him till our faces were very close together,—the big lusty fellow! till we were looking into each other's souls through each other's eyes.

"Say it!" he commanded, compelling me with his gaze and touch.

"I forgive you, Ned," I barely whispered. Then he put his arm around me and kissed me. It may be that he kissed me more than once, old chum; my recollection is a little hazy.

And, for the moment, every care and worry left me; and I was a-flutter with bliss and happiness.

"Marjory," he whispered tenderly, "I love—"

He had just got that far, Nell, when I gave a little screech and jump and pulled away from him. The thought that I had lost him fifty thousand dollars—just think of the sum!—struck me like a chill wind in the face. For the first time the full enormity of my blunder appeared to me and appealed to me. Fifty thousand dollars! Ned could never forget it, he would always remember it against me; let him strive as he would, the thought of the loss of that much money would always be with him. And I had done it; I had caused him to lose it!

"What's the matter, Marjory?" he asked in keen and quick concern.

I burst into tears. He tried to caress me, to ascertain what ailed me; but I drew farther away from him, and refused to be consoled. Oh, I was so nervous, so miserable, so unhappy! And right when I ought to have been rejoicing over his declaration of love, Nell Adams—think of that!

After a little boohoo, I calmed myself and told Mr. Ned—my Ned!—just how I felt about the matter. He tried to laugh me out of the notion—the big good-natured boy!—but I could see he didn't feel much like laughing; it was an effort for him. What man can laugh unrestrainedly, that has just lost fifty thousand dollars!

"Now, Marjory;" he said to me, "not another word of the kind—on the subject. Of course fifty thousand plunks[3] is quite a sum,"—I winced, Nell!—"but I think what I've got in exchange for it, as it were, if I have got what I think I've got,"—beaming upon me, "is worth the price. It's true"—his face momentarily clouding,—"I'm completely cleaned out,"—again I winced! "for I've got to lose the whole thing myself; I won't let father lose a cent of it. But I can start in at the bottom of the ladder again,"—once more I flinched and shuddered, and felt the blood flowing cold through my heart! What blundering, thoughtless, cruel animals men are, Nell Adams!—"and maybe, if the rungs aren't too slippery, I can climb—"

"Oh, don't!" I wailed dismally, weeping afresh. "Don't say any more, Mr. Ned—Ned! Don't—don't—don't! And I'm nervous—I'm sick; I can't think of work to-day, and I want to go to my rooms, and rest and sleep—and never—never wake up!"

"There—there!" he said soothingly. "I see you're all upset. Well, go to your rooms; and don't come back till to-morrow, if you don't feel like it. You'll be all right by that time, Marjory."

He put his arm around me and tenderly kissed me; but I didn't appreciate his caresses. I was too wretched! And I went shuffling and stumbling from the office, my eyes blinded with tears!

---

3 Plunk - to set down suddenly

Chapter 14

I WENT straight to my rooms, threw myself upon my bed and tried to compose myself to sleep. But a half-hour's miserable struggle with my tense nerves convinced me that my resolves and re-resolves and efforts and renewed efforts were worse than useless; and I got up to think the thing all over—to fight the battle out on my feet.

Up and down and round and round, I paced and pouted—like a naughty kid locked up for punishment!—looking out this window and then out that, and sniffling and knuckling my fists into my eyes. I was simply desperate, Nell mine—nervously insane and insanely nervous. But at last I quieted down, and sat down to think—to think rationally, I flattered myself.

What had I done! Lost Ned fifty thousand dollars? I didn't believe it; but he did. Aye, there was the rub! And, of course, he might be right. And if he were—oh, if he were! Well, it was done, if it was done; and I couldn't help it—now. But could I ever go back to that office to work? The mere thought of doing so made me shudder! No, I couldn't—and I wouldn't! But what would I do? I'd just pack my things and run away; that's what I'd do. But Ned loved me—Ned loved me! And he had forgiven me and assured me he didn't care for the loss of the money. But I knew he did—oh, I knew he did! And I couldn't go back—I couldn't! wouldn't! No, I'd run away—away off where Ned would never find me, would never hear of me again. But, oh!—oh!—I loved Ned! And could I go away and leave him—and never see him again? Ah! could I—could I? I must—that was all there was to it!

And, Nell Adams, I got out the new suitcase I had bought a few days before,—a bargain I had picked up!—and resolutely began to

170

pack my few things!

But where was I going? It didn't matter. Anywhere! Anywhere, to get away from Columbus! Anywhere! Chicago, Cincinnati—anywhere! I tell you, old chum, I was desperate—irresponsible, I guess.

When I had tumbled my meager effects into my suitcase,—ruthlessly tossing aside everything of little value,—I snapped the catches and turned the key; and heaved a sigh of partial relief. I had come to a decision; and I felt a little better. Then I bathed my face and smoothed my hair, and put on my hat and wrap. Finally I glanced at my watch,—it was eleven-forty-five, I remember,—took a last look at my cosy rooms, and caught up my suit-case and scooted down the stairs. And a few minutes later I was on a car and on my way to the Union depot.

The car stopped, and I got off and hurried to the sidewalk. I was so strung up I couldn't do anything except with a rush. The big depot was before me—forbidding, depressing; and I trembled, and shrunk within myself. The dusky, gloomy arches made me shiver; the smell of smoke and steam made me faint. But I stoically held on my way; and soon was within the vast waiting-room—and utterly lonely and sick at heart in the stirring throng.

Directly to the intelligence-office I went, and inquired—dry sobs interfering with my speech:

"When does the—the next train leave for—for Chicago?"

The answer I received did not accord with my desires; so I asked:

"And when does the next train leave for Cincinnati?"

The young man behind the desk looked up at me, curiously, admiringly, a telephone receiver to his ear, and returned:

"Over which road?"

"Over any road," I replied.

"There'll be a train over the Big Four about one-thirty-five; it's the nine-fifty-five behind time—delayed by a wreck."

"Thank you," I murmured, and turned away.

I had made up my mind to go to Cincinnati.

I bought my ticket; then dropped into a seat near the center of the great room, my suit-case at my feet, and gave myself up to idle

thought and purposeless observation—as nearly as I could. Oh, how
lonely—how lost I felt! The people kept coming and going—coming and going, and jostling and elbowing, and talking and gesticulating; and, as one in a dream, I stupidly watched them and listened to
them. I wondered carelessly, dumbly, where this one lived and what
that one's business was; and I wished I could quit seeing them, quit
hearing them—wished I were in some cabin in the trackless woods,
all by my little lonesome self, Nell. For I was so tired, so—so homesick; and, all at once, I found myself thinking about old Chesterville
and its quiet streets, about Jack and Aunt Dodo. And my lips would
quiver and the dry sobs would come; and I felt myself longing to go
back to the old place—to the old forms and faces.

That made me mad, Nell Adams—to find I was still such a silly baby!—and I angrily shook myself; and immediately resolved I
wouldn't go back there—and I wouldn't ever see Ned again—and
I wouldn't ever see anybody again, that I had ever known. No, indeed! I was going to lose myself and my identity in some big city,
bigger than Columbus—Cincinnati, probably. Yes, Marjory Dawes
should die, and Sarah Grimes should die; and neither should be res-
urrected or remembered.

And then I found my eyes moist with tears of self pity; and I was
madder than ever—mad in good earnest, I tell you. I just stamped
my foot and vowed I wouldn't; and I didn't—any more.

I kept watching the clock and wishing my train would come.
The hour hand passed one; and I began to listen to the train-crier every time he came in. Then, all at once, my attention was arrested by
a young woman entering the room from the direction of the street. I
couldn't help but observe her as she came tripping along, swinging
her suitcase and swelling with self-confidence and self-assertiveness; for her plaid coat closely resembled the one I had on and her
hat was very much like my own. That much I noticed as she passed
me on her way to the ticket-window; also, I noticed that she gave me
a swift glance—and smiled a peculiar little smile.

I watched her buy her ticket, idly, numbly speculating as to who
she was and where she was going. When she turned from the window, she surprised me by coming directly to me and taking a seat at

my side.

"I thought I'd sit down here and make your acquaintance," she said in an easy, natural way, with a smile that lighted her whole face—and completely disarmed me. "We might be twins—judging from the similarity of our dress and not from the similarity of our looks. I noticed you as I passed you—how much your coat and hat are like my own; and I had to grin."

She laughed a little laugh that was pleasant to hear.

"Yes?" I succeeded in saying, trying to show interest.

"And I declare!"—exclamatorily.

"What?" I inquired.

"Why, our suit-cases are just alike."

She clapped her gloved hands gleefully.

"So they are," I admitted apathetically. I wished she would move away and leave me to my gloomy self and gloomier thoughts.

She was about my size; but didn't look at all like me. Her eyes were blue; her hair auburn and fluffy; her nose roguishly tip-tilted and blessed with a few freckles.

"Which way 're you traveling?" she said.

"By rail," I replied coldly.

"Good!" she giggled. "But where are you going?"

What impertinence! But, somehow, the frank smile accompanying the question robbed me of resentment.

"I'm going to Cincinnati," I answered.

"Going on the next train—the Big Four?" she persisted.

"Yes."

"So am I—as far as Dayton. It's a good thing for me the train's late; I—I—well, it just happens to suit me."

Then she sat silent, restlessly plucking at the buttons of her coat. I quietly observed her. Apparently she was absorbed in thought; but I soon learned that she was alert, watchful—aware of all that was going on about her. What was the meaning of her strange actions? Who was she? I was interested; and I lost myself and my troubles in hazy speculation.

Suddenly I saw her give a little start and shoot a swift, sly glance toward the news-stand in a far corner. I leveled my gaze toward that quarter; but noted nothing of an interesting or exciting nature, except—except—yes, a man was leaning against the angle of the wall and furtively observing us. Observing us—her—me? Who was he watching? I couldn't tell; but I wished I could. He was a little wizzened man, very dark; and he was enveloped in a long shaggy overcoat and wore a nappy cap pulled low over his eyes.

Again I turned my attention to my companion. She grinned at me—a pert and reckless little grin.

"See him?" she whispered, barely moving her lips.

"See whom?" I breathed softly in reply.

"That man over by the news-stand."

"Yes. Why?"

"Darn him!"

"What!"—pretending to be shocked.

"Yes, darn him!"—her eyes dancing.—"He's watching me."

"Ah?"

"Yes, he is."

I didn't know what else to say, Nell ; so I said nothing. My companion was silent a moment; then she whispered:

"What time is it, please?"

"One-twenty," I answered, glancing at the clock upon the wall. I didn't offer to consult my watch; and my companion noted the fact, smiled a contemptuous smile—and tittered:

"Oh, you needn't be afraid! I'm not trying to swipe your watch. I'm not that kind—any more than you are."—Then, abruptly:—"Say!"

"What?"—coldly, calmly.

"Will you do something for me?"

"I don't know. What do you want me to do?"

"I want you to throw that man off the track."

"Off the track?"

"Yes; off my track."

"Off your track?"

"Yes. He's followed me down here; and he's spying on me. No!"—smilingly shaking her head, —"I can't tell you why he's doing it; that's a secret. But I want to take that Big Four train, for

Dayton; and I don't want him to know it. Now, will you help me to throw him off my track?"

"I—don't—know,"—thoughtfully. "Is—Is—he—"

"Yes, he's a private detective."

"And?"

"No; I haven't committed any crime—yet, at any rate. You needn't be afraid; you won't get into any trouble. Will you help me?"

"How can I?"

"I'll tell you. That fellow doesn't know me; he's just spotted me by my clothes, I'm certain. And this very moment he's puzzling his head which one to watch—me or you. See? Now, I've got to throw him off the track—or not take the train. Here's my plan; not a very good one—but all the one I can think of. You take your suit-case and leave the place, as if you were going up street. Maybe he'll think you're the one he's been sent to watch—think you've given up going on the train, and will follow you. And, if he does, that will give me a chance to slip into the lunch-room and hide till the gates are thrown open. Then maybe I can slip out with the crowd, without him seeing me. Catch on?"

"Yes. But what shall I—"

"You'll just turn the corner, as soon as you get outside, and come back in here. If he follows you, he'll see you do it; and he'll know at once, of course, that you're not the one he's after—know we've tried to trick him, and he'll drop you and begin to look for me. If you're going to do it, though, be off; for we've only got a few minutes."

I hesitated a fraction of a second; then caught up my suit-case and made for the exit toward the street, looking neither to the right nor the left. Don't ask me why I did it, Nell Adams! Did you ever know me to be able to give a reason for my erratic decisions and actions? I decided on the impulse of the moment—that's all; why, I don't know.

As soon as I was through the doors, I turned the corner to the right and sauntered leisurely along to the side entrances. There I stopped a moment and looked down upon the tracks—and glanced over my shoulder to see if the man in the shaggy overcoat had followed me. But he was not in sight. So I pushed open a door and re-entered the waiting-room.

One comprehensive look showed me that our ruse had failed—signally, utterly. The detective still stood leaning against the angle of the wall—grinning a nasty, sarcastic grin; and my companion still sat where I had left her—in a dejected, huddled heap.

"It didn't work," I whispered as I dropped upon the bench at her side.

"No," she murmured, slowly shaking her head; "and I've got to give up going—on this train, anyhow. I thank you, just the same."—Then, perkily:—"Darn that man!"

Nell, bad as I felt—for her and for myself—I had to laugh! She caught the infection, and began to giggle; and we both buried our faces in our handkerchiefs and teeheed outright.

"I might as well be off," she said, wiping her eyes; "that detective means to stick to me—like lint to a wool skirt. There's your train coming now, I guess; and I wish it were mine. But better luck next time. Well, goodbye—and good luck to you."

"Goodbye," I responded, giving her my hand.

She seized her suit-case, gave me a parting smile and left me—going toward the street exit; and the detective grinned and shuffled after her—keeping a few yards behind her.

My train rolled in; and the crier called it. I ran the gauntlet of gatekeepers and guards, tripped down the steps, and scrambled aboard and secured a comfortable seat. Away we went, running like mad—making up lost time. The scenery flitting past my window was not inviting; so I cuddled down, with my head upon my arm and my arm upon the sill, and quickly fell asleep.

"Dayton!"

It was the brakeman bawling; and I awoke with a start—and sat up with a jerk.

"Dayton!" the smut-faced fellow repeated.

I rearranged my hair and readjusted my skirts, and yawned—really gaped a prolonged and spasmodic gape, Nell!—and looked through the window at the panorama of shabby houses and vacant lots and gaudy bill-boards. Why is it, I'd like to know, that every railroad enters every city on said railroad's line, through said city's most uninviting and disreputable suburbs? Echo wails—"why," Nell Adams!

We rolled into the attractive little union depot. Abstractedly I sat gazing out at rumbling trucks and tumbling trunks, and people hurrying this way and that—apparently without order or purpose; and my thoughts were far, faraway—and sad enough. Then, of a sudden, my attention was attracted and held by a man peeping through the iron fence separating the depot enclosure from the tracks. He was looking straight at me. Our eyes met; and immediately he beckoned me. At least I thought he was beckoning me; he was beckoning somebody, sure—and he was looking right at me. The impudent scoundrel! I wouldn't pay any more attention to him; and I turned away my face—and then peeked at him slyly, out of the comers of my eyes!

Well, of all things, Sweet Nell! As soon as he again caught my glance, he began to beckon me, impatiently, frantically, grimacing and vigorously nodding his head. What on earth ailed the fellow? Was he drunk or crazy—or both—or what? And did he mean me—or somebody else in the car? I turned to look. No, there was no one behind me. Then he must mean me. But what did the silly man want—what could he want?

Once more I granted him my attention; and once more he made a beckoning motion with his hand and grimaced and nodded—more frantically, more wildly, than ever. Then he pointed toward the gate, and then at me—and threatened to jerk his head off, he nodded so rapidly.

Unconsciously, almost, I touched my breast with the tip of my fore finger and slightly inclined my head; and the fellow went daffy with delight, apparently, and bobbed till his derby hat fell off. He was a big, pursy, red-faced man; and I fancied I could hear him grunt as he stooped to recover his headgear. Keeping an eye on me and motioning me to come, he moved toward the gate. It was plain enough what he desired. But what did it mean; and what should I do? Passengers were crowding into the car. I was in a stew, I tell you, Nell!

Then a thought, an idea, came to me—like a flash of white light in dense darkness. Ned had learned of my departure from Columbus, had ascertained what train I took, and had telegraphed or telephoned someone at Dayton to entice me off the car and hold me until his arrival. That was it—that was it, exactly! Well, it wouldn't work, I assured myself. I wasn't going back to Ned—dear Ned!—my Ned—then or ever; I was going on—on—on! But maybe Ned would do something desperate if he didn't get me back—if I didn't go back. The thought was complimentary but disquieting. Maybe—maybe he would commit suicide. That thought was flattering but startling. Oo-h! Maybe he had committed suicide—and Mr. Durbin had sent word to have me taken from the train. And that thought was idiotic but alarming, dreadful, maddening. In a moment I had convinced myself that that was just what had happened; and in another moment I had my suit-case in my hand and was making my way from the car. Call me silly, foolish, crazy—what you will, Nell; I was all that, and more—I admit it. But I couldn't help it. I had wearied and worried till I hadn't any sense left.

As I descended the steps of the car, the bell began to ring for the train to start. I saw the big pursy man at the gate, nervously rubbing his palms together and shuffling his feet.

"Miss Dawes?" he whispered inquiringly, bending toward me as I came up to him. At least that's what I thought he said.

I nodded; and he snatched my suit-case from my hand, caught me by the arm and unceremoniously hurried me toward the open space at the far end of the depot. I was shaking so I could hardly walk. My suspicions were confirmed—my surmises were correct, then; Ned or Mr. Durbin had sent word to have me stopped. But, oh!—had Ned done—done something awful?

"Did-did you hear from Columbus?" I ventured to ask my portly conductor.

"Sure!" he muttered, according me a wondering glance. Then he stopped suddenly, scowled fiercely and growled:

"It's all right to be cautious, young woman; but you came pretty near being too d—well, overly cautious. I thought I was going to have to appeal to the gate-keeper to let me through—to get you off the train. And that might have balled up things good and proper; for the other side's next—and on the watch. Why didn't you come as soon as I motioned to you?"

I didn't know why I hadn't come as soon as he beckoned me, Nell—as I didn't know why I had come at all; and, in addition—and far more important, I didn't know what in the world he meant by his hints in regard to caution, and all that. And I felt like telling him so, frankly; but something prompted me to keep mum on that particular point. So, instead of replying to his question, I queried cautiously:

"Was it Ned you heard from—or—or his father?"

"Huh!" he chuckled, shaking his head. " I don't know anything about Ned or his father—or his sisters and his cousins and his aunts. All I know is the boys just sent me down here in an auto, to get you, young woman."

"The boys!" I gasped, trying to draw away from him. "What boys—who—what do you mean?"

"Oh, come off!" he grinned. "You're fly, all right; but there's no need in trying to fool me. You know who sent after you. Here's the auto. Let me help you in."

"But—but—" I tried to object.

"In you go," he broke in upon me.

And with the words he whirled me around and gave me a boost that landed me plump in the rear seat, on the far side of the vehicle. Then, before I had recovered sufficiently from my surprise and shock, to say a word in protest, he had piled himself at my side—with my suit-case upon his knees.

"All ready," he said to the chauffeur, giving that individual a curt nod.

"Where are we going?" I cried.

"Shut up!" my companion growled. "Don't attract attention to us; keep still. And what's the use of keeping up the game? You know what's what—and where you're going."

I just gave up, Nell mine, and sank back in dumb and stoical despair. I didn't care what it all meant; I didn't care what became of me! I was too far exhausted, nervously and mentally, I guess, to realize anything fully—to do anything but dully wonder.

Up the broad and beautiful business thoroughfare we sped, and far out into the residence section. At last we stopped in front of a big house set well back in a grove of trees. Its walls and chimneys were of dark-red brick. An iron fence with an arched gateway surrounded the grounds; and a broad flag walk and well-worn stone steps led up to the front door of the venerable pile. I gave an involuntary shiver, Nell; the building looked like a private hospital for dope fiends or an asylum for insane folks!

"Here we are," my companion muttered, speaking for the first time since leaving the depot.

He rolled over and dropped to the ground. Then he grabbed me,—literally grabbed me!—and snatched me out of the vehicle,—as if I were a bit of baggage!—and set me down with a thump.

"Now, get away from here," he called to the chauffeur; "and mind you forget all about this. Understand?"

A pair of black goggles turned in the direction of the speaker and a leather cap bobbed; that was all. Then the auto rolled away.

Again my conductor caught up my suitcase and caught me—helpless me, Nell!—by the arm.

"What—where—where are you taking me?" I cried, dimly divining that something was desperately wrong.

"Oh, the devil!" he grunted roughly. "What is the use of pretending? Come on!"

He hurried me along. Apathetically I submitted; and soon we stood in the upper hall of the building, and my conductor was rapping upon a closed door.

"Who's there?" demanded a coarse voice within.

"Me—Murphy," answered my guide.

A key turned in the lock; and the door swung partly open. I caught a glimpse of a lamp-lighted room with its blinds close drawn, and of a hairy face peeping out at us. Then the door swung wide; and my conductor pushed me across the threshold. Dimly I saw a number of men sitting before me; dumbly I heard the door shutting behind me!

Chapter 15

YES, there I was,—little lone, lorn Marjory Dawes!—facing a roomful of strange men. I blinked and winked, and rubbed my eyes. The air was hazy with tobacco smoke and redolent[1] with liquor. The men sat staring at me, sprawling in various attitudes and placidly smoking; and not one of them spoke, not one of them offered me a chair, even. And I was ready to drop in my tracks!

What awful blunder had I committed; what awful situation had I got myself into? Was I dreaming or daffy? Why had the man called Murphy enticed me from the train; and why had I yielded to him? And why—why—why!

My heart throbbed—and threatened to stop; my head thumped—and threatened to burst. Oh, dear—dear—dear! I wanted to scream; and couldn't make a sound! I wanted to turn and fly from the place; and couldn't move a foot! I was dumb, numb—palsied, petrified!

Murphy pushed past me, flung my suitcase upon the floor and panted pompously:

"Here she is, fellows; and here's the stuff."

The other men just nodded and grunted ungraciously; that was all the response they made.

Then a side door opened, and a tall, stoop-shouldered, hatchet-faced young man entered briskly, a roll of papers in his hand. Catching sight of me, he stopped with a jerk. Then he swept the assembly with his eyes, and cried angrily:

"What ails you unmannerly devils? Can't you see there's a lady present? Throw away those cursed cigars, and open the door and let

---

1 Redolent - strongly reminicent or suggestive of

the smoke out. Bosworth, give her a chair. You're a bunch of sweet-scented posies—you are!"

The men silently, sullenly obeyed his orders. I dropped wearily into the chair offered me. The young man went behind a roll-top desk in the corner, and there busied himself for a few moments. Then he came around in front of me and said:

"Well, I see you got here."

I looked up at him. He was smiling a complacent, self-satisfied smile that exasperated me, maddened me.

"Got here!" I snapped. "I was brought here."

"Brought here?" he grinned, intertwining his slim beringed fingers and teetering back and forth upon heels and toes. "Of course; Murphy brought you from the depot. But you got that far yourself, didn't you, Miss Graw?"

Miss Graw! I fairly jumped, Nell Adams! And the young man looked at me in stupid amazement. Miss Graw! A shaft of light punctured my thick skull, entered my dull, dark brain; and in a fraction of a moment everything was bright and clear as noonday—everything was plain and simple as a-b-c. Miss Graw! That was what the pursy and persistent Murphy had called me at the depot, then; and not Miss Dawes, as I had thought. And the Miss Graw they were expecting—and the Miss Graw they thought me—was the young woman I had met in the depot at Columbus. Oh, why hadn't I thought of that at once—when Murphy first beckoned me! How stupid I had been—how unpardonably, idiotically stupid! And what horrible fix had I got myself into? Oo-h! And how was I to extricate myself? Should I speak out, make them aware of our mutual mistake, our mutual blunder—Murphy's and. mine? Or should I keep still—trust to blind luck? Oh! what should I do? I didn't know—I couldn't even guess; for I hadn't the faintest idea of why they were expecting Miss Graw—of what was her mission. Nell Adams—Nell mine! Was ever another poor silly girl in such a predicament!

But I saw I must do something—say something; for it was plain the young man was puzzling over my prolonged silence, and the other men were looking at me, curiously.

"Yes, I—I got here, I—I suppose," I murmured, in a voice

barely audible.

"You didn't have any trouble, did you?" was the next question.

"N—o," I responded faintly, I—I guess not."

"Guess not," he laughed. "Don't you know?"

"I had a—a little trouble," I ventured.

"You did?"—excitedly.—"Where?"

All the other men sat up—and began to take notice.

"At Columbus," I answered.

"Indeed!" the young man exclaimed; and his elders all gravely listened.

"Yes," I nodded.

"What was it like—what happened?" my inquisitor demanded eagerly.

"A detective was watching me."

"A detective?"

"Yes; a man, at any rate."

"Ah!"—sharply.

And several other "ahs" and sundry other exclamations sounded throughout the room.

"Describe the fellow," the young man pursued.

"He was a little man with dark shriveled features," I said; "and he wore a loose shaggy overcoat and—"

"Gargle!" grunted Murphy. "Just his description exactly."

"That's who it was!" chimed in several others.

"Well, what did he do?" inquired the young man.

"He didn't do anything," I replied.

"No?"

"No; he just watched me."

"He didn't offer to arrest you—or anything like that?"

"No."

"Did he see you leave the depot—did he know what train you took?"

"I think not."

"Why didn't he—if he was watching you?"

"He wasn't watching me then."

"Oh! How was that?"

"He had left the depot."

"You don't say!"—evidently greatly surprised at my statement.—"Why, I can't understand why he should do that—when he had his eye on you. Did you throw him off the track some way?"

"No."

"Maybe he wasn't watching you, at all."

"Maybe he wasn't."

"Well, what made you think he was?"

"He was watching me or the girl with me."

"The girl with you? What do you mean?"

"There was a girl sitting beside me."

"Oh!"

"Yes."

"And you don't know whether the man, Gargle, was watching you or her—is that it?"

"I guess he must have been watching her."

"What!"

"Uh-huh."

"Why, you said a moment ago he was watching you."

"Did I?"—innocently, sweetly.

"Did you? To be sure you did. You seem to be sadly mixed up, some way. Let's see if we can't get this thing straightened out. It's important that we understand it—understand whether you were watched by Gargle; and, if so, whether he learned your destination. Now, what makes you think he was watching the other girl?"

"She said he was."

"She did?"

"Yes."

"What was he watching her for?"

"She didn't say."

"Who was she?"

"I didn't know her."

"And she didn't tell you her name?"

"No."

"Was she waiting for a train?"

"Yes."

"What train?"

"The one I came on."

"And did she come on it?"

"No."

"No?"

"No; she said she couldn't come on it—because the man was watching her."

"Huh!" snorted the man called Bosworth, evidently perplexed and concerned; and "huh!" seconded several of the others.

"Shut up, you fellows!" the young man cried crossly. Then, to me: "What became of that girl—that young woman?"

"She left the depot."

"Then what did Gargle—the man—do?"

"He followed her."

"Well, don't that beat the devil!" ejaculated Murphy; and several of his cronies expressed their opinion that it did.

"Say!" cried the young man, exasperated. "Can't you fellows keep still?"

He nervously patted his foot and was thoughtful, for a few seconds; then he looked at me,—quickly, sharply,—and said:

"Did that young woman look anything like you, Miss Graw?"

"No, she didn't," I replied.

Nell, you'll wonder what I hoped to accomplish by my deception and circumlocution. I don't know; I've never been able to find out. I guess I was just sparring for an opening—as our sporting friends say. I guess I didn't want those men to know what a little fool I had been, to get off the train and come there; guess I just wanted them to go on thinking me Miss Graw. Then, I scented mystery; and, I suppose, my insatiate curiosity—the bane of our sex, you know!—impelled me to attempt to stick my nose into it.

The hatchet-faced young man persisted:

"Well, was she dressed like you?"

"Yes," I admitted; "she wore a coat and hat very much like mine."

"Huh!" grunted the man called Bosworth; and "huh!" grunted two or three of the others.

Murphy cried: "Boys, Gargle spotted the wrong girl!"

"That's what he did!" chorused several of the others.

Then they all burst out laughing; and laughed—and continued to laugh, boisterously, uproariously. And the young man joined them; and I sat and smiled at the applause I was receiving—and studied what I should give them for an encore.

"Say!" my inquisitor grinned gleefully. "You're all right, Miss Graw—you are! Orlanger couldn't have picked a better girl for the job."—I wondered who in the mischief Orlanger could be!—"You just sat still and let Gargle tag off after the wrong party. That was good—good! But,"—his face clouding and puckering,—"I wonder who the other girl could be, hey? And why was she expecting to be watched—and afraid to take the train? Well, it doesn't make any difference to us; you're here—and Gargle didn't hound you. You brought the—the stuff with you, of course?"

"I brought some stuff," I replied.

"Some? Didn't you bring it all?"

All the men were very alert and, apparently, very much concerned. I hardly knew what to say.

"Didn't you?" the young man persisted.

"Why, y-e-s, I—I suppose I did," I answered.

Breezy sighs of relief and satisfaction sounded throughout the room.

"Well, what makes you act so queer about the thing, Miss Graw?" the young man pursued.

"Nothing," I explained; "I guess I'm just tired—and hungry."

"That's so, no doubt," he nodded. "You haven't had any supper, of course."

"Nor have we," interjected Bosworth, with a short laugh.

"Nor I haven't had any lunch—any dinner," I volunteered.

"Heavens!" ejaculated another of the group, feelingly rubbing his stomach.

"Say, Harris!" Murphy cried. "Call Rotterden out. Let's get this thing over with; the young lady wants something to eat—and I'm hungry as a famine myself."

"Yes, call the old man out, Harris," seconded a number of the others.

"All right," assented the young man, Harris; and he strode to the side door, threw it open and called: "Rotterden, the young woman's got here—with the stuff. Can't you drop that work and come out?"

"The young woman?" rumbled a rough voice from within. "Oh! Miss Graw, eh? Good! I'll be through with this in a little while."

"But she hasn't had anything to eat since morning," Harris suggested,—rather timidly, I fancied,—"and she wants to deliver the stuff and get away."

"All right,"—a surly growl, —"I'll be out in a minute, then."

Sweet Nell Adams—dear Nell Adams, right then I knew my exposure was imminent—was coming. How or why I knew it I hadn't the faintest idea—and haven't now; but I knew it. And I trembled—and wished I was anywhere but where I was; and I condemned myself for a consummate little dunce—for concealing my identity as I had done, for coming there at all. And I was ashamed of myself—and my cheeks burned; and I was angry at everybody else—and my bosom heaved. Oh, Nell—Nell! I was in a fix; and I knew it!

The side door swung wide, and a little man in shiny black bustled into the room. His head was bald as a toy balloon; his features were almost concealed by a bristly, frizzly black beard. He came up within a few feet of me; and, peering through the thick-lensed glasses astride his aquiline[2] nose, he gave an ungracious grunt of greeting. Then he sprang back a step or two and cried:

"Why—why, who's this?"

"It's Miss Graw," Harris replied wonderingly.

The little man let out a savage growl and fairly jumped up and down—glaring, mouthing and gesticulating[3], in mad rage; and his associates looked on in awed silence and growing alarm.

"What's the matter?" Harris ventured timidly. "What's the matter, Rotterden?"

"Matter!" stormed the little man.—"Matter! Who brought that girl here?"—dramatically pointing a finger at me.

---

2 Aquiline - like an eagle
3 Gesticulating - use gestures instead of speaking

"I did," Murphy volunteered.

"You did!" Rotterden snarled. "You did! Well, what did you do it for? Trying to butt into trouble—and lead us all in with you? That,"—indicating me, with withering contempt and infinite disgust, —"isn't Miss Graw!"

Instantly all of them were upon their feet—all talking and gesticulating at once.

"Well, who the devil is she, then?" shouted one man.

"That's it!" voiced several others. "Who is she, then?"

"Ask Murphy!" yelled Bosworth.

"Ask her!" bawled another man.

"Aw, throw her out!" came a voice from behind me.

"That's the stuff!" answered another voice. "Put her out!"

Nell Adams, how would you have liked it—to be in my shoes at that moment? And to think I had brought it all upon myself—by my own silliness!

Harris—the stoop-shouldered, the hatchet-faced, the weak-looking!—was the only one who remained self-possessed.

"Here!" he commanded authoritatively. "Sit down—and be still, you fools! Sit down, I say! Do you want the police in here? If you don't, stop your noise—keep still. That's better. Now, listen. We've got to untangle this thing. Shut and lock that door. Now, listen—listen! You can't all talk at once. Let Rotterden or me do the talking."

"You do it—go on," the little man panted, weakly sinking into a chair.

Harris faced me and demanded sharply, sternly—while the others almost held their breaths:

"Now! miss, what are you doing here?"

"I don't know," I replied meekly enough.

The young man keenly searched my face; I guess he thought me crazy, Nell—and he had reason on his side. Then he whirled round to Rotterden and said:

"You know to a certainty she isn't Miss Graw, do you?"

"Of course I do," the little man muttered.

"I saw Miss Graw in Orlanger's office, just last week."

"Well, do you know this girl?"

"No, I don't: but I'll bet she's been sent here by the other side. Murphy's a fool; he's made a mess of things."

"I couldn't help it," Murphy began in his own defense, "I—"

"Shut up!" the young man cut him off. And again he turned to me, and said: "Now, miss,"—coldly, determinedly, "you've got to answer my questions; and you'd better answer them straight. Understand?"

I nodded.

"Well, what are you doing here, then?"

"I tell you I don't know," I replied truthfully.

"What did you come here for? Put it that way."

"I didn't come here; that man there,"—indicating Murphy,— "brought me here."

"From the train?"

"Yes—of course."

"Well, where did you come from—what place?"

"Columbus."

"What's your name?"

"Dawes—Marjory Dawes."

Murphy uttered a sharp "huh!" and grinned a sickly grin.

"Why did you come to Dayton?" Harris pursued.

"I didn't come to Dayton," I tried to explain; "I was on my way to Cincinnati."

"What did you get off here for, then?"

"Because that man,"—again indicating the collapsed Murphy,— "beckoned me to get off."

"Oh!"—incredulously, sneeringly.

"Yes, sir."

"That sounds pretty thin to me."

"I don't care if it does,"—angrily.

"You don't?"

"No, I don't."

"Did you think you knew him?"

"No; but I thought he knew me."

" Indeed!"—nastily.

"Yes, I did,"—stiffly.

"Are you in the habit of getting off trains to meet every man you think knows you—every man that nods and smiles at you, hey?"

Oh, he said it so insultingly, Nell Adams! And tears of mortification came to my eyes.

"Here, Harris!" Murphy cried hotly. "None of that—curse you!—or you'll have me to reckon with. Let me do a little talking. I believe this girl's all right; just let her explain. I know this: I had a devil of a time getting her off the train; I motioned and motioned till I got tired—till I thought I'd have to board the train and drag her off. Let me ask her a few questions."

Then, to me: "Miss—Miss Dawes, when I called you Miss Graw what did you think?"

"I thought you called me Miss Dawes," I answered frankly and honestly.

He nodded and smiled encouragingly; then he went on:

"And what did you think I wanted of you—when I motioned to you to get off the train? Tell us all about it."

"I was running away from—from a—a party in Columbus," I stammered, "and I thought maybe they—he—or his father—had telephoned or telegraphed some word to me; and I got off the train to learn what it was."

"Just so," Murphy said, beaming upon me. Then, to his associates: "Boys, I think she's all right—think she's telling the truth; for she mentioned something of the kind—something about word from somebody I didn't know anything about—as we got into the auto. I think she's telling the truth—think she's all straight, boys."

"She may be," Harris said placidly, "but I don't think so. I'll ask her a few more questions, anyhow. Miss Dawes, you call yourself!—why did you pretend to be Miss Graw?"

"I didn't," I denied; "you just called me that."

"Well, why didn't you let us know our mistake—at once?"

"I—I didn't want you to know who I was, I—I—"

"Of course you didn't!"—triumphantly. "But why?"

"I didn't know—know what you were expecting of Miss Graw, and—and I wanted to find out, I—I guess."

All the men looked very sober; and Murphy gave a little groan.

What had I done? I couldn't understand the cause of their sudden gravity.

"That's just what I thought," Harris said icily; "you wanted to learn all about Miss Graw's mission to us. Now, who sent you here?"

"Nobody," I replied.

"Take care. You'd better tell me the truth."

"I am," I insisted. "Please let me go now; I want to get some supper—and go on to Cincinnati."

"You can't go yet," he muttered stubbornly; "and you can't go at all till this thing's straightened out satisfactorily. What—"

But just then the telephone bell rang in the adjoining room. Harris left me and went to answer it, closing the door behind him. In a minute or two he returned and remarked:

"That was Orlanger, boys. He says Miss Graw was shadowed at the Union depot, by Gargle, and that she can't get here till later—to-morrow, maybe."

Then, to me, abruptly: "How did you know she was shadowed?"

"I saw the man watching her," I murmured, sighing wearily, "just as I told you."

"Yes; and then you thought you'd come on here and pretend to be Miss Graw, and find out all about her business with us. Now, didn't you?"

"No, I didn't,"—peevishly.

"No?"—tauntingly.

"No."

"And nobody told you to come here?"

"No."

"Nor suggested such a thing to you?" The persistent pest!

"No."

"You just came here by chance?"

"I tell you I didn't come here,"—irritably.

"Well, you just got here by chance, then?"

"Yes, I suppose that's it. And now I want to get away."

"We're not quite through with you yet. How did you know Miss Graw was coming here?"

"I didn't know it."

"Oh!"

"No, sir, I didn't."

"You know now we were expecting her—and that Murphy took you for her, don't you?"

"Yes, of course."

"Do you know what business she—what she was coming here for?"

"I do not."

"Don't know a thing about it?"

"Not a thing. And I tell you I want to get away from here; I'm hungry—nearly famished."

"Well, I guess that's all the questions I have to ask you."

I got upon my feet, preparatory to taking my departure.

"Wait a moment," said Rotterden, the little frizzly man; "sit down. I want to ask you a question or two."

I dropped back into my chair, catching my breath; I was about ready to cry.

"Where are you going from here?" he inquired.

"To Cincinnati, I told you," I replied crossly.

"You say you're running away from Columbus?"

"Y-e-s."

Now what was coming?

"Who are you running away from?"

"My—my employer."

"What for?"—sharply; suspiciously, impudently.

"None of your business!" I retorted. I was out of patience, old chum.

Several of the men grinned; and one or two chuckled audibly. The bristly little man's bald head flushed clear to the back of his neck.

"Don't get gay, young woman!" he snarled. " You're not out of the woods yet."

Nell, I flew mad as a wet hen—all in a second.

"You're a despisable little beast!" I screamed. "Shame on you—to try to bully a defenceless girl! Oh, I just wish Ned were here! He'd settle with you—with all of you!"

"That's the stuff!" Murphy muttered sotto voce. "Give it to him; I'll back you!"

"Who's Ned, Miss Dawes?" inquired Harris, grinning his nastiest.

"He's Ned—that's who!" I screeched, in reckless and utter abandon. " My Ned! Mr. Edward Durbin of Columbus, my employer; and I'll—"

Nell, I never finished that sentence. At the mention of my employer's full name, every man again excitedly sprang to his feet; and pandemonium broke loose. I sank back in my chair—amazed, dismayed, overwhelmed. What was the matter? What had I done— oh! what had I done? All I could see was a lot of waving arms, stamping feet, bobbing heads, rolling eyes and working mouths; and all I could hear was a rumble and grumble and jumble—something like this:

"It's a shame!—Bah!—she's a spy!—She's an innocent little fool!—Ned Durbin!—Leatherlips club!—Her employer!—Sent her! Didn't!—Did!—You're a fool!—So're you!—Let 'er go!—Won't!—Ruin everything!—Lock 'er up!—Never!— Police!—Hell!—Lose election!—Nonsense!—Us boys!—Get us in trouble!—Yeah!—You're a liar!—You're another!"

Nell, I couldn't make anything of it. Do you wonder? It was worse than a South American revolution!

Finally Harris, by frantically waving them to silence and commanding and beseeching them to come to their senses, succeeded in restoring a semblance of quiet—though the rumblings and grumblings and mutterings and sputterings went on. Then he came up to me, took me roughly by the arm and said:

"Here. I'm going to lock you up in the adjoining room, till we get this thing settled."

"Well, you're not!" I cried, jerking away from him.

"I'll be cussed if you lock her up!" Murphy shouted, cracking his fists.

"That's the stuff!" abetted Bosworth. "I'll stand by you, Murphy!"

"And I'll stand by you, Harris!" yelled another man. "Lock 'er up!"

The hullabaloo promised to break loose again; but Harris quickly explained:

"Listen, you hot-headed fools! Listen! I'm not going to harm her—"

"You better bet you're not!" Murphy interjected.

"Shut up!" bawled two or three.

Harris continued: "I'm just going to shut her up in the other room, while we talk this thing over. She mustn't hear what we have to say; she's heard too much already, and—"

"That's what she has!" snarled Rotterden.

Harris concluded: "And she mustn't hear any more. Do you fellows want to queer the whole game? Say! If you don't, let me have my way; and keep still. When we've talked the thing over, I'll stand by whatever's agreed upon—so will Rotterden. Now, be reasonable. We're in a devil of a box; and we've got to get out of it, some way."

Then, to me: "This way, Miss Dawes—for only a few minutes."

"And then will you let me go?" I questioned shrewdly.

"You bet he will, Miss!" Murphy answered me.

I nodded my willingness to be made a prisoner; and Harris hastily bundled me and my suit-case into the adjoining apartment. Then he banged and locked the door; and there I was, Sweet Nell of old Oberlin, poor little, pretty little Marjory Dawes of Chesterville!—in durance abominable, a victim of my own silliness! Did you ever—ever—oh, Nell, there's no use in saying another word!

Chapter 16

I DROPPED limply into a chair, Nell, and covered my face with my hands. Oh, how miserable I was—how abjectly and utterly miserable and lonesome and homesick! I wanted Ned—my Ned; I wished for Jack—dear old Jack! I longed for Aunt Dodo, you—Sweet Nell!—Mr. Durbin, Colonel Wells—anybody and everybody I had ever known and loved! And the tears would and did come; and I had a good big cry! Then I felt much better; and I wiped my eyes and began to look around me—and listen to the confused buzz and murmur of voices in the room I had just left.

My place of detention was about the size of the apartment adjoining; and, like its fellow, had a door opening into the hall. It contained a long table, a small safe, a bookcase and a number of chairs. The floor was carpeted; and there was a telephone upon the wall.

I wondered what chance of escape there was; and I arose and began a tour of inspection. The door opening into the hall was locked, and the key was gone. No hope in that direction, I decided. Next I went to the two windows. Both looked out upon a black abyss—no convenient portico or other aid beneath them. I gave up and returned to my chair—helpless, hopeless. Then my gaze rested upon the telephone; and I gave a start—and a little shiver of joy. Ooh! I felt prickly and queer all over, then hot, then cold again—all in a few seconds. Why not call for help—why not? The hubbub in the other room was so great my jailers wouldn't hear me talking, I was sure. Yes, why not call for help! But whom—whom would I call? The police station? Oh, I didn't want to do that! And probably they were in with these political tricksters—or whatever they might be—

at any rate, I reasoned. No, it wouldn't do to call the police. Oo-h! Why not call Ned—my Ned!—up at Columbus? Of course it would take him quite a while to get to me,—I had no idea how long!—but what else could I do? Yes, I'd—yes, I would? I'd make the attempt, anyhow!

I went over to the phone and took down the receiver.

"Number?" central said promptly.

"I want Edward Durbin, Chittenden Hotel, Columbus," I replied tremulously. "Yes, Durbin; D-u-r-b-i-n. Yes, Edward. Whom for? Oh! who for. Mr. Rotterden,"—with quick inspiration.—"Yes, Mr. Rotterden. And hurry, please; it's very important. No, I'll hold the phone. No matter; I don't mind the wait. All right."

I meant to prevent the ringing of the bell if possible; so I stood leaning against the wall, the receiver to my ear. I was quivering from head to foot—with hunger, weakness and excitement. The uproar in the other room was increasing. Their voices sounded more and more animated, more and more excited; hoarse tones contended with shrill tones, and oaths with exclamations. I could hear the shuffle and stamp of feet, the bump and bang of moving furniture. Oh, what was going to happen—how was it all going to end! And why didn't I get Ned—why didn't I! Oh, dear—dear!

"Hello!" said a voice in my ear.

"Hello!" I murmured in reply.

"Here's Columbus; here's Mr. Durbin. Hello, Mr. Durbin!"

"Hello!" came a voice that I recognized as Ned's—dear Ned's! And I danced up and down, in joy!

"Hel—hello!" I answered. "Hello, Ned!"

"Well, who is it?" he demanded gruffly.

"Why—why, don't you know?" I replied. "It's—It's me!"

"Me?"—crossly.—"Well, who's me!"

"It's Marjory!"—ever so faintly.

"What!"—excitedly, almost incredulously.

"Yes, it is, Ned."

"Is that so? Where the mischief are you?"

"Out here—or down here—at Dayton."

"What!"

"Yes, I am."

"What in the nation are you doing down there?"

"I—I ran off from you, you know."

"Yes, I know—I think I do; and I've been hunting you all the afternoon."

"You have?"—in a tone of keen gratification.

"Yes, I have! Don't let me know that you feel so good over the fact, please; it hasn't been any fun for me. Now, what are you doing down there?"

"I'm not doing anything. I'm—I'm a prisoner, N-e-d!"

"A what?"

"A prisoner."

"A—a—I can't understand you, I guess. What did you say?"

"I say I'm a prisoner. Understand?"

"No; spell it."

"P-r-i-s-o-n-e-r," I spelled slowly and distinctly.

"A prisoner?" he fairly yelled.

"Yes; I'm locked up."

"What in the name of common sense do you mean, Marjory Dawes?"

"Just what I say, Ned Durbin!"—peevishly.—"I'm a prisoner, I'm locked up in a room; and I want to get out. I haven't had anything to eat since morning, and—"

"Well, hold on a minute!" he bawled.

"What have you done to get locked up?"

"Why, nothing/" I replied snappishly. "What a silly boy you are, Ned!"

"What're you locked up for, then? Who's locked you up—the police?"

"Nonsense, Ned Durbin!"—in keen disgust.

"Who then?"

"I don't know," I tried to explain; "some political gang of some kind. They thought me somebody else—some other girl, and coaxed me off the train and brought me to this house; and then, when they found out their mistake, they locked me up in this room and—"

"I understand!" he broke in on me. " I understand!"—

excitedly.— "They thought you Miss Catherine Graw—on account of your clothes. Well, we've got Miss Graw shut up here; but nobody knows it but a few of us. Now, where are you? What's the number?"

"I don't know, Ned; but it's a big brick house away out in the suburbs, and—oh, Ned! Ned!"

"Yes! Yes!"

"The men are in the next room—right now—quarreling over what they'll do with me. Oh, come—come quick!"

"I'll get there as fast as steam or electricity can carry me," he answered heartily; "and I'll find you—never fear. Don't be worried; those men won't dare to harm you or offer you any indignities. Goodbye, now; I'll be with you in a few hours, at the most. Say!"

"Well?"

"You don't find it so nice running away from me, do you?"—The mean fellow! He was laughing!—"You find you still need me in your business, don't you? Ta-ta! So long!"

Just then, from the other room, came the alarming sounds of hoarse oaths, and smashing blows and crashing furniture. Evidently the wordy consultation had ended in a free-for-all melee.

"Ned!" I almost screamed in the receiver. "Ned!"

But he was gone! Oh, Nell—Nell Adams!

Weak and trembling, I dropped down into a chair. The sounds of struggle and conflict went on. Then I heard the bang of a door; and presently I heard someone fumbling at the lock of my own—the one leading to the hall. I sprang to my feet, in fear—not knowing what to expect. The door swung open; and there stood Murphy, panting and perspiring. His clothes were dusty and awry; his cheek was bruised and his nose was oozing blood. I could do nothing but silently gawk at him, Nell. The sounds of battle still continued.

"Come on!" the pursy fellow wheezed. "I got the keys—and locked—the cusses in. Let 'em—fight it out! I got—you into this—muddle, and I'll—get you out. Come on."

He stooped and caught up my suit-case, and lurched through the doorway into the hall; and I closely followed him. Down the stairs we hurried and out upon the street. My deliverer waddled in advance of me, puffing laboriously. Under an arc lamp at the nearest corner he stopped and said:

"Here's the car line; you can take a car here that will carry you right to the depot."

"Oh, thank you ever so much!" I murmured feelingly.

"You don't owe me any thanks," he said, shaking his head; "but I want you to promise me something."

"What is it?" I asked.

"I want you to promise me that you'll leave town as soon as you can, for wherever you want to go; and that you won't mention your evening's experience to anybody. Does that go?"

"Y-e-s, I guess so," I answered thoughtfully; "I won't say anything to anybody here, anyhow."

"I don't want you to say anything about it to anybody anywhere," he said quickly.

"Oh!" I objected. "I'll have to tell Ned all about it."

A car was coming in the distance.

"That's your car," my companion muttered. Then, briskly: "Who do you mean by Ned? You don't mean Ned Durbin, do you?"

"Of course," I made answer.

"Oh, the devil!" he exclaimed roughly.

"You mustn't tell him—of all men."

"Why?" I inquired ingenuously.

"I can't tell you why. But you mustn't tell him; you'd get me— all of us into trouble. But you won't see him, will you? Didn't you say you were on your way to Cincinnati?"

"That's what I said—yes." The car was drawing near.

"Well?"—in evident concern.

"Well, I don't think I'll go there now. While you men were deciding my fate, I phoned Ned; and he's coming down from Columbus, after me."

His jaw sagged slowly, and he stared at me—open-mouthed. I gave a little laugh and moved to the curb; and the car came to a stop.

"Give me my suit-case," I said.

"I've a notion not to do it," he growled wrathfully; "I've a notion to grab you and take you back. Confound you! I'm almost convinced that Durbin did send you down here."

But he walked out to the car with me and assisted me up the steps.

"Good night," I cried gaily, waving my hand.

"Good night," he muttered sullenly.

Then he turned and waddled away; and just then a man emerged from the shadow of a tree and ran to catch the car. I went inside and dropped into a seat; and the man stood upon the rear platform and peered through the glass in the closed door.

When we reached the depot, I got off and went at once to the lunch-room; I was nearly famished. Ten minutes later, feeling much refreshed—feeling that life was again worth living, Nell!—I sauntered into the waiting-room. Which way would Ned come, I wondered—by steam road or electric? Well, I had better wait at the depot till the next train came in from Columbus, anyhow, I decided. But how long would that be? I'd go and inquire. I started to carry out my resolve; but midway of the room I came face to face with the man who had come in from the suburbs with me.

"I want you," he said quietly, smiling inscrutably.

I was startled, mystified—for the moment, Nell, of course; but I was not at all alarmed—and but little concerned. My stomach was full of warm food and, consequently, my heart—or is it one's head?—was full of courage. Then, too, I was armed and fortified with the knowledge that Ned was coming to my rescue—no matter what might happen to me; and I replied stiffly, coldly:

"Sir!"

"I want you," he repeated coolly; "want you to go with me."

I looked straight up into his face without flinching from his direct gaze. He was a middle-aged man, smooth-faced, muscular, and not unattractive.

"I don't understand you," I said.

"Oh, I guess you do!" he smiled.

"You must be laboring under a mistake in identity," I suggested.

"Not at all," he grinned. "Come on with me."

"But I won't."

"Oh, yes you will!"

"Why should I?"

"To prevent a scene."

"To prevent a scene?"

"Yes. If you don't come with me, without resistance, I'll be compelled to call a policeman. That would be embarrassing, wouldn't it? Listen. You've been closeted with Rotterden and Harris and their gang; I tracked you out there—and I shadowed you back here. Now you must come with me."

"Where do you want me to go?"

"Up to Judge Montford's house."

"What for?"

"The judge and some of the boys want to interview you."

Some more "boys," Nell Adams! I didn't relish the thought of making their acquaintance!

"What do they want to interview me about?" I temporized.

"They'll tell you when you get there; I presume you can guess, though. Come on."

"But I want to know now," I insisted.

"I think you can guess," he chuckled. "However, I don't mind saying this: you're not going to be harmed in any way, nor prosecuted nor imprisoned—if you'll come along quietly and tell us all you know."

"Know?" I snapped irritably. "Know about what? I won't go a step till you tell me. There!"

He silently searched my face for several seconds—for signs of weakness, I suppose; then he said:

"They want you to tell them about what you brought down from Columbus, for Rotterden and his ring."

"That's easily answered," I smiled; "and I'll answer it right here—to you. Then I won't have to go with you. I didn't bring anything."

He shook his head impatiently.

"That doesn't go," he muttered. "Come on; I can't fool away any more time."—Then, with a shrewd grin: "I guess you're hoping for a chance to slip away from me; but you won't get it. Come on."

"I've got to, have I?"

"Sure."

"All right," I said, thrusting my suit-case toward him.

He appeared surprised; but whether at my readiness to accompany him or at my assurance in forcing my baggage upon him, I couldn't tell.

"I needn't keep a restraining hand upon you, need I?" he questioned.

"No," I replied curtly, sharply.

"All right."

Side by side we walked out of the depot.

"Here's our car right this minute," he remarked in a tone of keen gratification.

We climbed aboard; and rolled away toward another residence section of the city. Nell, I was rather enjoying myself and my kaleidoscopic experiences. Little Marjory Dawes was becoming such an important personage! I tried to strike up a conversation with my new conductor—hoped for a mild flirtation, almost!—but he was as glum as the portly and pursy Mr. Murphy had been.

Our ride was a short one; and a few moments after alighting from the car, I found myself in the well-lighted parlor of a fine residence—and again surrounded by a crowd of men. But these men, without exception, apparently, were well-dressed and polished gentlemen. At any rate, they were well dressed; and they arose to a man, on my entrance, and remained standing till I was seated.

Then a big-boned, elderly man—with square and heavy jaws, and stubby iron-gray mustache, and wiry iron-gray hair combed pompadour, and wearing an iron-gray suit!—wheeled his chair in front of me, leaned forward with his elbows upon his knees, and began slowly and soberly:

"My dear young woman, I desire to begin the little talk I hope to have with you, by begging your pardon for bringing you here— especially, for bringing you here at such an hour and in such a manner. But I think you'll readily understand that we had no choice in the matter. Now, I'll just preface the questions I mean to ask you, by saying you know some things that it's absolutely necessary that we learn; and if you'll kindly and sensibly tell us all you know— without equivocation or reservation—we'll soon be through with you and you can go on your way, rejoicing."

He paused, and smiled affably.

"Yes, sir," I murmured, also smiling. He was such a nice old fellow, Nell mine!

"That means that you'll answer my questions?" he queried.

"Yes, sir."

All the other men kept respectfully silent.

"Very well," my new inquisitor proceeded.

"Now your name is—is—",—consulting a slip of paper he held in his hand,—"is Catherine Graw, is it not?"

"No, sir," I twittered sweetly.

"What?"

I smilingly shook my head.

There was a stir among my auditors.

"Your—name—isn't—Catherine—Graw?" the nice old gentleman said slowly, huskily.

"It is not," I answered composedly.

"Why, Hobson,"—turning to the man who had brought me,—"what's the meaning of this?"

"I don't know, Judge Montford," the fellow admitted, evidently puzzled. "All I know is that she's the young woman that was closeted with Rotterden and Harris and their gang. I'm dead sure of that; I trailed her out there, and I saw Murphy put her aboard a car to send her back into the city, and I rode on the same car with her—and I got her at the depot and brought her here. That's all I know."

"And you say your name isn't Catherine Graw?" the judge inquired, again turning to me.

"I do," I replied.

"Your name isn't Graw, at all?" he pursued.

"Not at all."

"Didn't you come from Columbus this afternoon?"

"I did."

"And didn't a man by the name of Murphy meet you at the depot, by arrangement?"

"Not by arrangement—no, sir."

"But he met you?"

"Yes, sir."

"And you went in an auto with him, to meet a number of men, didn't you?"

"I didn't know whom I was going to meet."

"You didn't? Take care!"

"No, I didn't."

"But you went with him?"

"Yes, sir."

"And you met a number of men?"

"Yes, I did; but—"

"Wait a moment, please. What is your name?"

"Marjory Dawes."

"That's the truth?"

"Yes, the truth."

"Dawes, eh? Well, that sounds a good deal like Graw; our informant got the names mixed in some way, I presume. Now, Miss Dawes, what did you bring from Columbus with you and deliver to Rotterden, or Harris, or any other of the men you met at that big brick house where Murphy took you?"

"Nothing."

"Take care—take care, now,"—smiling and shaking his head, kindly but deprecatingly.

"Nothing," I repeated. Then, with sudden inspiration and resolve: "Judge Montford, let me tell you all I know—everything."

"I'll be only too pleased to listen," he smiled.

I detailed my tale of unusual misadventure, from its beginning in the depot at Columbus to its seeming ending in the depot at Dayton; and my auditors gave breathless attention. And when I had concluded my recital of wonderful misunderstandings and mishaps, they sat staring at one another in open-mouthed amazement and incredulity.

But I didn't say a word, Nell, about my phoning to Ned; nor did I mention his name. I don't know why I didn't; it was just an instance of over-precaution and foolish timidity, I guess. But this I do know—now: had I mentioned his name, as my employer, it would have saved me all further annoyance.

Judge Montford, apparently, was the first to recover from the astonishment my story occasioned.

"Well, gentlemen," he said placidly, "are we to give credence to Miss Dawes' statement—or what are we to do?"

Nobody responded for a few moments; each man silently and interrogatively looked at his neighbor. Then Hobson spoke up—timidly and half-apologetically:

"Judge, may I say a word?"

"Certainly," was the gracious permission.

"I think you've forgotten a part of what Gargle phoned us: that when he was in Orlanger's office he got a chance to scratch his name on the valise he thought Miss Graw, or Dawes, or whatever her name is,—would bring with her. I believe I'd examine that valise there; it might help us to settle the question."

"Not a bad suggestion, Hobson," the judge drawled musingly. "By the way, gentlemen, it's a little odd we haven't heard anything more from Gargle; you remember he was to phone us again as soon as Miss Graw,—as he called the party,—left Columbus. His silence, to my way of thinking, is rather confirmatory of Miss Dawes' story."—All the while he was closely examining the outside of my suit-case, turning it round and tipping it this way and that.—"Then another thing in proof of Miss Dawes' veracity is the fact—why—why—why!"

He paused—stopped speaking; and I held my breath, as did all the others.

"Why," the judge announced, with all the solemnity of an oracle of doom, "here's Gargle's name on this valise—right here on this corner, scratched with a pin, evidently. G-a-r-g-l-e. Well—well!"

And be leaned back and looked me full in the face, pityingly shaking his handsome head.

Sweet Nell of old Oberlin, I was utterly dumbfounded. I bent down and looked at that confusing, accusing and convicting name scratched upon one end of my suit-case—and, for the moment doubted my own identity; and wished Ned would come and change my name at once—that I might know myself!

"Well—well!" Judge Montford repeated, still deprecatingly

wagging his head.

And I knew he considered me an artistic but conscienceless liar. The red mantled my face; and I cried—nervously, shrilly:

"It isn't mine; this case isn't mine!"

"My dear girl," he replied soberly, feelingly, "I wouldn't say it—I wouldn't say a word more; you'll only make a bad matter worse, perhaps. I'm very sorry, but—"

"But it isn't mine, I tell you!" I interrupted indignantly. "It must belong to that girl I met in the depot at Columbus—Miss Graw, or whatever her name is; she must have taken my suit-case, when she left me in such a hurry, and left her own. At any rate, it isn't mine. That detective's name couldn't be on my suit-case—just couldn't! He never had a chance to put it there."

The judge earnestly searched my face. His associates were growing restless.

"Just a few moments more," he said to them, with a wave of his hand. "Let's be sure of our ground." Then, to me: "What would be in your suit-case, Miss—Miss Dawes?"

"Why, my clothes, of course," I answered promptly.

"Did you pack it full?"

"Yes certainly."

"Didn't leave room in it for anything else?"

"No, sir."

"Let's examine this case and see what it contains, then," he suggested.

"Very well," I consented readily. "But maybe it's locked."

" No doubt," he replied, smiling inscrutably. "But try your key upon it."

I did so, Nell—boldly, confidently, being dead sure my key wouldn't work the lock. Judge of my surprise when, after a slight catch or two, it turned easily and the case sprung open!

But I didn't have time to think of what it meant—that my key should open the locked baggage of a stranger. The two halves of the case fell apart and—there exposed to the gaze of the surprised lot of us were a number of packages of printed matter and a number of rolls of bank bills.

I gave a little screech—and sank back in my chair, my heart fluttering. The men got upon their feet and craned their necks to see, uttering grunts and exclamations.

"Why—why!" the judge ejaculated, accusingly eyeing me.

Instantly I roused myself. "Can't you see," I cried, "that that proves what I said—that the case isn't mine? Can't you see that it's Miss Graw's—and that those other men knew I wasn't Miss Graw, and thought the case mine, and didn't open it? Can't you see? Can't you see?"

"That's a fact," said one man; and two or three of his comrades nodded approval of the statement.

"That's so" muttered another; and "that's so" echoed several of his companions.

I felt easier.

"Well, we've got 'em dead to rights—and got their stuff," chuckled Hobson, rubbing his palms together and bobbing his head.

"Say!" cried the judge. "That's the truth, isn't it?"

Then they all laughed, and slapped one another upon the back and capered about the room; and chuckled and sputtered, and coughed and choked—and did it all over again, till their features were aquiver and their eyes were moist with tears.

"Can't I go now?" I suggested to the judge, when the hubbub had somewhat subsided.

"My dear girl," he said gravely, laying a hand upon my shoulder, "I'm afraid we'll have to hold you; I don't know—but we may need you."

"Need me?" I cried fretfully, my patience worn threadbare. "What for?"

"Never mind—never mind!" he murmured soothingly. "Maybe we won't need you at all; but you'll have to stay a little longer—till we talk the affair over."

"Oh dear!" I half whimpered. "I wish Ned would come and take me back to Columbus; I'm tired to death of this town."

"Ned?" the judge questioned.

"Yes, Ned," I replied petulantly; "Ned Durbin. If he was here—"

"Ned Durbin?" the judge interrupted. "Young Ned Durbin—the

real-estate man?"

"Of course," I yawned behind my hand; "he's my employer."

"Why, girl—Miss Dawes!" the dear old fellow laughed, pinching my arm. "Why didn't you tell us that long ago—that Ned Durbin's your employer? We'd have known at once you were all right; would have had no doubt of your story. Did you say he's coming after you?"

I answered in the affirmative; and told him about my running away from Ned and about my phoning him to come to my rescue. He laughed heartily; and the other men joined him. I felt very silly, Nell; but I felt very happy, too—for Judge Montford was saying:

"Well, Mr. Durbin can't get here till after midnight—the best he can do. You come with me, Miss Dawes. I'll turn you over to Mrs. Montford; she'll mother you and look after you. I can see you're completely fagged[1] out. Come with me."

And a half-hour later, Sweet Nell, I was tucked up in the whitest little bed in the neatest and sweetest little bedroom—and was fast asleep.

Early next morning Ned phoned me from the hotel where he was stopping. Judge Montford had met him at the train and told him where I was. After breakfast he came around to see me. I met him in the parlor; and he just stood and grinned at me, in silence—in unholy I-told-you-so amusement.

The mean impudent man!

"Ned Durbin," I said loftily, "if you don't stop that, you'll go back to Columbus alone. Now!"

And then he—he—well, you can guess what he did, Nell.

An hour later we were aboard our train and speeding toward the Capital city. Ned tried to talk to me; but I was silent and pre-occupied—thinking, thinking. Was I doing right, going back with him? Did I really desire to go back with him—considering what I had done? Would he—could he—ever forget the loss of his money? Would he—could he—truly forget the deplorable blunder I had made, and forgive me?

He roused me from my bitter reverie, by asking:

---

1 Fagged out - tired, exhausted, physically exhausted

"What are you thinking about, Marjory?"

"Nothing—much," I murmured.

"Yes, you are; and I can tell you what it is."

"What?"

"You're wondering why you ran away from me."

"Well, I'm not!" I cried indignantly. "I'm wondering why I'm going back with you—why I ever sent for you."

"Oh!" he laughed. "I can answer all such easy questions as that."—He was grinning like he was enjoying himself greatly!—"You sent for me because you found out you weren't able to take care of yourself; and you're going back with me for the same reason."

My face reddened with anger—I felt it; and the big rude fellow at my side just hawhawed[2].

"Indeed," I quavered, tears in my voice and eyes, "you're very kind, Ned Durbin."

And I turned my back upon him and sat blinking out the window.

"Now—now!" he said coaxingly, tenderly. "Marjory, look around here."

But I made no move to comply with his request.

"Marjory," he whispered.

I gave no heed.

"Marjory," he repeated.

"What?"—tearfully.

"Look around here."

"I—I can't."

"Yes, you can. Wipe your tears away; I want to talk to you. I've got something interesting to tell you."

I dried my eyes—with repeated little jabs of my handkerchief; then turned to him, silently, questioningly.

"I'm telling you the truth," he said soberly, earnestly. "You have found you can't do without me; and I've found I can't do without you."—I was comforted at once, Sweet Nell!—"Now, I want you to tell me why you ran away from me."

"Why, you know—Ned," I breathed softly, snuggling a little closer to him.

---

2 Haw haw - a deep especially loud boisterous laugh; guffaw

"No, I don't," he smiled.

"Surely you do."

"Surely I don't—sweetheart."

"Why, I ran away because—because I lost you all that money, of course."

"What money?"—grinning provokingly.

"What money! You know, Ned—dear."

"You didn't lose me any money, Marjory."

"Ned!"

"You didn't. Listen, sweetheart,"—joyfully.—"You didn't lose me any money; you made me money."

"Why—why—"

"Listen! When you said you had a headache, yesterday, and left the office, you hadn't been gone more than half an hour till a fellow came in and wanted to buy the Klein tract. He offered me fifty thousand dollars: but I knew at once he was the agent of the Transylvania people, and I just laughed at him. In the end I sold it to him for a clean hundred and fifty thousand. So you see, Marjie, you made me seventy-five thousand instead of losing me fifty thousand. You were right all the time; I was wrong. The word was sent out from the Transylvania—for effect; my friend I met at Newark was misinformed; the Journal was mistaken—as you insisted. And now—"

He stopped and beamed upon me—devouring me with his eyes, Nell.

"And now?" I whispered faintly—but encouragingly.

"Now," he resumed, "you must help me to spend it, Marjory."—Oo-h! Delight, Nell Adams! It had come at last!—"You must marry me, Marjie; and we'll take a flight abroad—and then come back and build us a nest. Eh?"

The big bold man! He slipped his arm around me—right there in the car.

"Don't!" I pleaded, blushing to the tip of my nose. "Please don't, Ned; somebody'll see you."

"Well, answer me, then," he laughed.

"Take away your arm—and I will."

"Answer me first."

"Answer you what?"

"Will you marry me?"

"Oh, Mr. Durbin, this is so sud—"

"Hush!"

"So sudden, I—"

"Marjory Dawes, answer me! Will you marry me?"

"Why, you said I must, didn't you?"

"Does that mean yes?"

"Y—e—s."

And then we talked and planned, and planned and talked, and enjoyed ourselves immensely—to the limit, Ned said.

But at last a thought intruded itself; and I inquired:

"Ned, what were those men down at Dayton—Rotterden and Harris and the rest—trying to do?"

He laughed: "They, with Orlanger of Columbus, were trying to buy and steal the election down there; trying to put in Rotterden as state senator. He has pledged himself to support some railroad schemes of Orlanger's; Orlanger's a lobbyist for the railroads. I don't suppose I can make you understand it all,"—he looked at me so fondly, Nell, I couldn't resent his implied lack of confidence in my keen discernment!—"and I don't know that it matters. I'll just say this: I'm president of the Leatherlips political club, and I got onto their game—and queered it. Now, let's talk about ourselves."

But what's the use of writing more, Nell mine? You've guessed the conventional and tiresome finale, "they married and were happy ever afterward," long ago. Yes, we married—Ned and I; married down at old Chesterville,—or should I say were married?—last Christmas. I forgave Jack and Aunt Dodo and Dorothy, of course; and blessed them and fate that Jack's marriage had made an exile of me. For had not said exile brought me Ned—my Ned?

It was at my own wedding that I again met Colonel Wells—my dear old Southron; and it was there he told me all about how he befooled the marshal at Conesville.

Ned and I went abroad immediately—to southern Europe and Egypt and the Holy Land, first, then back by the way of Berlin and

Paris and London. We were gone six months, and spent six thousand dollars; and brought back a whole shipload of foreign trumpery[3] to litter up our new home.

And now, Nell Adams, as soon as you've read this—no, don't stop to read it; it'll take too long!—pack your things at once and come to see me—out here on Bryden Road. Maybe I'll give you Daddy Durbin as a husband; he's awfully nice. Then—oh, I've got a secret to tell you; and I haven't got the courage to put it down in cold, unfeeling black-and-white!

MARJORY

---

3 Trumpery - tawdry finery

Writings of James Ball Naylor

Collected Verse

1893   *Current Coins Picked Up at a Country Railway Station*, S. Q. Lapius, Columbus, Ohio, Hann & Adair, Printers and Bookmakers.

1896   *Golden Rod and Thistle Down*, S. Q. Lapius, Columbus, Ohio., Hann & Adair, Printers and Bookmakers.

1906   *Old Home Week*, C. M. Clark Publishing Co., Boston, Mass.

1906-1907 *Old Home Week*, C. M. Clark Publishing Co., Boston, Mass. Governor Rollins Version, (double copyright).

1906-1907 *Old Home Week*, C. M. Clark Publishing Co., Boston, Mass. Mayor Fitzgerald Version, (double copyright).

1907   *Songs From the Heart of Things*, New Franklin Printing Company, Columbus, Ohio.

1927   *A Book of Buckeye Verse*, Tucker-Kenworthy Co. Press, Chicago, Ill.

1935   *Vagrant Verse, Morgan County Herald*, McConnelsville, Ohio.

1968   A *Second Book of Vagrant Verse*, Preface by Lucile Naylor, D. W. Garber. (One copy only).

2011   *Vintage Verse*, Edited and Annotated by Theresa Marie Flaherty, Turas Publishing, Corpus Christi, Texas.

Serialized Writings

1896-1897 "Beggars Awheel," *Ohio Farmer*, December 3, 1896 to January 21, 1897.

1897-1898 "In the Days of St. Clair," *Ohio State Journal*, December 5, 1897, to February 27, 1898.

1898-1899 "Under Mad Anthony's Banner," *Ohio State Journal*, November 27, 1898, to March 5, 1899.

1900-1901 "The Sign of the Prophet," *Ohio State Journal*, October 28, 1900, to February 10, 1901.

1904   "The Witch Crow and Barney Bylow," *National Magazine*, V. 21, No. 3, December, 1904 through V. 22, No. 1, April, 1905.

1905   "The Little Green Goblin of Goblinville," *National Magazine,* V. 22 and 23, September and October, 1905.

1906   "From Jim to Jack; Letters to an Old Time Schoolmate," *Ohio Magazine*, V. l, 1906.

1907-1908 "A Counterfeit Coin," *Ohio Magazine*, Columbus, Ohio, Vol. 3 and 4.

1926   "Physicians of Morgan County," *The Weekly Herald*, January 21, 1926 through March 4, 1926.

1927   "Rambling Reminiscences," *Morgan County Herald*, McConnelsville, Ohio, March 29, 1927.

1939   "Straight Sticks from the Brush of Old Morgan County," *Morgan County Herald*, McConnelsville, Ohio, June 15, 1939 through September 7, 1939.

Novels

1899   *Under Mad Anthony's Banner, Ohio State Journal,* Chauplin Press, Columbus, Ohio, 1899.

1901   *Ralph Marlowe*, Saalfield Publishing Co., Akron, Ohio.

1901   *The Sign of the Prophet*, Saalfield Publishing Co., Akron, Ohio.

1902   *In the Days of St. Clair*, Saalfield Publishing Co., Akron, Ohio.

1903   *Under Mad Anthony's Banner*, Saalfield Publishing Co., Akron, Ohio.

1904   *The Cabin in the Big Woods*, Saalfield Publishing Co., Akron, Ohio.

1905   The *Kentuckian*, C. M. Clark Publishing Co., Boston, Mass.

1907   *The Scalawags*, B. W. Dodge and Co., New York.

1908   The *Misadventures of Marjory*, C. M. Clark Publishing Co., Boston, Mass.

2011   *Ralph Marlowe*, reprinted with additional material, edited and annotated by Theresa Marie Flaherty, Turas Publishing, Corpus Christi, Texas.

Children's Books

1906   *Witch Crow and Barney Bylow*, Saalfield Publishing Co., Akron, Ohio.

1907   *The Little Green Goblin*, Saalfield Publishing Co., Akron, Ohio.

1909   *Dicky Delightful in Rainbow Land*, Saalfield Publishing Co., Akron, Ohio.

Pamphlets

1907   *From Jim to Jack*, Herald Printing Co., McConnelsville, Ohio.

1911   *Across the Miles*, Rustcraft, Kansas City, Mo.

1911   *UCT Booklet*, United Commercial Travelers, Zanesville, Ohio.

1911   *Angelina's Ardent Lovers*, Advertising Poem.

1912   *For You*, Rustcraft, Kansas City, Mo.

1912   *If You Were Here*, Rustcraft Co., Kansas City, Mo.

1912   *The Old Time Friend*, Rustcraft Co., Kansas City, Mo.

1921   *Old Morgan County*, Poem, Herald Printing Co., McConnelsville, Ohio.

1921   *The Muskingum Valley*, Malta, Ohio, June, 1919.

1927   *Rambling Reminiscences*, Herald Printing Co., McConnelsville, Ohio.

--   *Flinch*, Advertising Poem.

Short Stories

1897   "Ben's Adventure," S. Q. Lapius, Copyright 1897.

1903   "Ol' Cap Mingo," *National Magazine*, V. 17, No. 4, January, 1903.

1903   "How Tom Evans Won his Wife," *National Magazine*, V. 17, No. 5, February, 1903.

1903   "The Mishaps of Ol' Andy Perdue," *National Magazine*, V. 17, No. 6, March 1903.

1903   "A Lucky Opal," *National Magazine,* V. 18, No. 4, July, 1903.

1903   "Sim Spike's Misadventures," *National Magazine,* V. 19, October, 1903 (reference to)

1903   "The Youthful Indescretions of Jim Whiss," *National Magazine,* V. 19, October, 1903 Reference to *Ohio Star*, August, 1909.

1906   "The Undoing of Old John Chaney," *Ohio Magazine*, V. 4., 1906

--   "Coming of Sawlus," S. Q. Lapius.

--   "Did It Pay?," S. Q. Lapius.

--   "Jud Trainor's Ghost," *Ohio State Journal.*

--   "Mamie's Prisoner," *Ohio State Journal.*

--   "The Diversions of Dicky Dare."

--   "The Blackmer Affair," S. Q. Lapius.

--   "The Mills of the Gods," S. Q. Lapius.

--   "One of Morgan's Men," S. Q. Lapius

--   "Spike from the Underground Railway," S. Q. Lapius.

--   "Story of a Skeleton," S. Q. Lapius.

--   "Stuff of Which Doctors are Made," S. Q. Lapius.

--   "Two Consultations at Mam Sterlings," S. Q. Lapius.

--   "Wild Tom," S. Q. Lapius

2012   *A Literary Playground - Short Stories* by James Ball Naylor, edited and anotated by Theresa M. Flaherty, Turas Publishing, Corpus Christi, Texas.

Newspaper Columns

1913   *The Ohio Star*, Marion, Ohio.

1913   "Sunshine Corner," *The Marion Star*, Marion, Ohio.

1915-1923   "Life's Vaudeville," *The Marion Star*, Marion, Ohio.

1920-1923   *The Chicago Journal of Commerce*, Chicago, Illinois.

1925-1928   *The Week.*

Political Sketches (Who's You in Ohio)

--	Allen Oh! Meyers
--	An'-drew Lightning Harris
1907	Charles Hungry Grosvenor
1907	Elmer C. Dover
1907	George Boss Cox
1907	Jon'ah McLean
1907	Joseph Beensome Foraker
1907	Kernel William Alexander Taylor
1907	May-Jar Charles Dick
--	Nickle-Us Longworth
1907	Theodore Energy Burton
1907	Tom Lofty Johnson
1907	William How-Hard Taft

Campaign Songs

1920	Republican Campaign Songs, Ohio Republican State Executive Committee, Columbus, Ohio.

Presented in Programs

1904	A Voice from the Past
1904	Down Upon the Rappahannock
1904	Flinch
1904	Follerin' the Fife and Drum
1904	My Skies are Seldom Gray
1904	The Fifer of the Buck Run Band
1904	The Girl Who Sings Popular Songs
1904	The Ol' Country Dance
1904	The Physical Culture Fad
1904	The Song in My Heart
1908	Foolin' Ma
1908	Song of the Motor Car
1908	The Cumberland Stage
1917	Old Glory, April 19, 1917
1917	Some Singers, June 4, 1917
1923	Minor American Singers, August 20, 1923
--	Boyhood Days
--	One Country, One People, One Flag
--	Pop Goes the Weasel
--	Snip, A Study of a Boy and his Dog
--	The Diversions of Dicky Dare
--	The Jester

The Millionaire Dude
When You and I Were Boys
Whistling Jimmy

Christmas Cards

Christmas in the Heart
From a Friend in Old Morgan County
Good Luck to You
Holiday Greetings
The Home Light
The Old Home Place

Broadsides

Bully Yankee
Call Him, Can Him and Cuss Him
Dr. John Goodfellow--Office Upstairs
Foolin' Ma
Gallery of the Immortals
Hands Across the Sea
My Laddie's Life Lesson
The One Flag
To Her Who Keeps My Dwelling Place
Ye Doctor's Life
Yours and Mine
What America Means

Unpublished Material

1908	Castle of Doors and Shutters, Children's story.
	The Fate of the Valley Belle, (A Barefoot Avenger), Story.
	Two Men and a Boy, Story.
	The Adventures of the Elephant, the Monkey and the Clown, Poem.
	The Cowboy and the Doctor, Comedy Sketch.
	Two of a Kind, Comedy Sketch.
1916	The Little Town of Toddville, Play.
	The Jackies, Play.
	One Country, Entertainment Program.
	When You and I Were Boys, Entertainment Program.

The Final Test
A Biography of James Ball Naylor

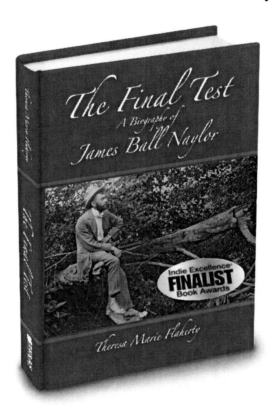

by
Theresa Marie Flaherty

ISBN: 978-0-9832342-4-1 Jacketed Hardcover $26.95
www.JamesBallNaylor.com
www.TurasPublishing.com
Also Available from Ingram - Amazon.com

Vintage Verse
by James Ball Naylor

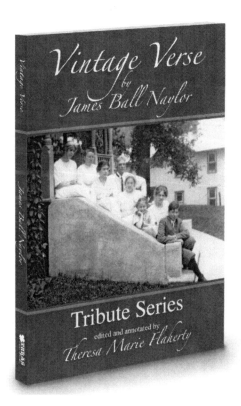

Edited and Annotated by
Theresa Marie Flaherty

ISBN: 978-0-9832342-8-9 Softcover $18.95
www.JamesBallNaylor.com
www.TurasPublishing.com
Also Available from Ingram - Amazon.com

Ralph Marlowe
by
James Ball Naylor

Edited and Annotated by
Theresa Marie Flaherty

A reprinted/reformatted edition of Naylor's 1901 best-seller
with additional material: a foreword, afterword,
contemporary reviews and period photographs

ISBN: 978-0-9832342-7-2 Paperback $23.95

www.JamesBallNaylor.com
www.TurasPublishing.com

Also Available from Ingram - Amazon.com

A Literary Playground
Short Stories

by
James Ball Naylor

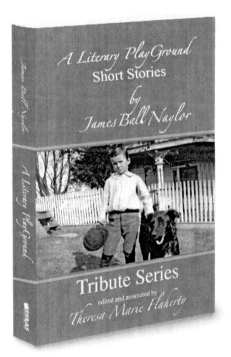

Edited and Annotated by
Theresa Marie Flaherty

ISBN: 978-0-9832342-2-7 Paperback $25.95
www.JamesBallNaylor.com
www.TurasPublishing.com
Also Available from Ingram - Amazon.com

CPSIA information can be obtained at www.ICGtesting.com
Printed in the USA
BVOW01s0101170914

367147BV00001B/4/P

9 780983 234234